T0195564

THE GRAND
ATTRACTION

ENOCH K. ENNS

authorHOUSE®

AuthorHouse™
1663 Liberty Drive
Bloomington, IN 47403
www.authorhouse.com
Phone: 1 (800) 839-8640

Published by AuthorHouse 04/04/2019

ISBN: 978-1-7283-0676-6 (sc)
ISBN: 978-1-7283-0674-2 (hc)
ISBN: 978-1-7283-0675-9 (e)

Library of Congress Control Number: 2019903965

Contents

Part III

Purpose

Part IV

Escape

From The Author...

A Preview Into Part V

Reminiscence...

PROLOGUE

"You may think you know the times. But they will change. Always have, always will. Even if it's going back to where and what it's been. You'll be surprised how often history revisits itself."
-Todd Whiggins, World-class Entrepreneur

"The Grand Mall defies all odds with its success. Even amidst a crippling economy, its appeal to any and all aspiring entrepreneurs makes its fever spread like wildfire."
-Reporter to the CityNews! Magazine

The Grand Attraction

The digi-screen flickered on the dash of the car—the driver ignoring the irregularities as traffic demanded more of his attention.

"Gooooooood morning, Cantedel city!" the broadcaster's voice stretched. Carls rolled his eyes from the wheel to his beautiful wife, Elairah.

The man continued: *"This is Randy Mitchell with your seven o'clock rundown of the haps. Traffic is busy, Westroad is backed up to the horizon again, and the Higharch is still your best way to work."*

Carls felt the leather grip of his steering wheel as the interstate wound to the right at eighty. *Like it did every morning for the past eight years.*

Not that making the Higharch freeway was what had led to the government's shutdown, just a million other choices like it.

"Joining me this morning is Fredrick Townsburgson, here to cheer our warm hearts with the state of collapsing governments."

Such a joker. *That one was getting old.* Elairah reached over and slid her finger up the volume bar.

"Yes, sir. It's been reported that late last night the Board met to finally conclude the contingency plan in lieu of the massive shutdowns. With so many of the once vastly-prominent corps failing from debt and deceit, they have approved the Committee of Professional Conduct. One of the more known businesses to be approved for this regulatory committee is ATR, as it oversees a growing need amidst the disarray of the auto industry."

She smiled at the mention—a certain pride in her eyes. That's where he worked: Auto Tech Repair. Once a medium-sized business off the corner of Décor Avenue and Wilson Chain, it now boasted a near-four hundred percent growth over the past three years. He'd been lucky enough to get

1

in before the government crumbled. With everyone else job-hopping so much, he naturally climbed the ladder.

He could now add *"supervisory management"* to his resume.

But resumes meant nothing anymore. Where you'd been, where you planned to go—no one cared. If you could get the job done, you were hired. If you couldn't, you were fired. Any business not promptly responding to its applicants found itself quickly stumbling off the cliff of economic bankruptcy. With the government blackout, the day-to-day folks were beginning to feel the amount of debt and hollowness of what once regulated and bailed out everything.

Now it was a flesh-to-the-wolves market.

In its wake, the Board—or what remained of closing operations for the authorities—had no choice but to elect new committees to help regulate and guide the rebirthing industries. These committees were of businessmen and women who, despite the oppression of once massive, lying corporations, now showed their true colors as dependable and promising.

The sun beat off his dash as he could just see the outer ridge of the Higharch overlook the vast city and ocean lining. Everyone was fleeing the mainland and heading to the shorelines almost as if hoping some ship would arrive to take them off-world—as the government had promised before.

"Remember the Virgin Star project?" Elairah gleamed. *She was thinking of it too.*

"Mmhm," Carls nodded, catching a glimpse of his three-year-old angel sleeping in the back seat. He smiled at her. *Little Joanna.*

"To live amidst the stars!" Elairah cheered, raising her fist in a mimic. Just like the commercials used to do. "Wouldn't it have been so cool to live on satellite cities? I wonder how close they actually were to finishing it…" Her gaze drifted off to the horizon again. Their view opened away from the sea as they made for the inland.

"Is this mall really like what they're saying?" she asked.

The Grand Mall—the one place thriving through the illusionary bliss of an economic reset. They say it was a city in of itself, packed with suites and hotels, amusement parks and countless extravaganzas. The place was teeming with entrepreneurs dying to get their hands on something luring.

"I don't know what really to expect of it," Carls answered plainly.

"Seems overhyped and yet vaguely plausible. I don't know, dear." Yet that was where they were headed for a much-needed recoup. It had been two and a half years since Carls had any sort of getaway with his wife. They were lucky enough to get a break in light of how much pressure his work was facing, let alone land a pass to the Grand Mall.

Courtesy of a new hire at ATR.

"Still don't know how I feel about him," Carls mumbled.

"Who?" Elairah asked, turning down the jumbled news reports.

"Bill," Carls elaborated, "from work. The guy who gave us these passes. Not even a month in and he felt spurred enough to give us what he could easily sell for a thousand of those e-Links or whatever it was he was addicted to. Found them everywhere at work."

Elairah perked to the mention. "What did they do again? What did he say they were for?"

"He claimed they heightened his senses. He said some kept him awake, others sped his neural processing or whatever, and others helped him remember more from the books he'd been studying."

"So, like a stimulant drug?" she conjectured.

"He swore up and down it wasn't illegal, but I don't know… he did pass every test we threw at him. Still don't know how."

"And he said he got it from the mall? For such a secluded resort, it's amazing he had so many e-Links. Never heard of them till you told me."

"Yeah, I'm surprised he has so many. And passes. He must have won the lottery there, or has an inside scoop. Either way, feels like more than coincidence. We'll see. I'm just glad we get to see what all the hype's about. And if it's even true."

What intrigued him the most about the mall was its venture to self-sustain its assets. Famous and ingenious innovators once employed and valued by the massive corps now crumbling had been given second chances from an arising multi-trillionaire. Who better to fund their expenditure than T.J. Lawrence—the world's richest, self-reserved man. Everyone knew he had a part in funding the mall's expansion and in selecting key assets to bolster its success. The man had enough wealth and wit to purchase immortality if he wished.

His ears tuned back to the station.

"Amidst the informing of the CPC, it was also announced that Noxis, the

3

last-standing mega-leader in internet regulation, has also filed and will be joining the list of closures."

Wait, what? Noxis?

Noxis was the sole provider of the codes ATR needed to reset the NAD chips on all the new makes of vehicles. With them down, there would be no more locks against hacking, let alone an easy way to remove the chips responsible for GPS tracking and manipulation.

Not a good sign for keeping communications open.

"Maybe Bill will have a bigger role if he's as good a tech as he claims. With Noxis down, we're hopeless in obtaining codes to reset NAD chips," Carls remarked. "Noxis made up over half our lead in the automotive industry."

Yet one more reason for the government to become so hated by the people. It had become involved with GPS monitoring and manufacturing. People were paranoid by how much the authorities owned their vehicles, and ATR had been built around the premise of removing the NAD chips responsible for tracking, listening, and altering people's vehicles. There was a point where the authorities could decide if you were going too fast or too slow, starting too quickly, turning too drastically, or stopping too irregularly.

Micromanagement at its worst.

They claimed it was to better prevent terrorists and felons from entering and escaping. At the push of a button, they could seize any vehicle, lock or unlock it, even tell it to go somewhere.

While all vehicles over the past thirty years had these chips installed, not all vehicles allowed for the removal. Most manufacturers were under contract with the authorities to incorporate the chips under the assumption of assisting law enforcement. To put a stop to high-speed chases in quickly-overpopulating cities. To put a dent in drug trafficking and smuggling. With Noxis filing out, they were about to lose the one insider they had for access codes to disable them. None of the other data collection corps had the keys used with NAD chips.

Which meant most new cars were about to be outdated. Or at least anything made within the last thirty years.

He glanced down at the cupboard, a picture of his two angels shone back at him. *His wife and daughter*—all he needed in life, no matter what came crashing down.

The report continued, but he swiped it off.

That also explained the flickering. If Noxis had already been shutting down, a lot more than just digi-screen displays were going to be affected. Most people were ditching their smart-devices right and left and looking for the antiques that had evaded the spy-tech. Everyone knew everyone was watching. Privacy was always infringed upon, which was more reason to fear once they learned of the government's involvement and ulterior motives.

Breathe, Carls, breathe, he reminded himself, merging off the freeway and onto the interstate.

Every new era was a rebirthing—a momentary bliss after the pain of labor. Yes, everything was crashing down and the ramifications of it all only just beginning to bloom. But the spring-time winds were soon coming over the shoreline. He was sure of it.

Everyone was sure of it.

For now, he would just have to focus on his family as he'd always done. They were finally taking a break.

He took another breath, looking over to his wife. She had nodded off to sleep with her hair bundled against the window. His angel in the back was also asleep. He looked at the knobs once covered by the digi-screen on the center dash. A smirk crossed his face. Even amidst such technological advancement, it always amazed him to see humanity step back to its roots.

To the soft rock-and-roll that still faithfully played across the waves.

Amazing how much a foundation the past laid.

Even more amazing was how excited he was to finally take his family on vacation and to see what was quickly becoming known as the pinnacle of humanity.

PART I

ILLUSION

"Long has man held captive the mind. Forever has he refused it wings. Wings to soar above the waves of doubt and selfish ambition. Wings to defy the terrain it was born upon, to reach to the clouds as it should."
—Willis Childs, Chief Engineer

The Grandeur Of Man

Carls was astounded at the sheer scale of the place. It towered high over the landscape. Regardless of still being underway, the structure was simply awe-inspiring. Even from afar, Carls could barely see the top of the enormous globe being constructed above it. *Almost as its own sun.*

Large marble pillars outlined the entrance with its massive panes of mosaics. Every inch of the parking lot was crammed with venturers. It took a solid thirty just to find a spot, let alone another ten just to reach the main doors.

Security guards stood firm above the steps, only allowing those with a pass. Carls had to weasel his way through the crowd of admirers, holding tight to his wife's hand, having a suitcase in another, with a weighted satchel across his shoulder, and a crammed rucksack upon his back. She also had a rucksack and Joanna tucked tightly within her arm.

It was cold outside. A certain chill seeped up from the drains of the lot. *He could only imagine how much AC a place like this took.*

The whole interior of the mall was outlined in obsidian—the cost of which was unfathomable. Carls could but stare at the entrance for a minute or two. The feeling was sublime, the atmosphere all the same. Clearly, the Grand Mall was man's proudest show of artistic design and architectural perfection. Even the floor upon which they entered was of colorful river rocks and marble.

He took notice of her smile.

"It's beautiful," she gleamed, tightening her hold upon him and rushing forward. "Do you see that?" Elairah called out with excitement.

Carls followed her lure toward the glistening fountain. She observed the ancient text and its translation beneath it: "*To test man's ability to exceed. To become what man might be. To be what he may.*"

Both their brows rose in confusion.

"Hm, I wonder what they mean?" she asked, making her way around to see if there was more. "Oh, here's the rest: *To free the limits of a once-captive mind and to captivate its freedom.*"

Carls looked at the large billboard behind them, showing but a glimpse as to what the mall had in store. They were at the south gate, in the Wehl'kom District. *Seemed fitting enough.*

The pass he'd been given was for a stay at Paradise Suites. They would head there to check in. Already he was loving the place. The sights, the smells, the sounds.

The atmosphere was filled with throwbacks to older days. Massive screens displayed the nearest attractions in cartoonish fashion. Even in passing, he noticed a shop selling retrofit TVs under the motto "*No one watches but you*".

Definitely a knock against the spy-tech of everything else made in the world.

Another billboard caught his attention. "*Welcome!*" the words bubbled upon the screen. "*Take a deep breath; you're in a new haven now! Welcome to the Grand Mall! Leave all your troubles and strife at the door, and we'll baggage it for you, free of charge!*"

It was one of those moments when one feels something is either entirely fake or truly everything it claims to be. Carls had yet to see one person not blown away at the attention to detail. One would think such a place would take thirty years to build—not the mere seven it boasted. To think it was still in development and yet so proudly open to entrepreneurship... *What else could they add?* Carls chuckled to himself.

"What?" Elairah took notice, a hint of laughter as well.

Carls could only appreciate her all the more. He loved his family. He loved his time with them. He loved that they were finally able to get away from the troubles of the real world and escape to a promising paradise.

Even Joanna was overflowing with curiosity to touch everything but managed to stay close and under her father's guiding hand. The first task on his mind was still to find the apartments. Sure enough, before them was a pillar of black marble, holding another etching of the place. They were able to find the apartments not but a hall and a turn away from them.

The Paradise Suites took up the whole length of the eastern hall—however small it might have been in consideration of the many others they had yet to discover. The suites rose to all three floors of the stone wall. The black plaque onto which the name was carved extended the width of the massive entrance. Locke quickly acknowledged that there was nothing short of magnificence in such an attraction. Any doubts he had of the place were quickly fading, if not already gone. *It had to be real.*

The lady at the desk kindly told them not to worry about carrying their luggage anymore, as they would do it for them as a part of the pass. He simply handed her the ticket and his keys and turned to his wife, saying with a smile, "What would you like to eat?" Maybe this trip was the perfect vacation for their family after all. Maybe Bill had been right: it *was* worth their while.

Taking out his camera, he asked a passing couple to take their picture. Surely, this was what he needed. What *she* needed. What *Joanna* needed. There was no mistake this was, without a doubt, the grandest attraction.

A Blink Of An Eye

They had finished eating and began to venture down the central hall again. He'd bought his daughter the largest lollipop on the menu for kids, and she happily gnawed away for the time, being atop his back. His wife led him through the countless shoe and purse shops, hopping from place to place. She could have spent a lifetime in each one had she not seen something of new interest in the store next to and then across from it. The place was almost too big to have any single starting point, thus they roamed. First managing to keep to the main floor until they came to an opening in the mall where light glistened from a large dome now four flights above them. It glistened through and down to the trickling fountain of a human-size seahorse wielding a golden trident. Etched into the plaque below it was the name Osgroth—the Guardian of Tranquility.

Joanna loved it, and it was all they could do to keep her from splashing in it. It was then they decided to take the escalator to the second floor.

"Oh, honey! Look there!" his wife shouted with joy, pointing at a clockwork store.

"No way! They actually have one!" he replied, already being rushed toward it. Elairah had a queer fascination with watches, or rather, clockwork of old. He knew he'd lose her in there if he didn't hurry up, so he grabbed little Joan and hurried after her. Indeed, the place seemed frozen in time— that period of history in which watches and the like were valued far more than in the twenty-second century. Large wood clocks filled the advertising windows, obviously successful in their work, seeing as his wife was already at the back of the store envying one of the watches from behind a glass retainer. When he reached her side, he too was able to see it.

There, about midway on the second rack, lay an Agarwood pocket watch with a golden chain.

"Oh, honey," she said, "*that* is my dream watch! I've always wanted one like it, and one of these years I hope to have one." She smiled at him, turning her attention to all the other displays she had at first overlooked.

Carls but glanced at the cost of it. "Maybe some time," he said, scoffing at the outrageous pricing. It was definitely more than he could bargain for, and he knew it wasn't necessary to purchase her love. She loved him regardless of what material things he had, and that was just one of the many blessings from her. He praised the Lord every day for a wife that cared nothing about wealth and fame, only loyalty and trust. And as a couple, they were honest with each other on everything.

"Look at this one, honey..." her voice trailed as she ventured about the shop.

"Daddy! Daddy!" his daughter cut in. "Can we go over there?" She pulled at his hand, pointing her little fingers toward a passing cart filled with stuffed animals and toys.

"We sure can," he answered her, easing to the front of the clockwork store. By the time they reached the entrance, the cart just turned down the hall and to the right. Carls waited for his wife to finally emerge and join him.

"Joanna saw a trader's cart with some stuffed animals. I saw it turn just down there. You wanna follow it?"

"Momma, please!" little Joan urged, reaching out to be held by her mom.

"Of course, we can!" Elairah said, reaching out to grab her from Carls.

"Then off we go!" he said hugging the both of them. "And quick! Before he disappears on us again!" And they were off in pursuit.

He knew the best memories of a child were in playing games with them. He himself even enjoyed the refreshing outlook of trying to make everything into a game of sorts. It made life more easing. It also helped him to smile in midst of troubling times and after a hard day's work. Many things could be learned through the eyes of a child, and he was but beginning to taste the true meaning of that.

They soon found that the trader's cart was no longer in their sight as they made that right turn. But little Joan's joy wasn't hindered in the least, for now it was hide and seek. She jumped out of her mother's hands and raced across the stone walkway, hand in hand with her father. Somehow, they'd managed not to run into anyone upon reaching the next turn in their pursuit.

"Ut oh!" Locke exclaimed playfully, looking from right to left. "Now which way did he go?"

"That way, daddy! That way!" his daughter shouted. Obviously, the lollipop was doing its work filling her with energy.

"Oh, dear," Elairah addressed, "you two go ahead! I'm going to have a look at some of the antiques we just passed down there. You two have fun, okay, Joan? You make sure you find that sneaky guy for me!"

"I will!" Joan assured, giving a rushed hug.

"Love you, dear," Carls said to his wife. "Be careful, and we'll meet up with you at the Osgroth fountain in an hour, ok?"

"You guys have fun," she bid them farewell, waving as they parted ways.

Carls could tell she was getting tired as her little steps were now inconsistent with each other. She still had all the energy of a three-year-old, but not the strength. They'd lost sight of the cart they had been chasing once again and now stood outside a record store.

"I think we lost him," he said playfully out of breath, taking a seat at one of the cross benches. He wasn't sure if she'd heard him or not, or if she even recalled what it was they were chasing. At the time, she was distracted trying to walk the floor lines as they bent from side to side. "Careful, Joan, we don't wanna run into anybody, so watch where you're going, please." His head dropped in *I-told-you-so* fashion as she tripped over her own feet, nearly tumbling into someone. "Sorry, sir," Carls said, turning his attention to little Joan. "Come back over here, Joan," he said calmly.

She came running towards him.

"Looks like you're getting tired—want me to hold you?"

"Nope!" she replied, just as blunt and innocent as all children are before getting distracted by something else.

"Ok, dear, let's start on our way back."

She was quick to his hand, and they began their walk in the way they had come. He hoped he would remember where exactly to go. He'd forgotten how vast the distance they'd covered was. But that didn't scare him, he was sure he would find it (after all, he was a guy, he couldn't get lost, right?).

"Hey, daddy, watch!" his daughter's voice cut back into his thoughts. He glanced down to see her hand outstretched. A look behind showed that she had probably been touching passersby.

"Oh, honey, we don't do that. We keep our hands to ourselves," he corrected, pulling her hand back in.

But the sudden jolt of her hand back out was a surprise to him. She tumbled once again to the side, crashing into another passerby. And that's when he noticed.

In the blink of an eye, a momentary flooding of disbelief filled him. "Joan!" he said rather strictly, reaching out and grabbing her, his heart pounding. Had that *really* just happened? Had she just fell *through* someone else? *What on earth just happened*, he said to himself. His eyes traced to whom the incident had occurred. Sure enough, static blurred from the knees down as the figure corrected itself. Nausea filled his head as he back-stepped. The man shot a scolding look towards him and kept moving. *What just happened?*

"Joan?" he panicked, realizing she was no longer in his hands. "Joan!" She was five steps too far from him, and he rushed to her. But before he could react, his body collided into a cart. Merchandise crashed everywhere as his flesh collided with the stone flooring. There was no mistake about it: that cart had just come out of nowhere. *Or had I just not noticed it?* Now nothing was making sense, and his mind reeled for explanations and reality. He looked up and—

His daughter was gone!

"Joan!" he yelled again. Back on his feet, he was leaping in every which direction, peeking around every corner for his little angel when, also out of nowhere, he felt a metal pipe thud into his forehead. He dropped senseless and unconscious to the floor.

What Happened? (Hide & Seek)

His eyes opened to a faded view of the corner block from which he had last looked behind. He still lay exactly where he had been struck, but everything looked different to him. *What happened?* he asked himself, lifting his body slowly from the cold floor. He saw the blood staining it; he felt the sharp shrills of pain and numbness. Whoever had hit him, there was no one now in sight to blame. But he couldn't tell much with his vision so ablur from the impact to his head. *Joan!* he remembered. *Where is she? What happened?*

He attempted scrambling to his feet but couldn't, so he sat in shock as his senses slowly began to return. Everything around him seemed vacant of life. The stores, the halls, the escalators—they were motionless. The tapping of feet, the mumbling of voices, and the feeling of body warmth—it was all gone.

Shivers trailed down his spine as he tried standing once more, this time successfully. Propping up against the corner block, he surveyed the second floor with more clarity. *Where is everyone? Where are the lights?*

The light. Last time he recalled, the place was gleaming with it, but now it seemed to be beckoning for security. Something was definitely wrong. *I must not be thinking right,* he told himself. He wobbled to the nearest bench and caught his breath, head toppling into his hands. *Joan…*he wept, *where is my little Joan…*

A sound echoed from behind him. He twisted his body to look. It had sounded like metal rattling on the floor. *Metal.* His heart was pounding. He prayed ever so dearly that it was all in his head. *If it is, then I can defeat this. I WILL awake and find my beautiful little girl running to embrace me….* and if it wasn't…

He stood from the bench, nerves breaking sweat from his skin. Every inch of him was shaking, but he still had control over his thoughts. Slowly, he inched toward the far end of the hall, eyes shot open to the dim lighting. The sound came again.

He had a hard enough time keeping focused, let alone stay atop his own two feet and did not notice the form bent over inside the corner store as he passed. He but concentrated on the one task: reach the noise, which he'd concluded to be down the hall to his right. Sunlight from above was of no use for depicting detail much farther than a couple meters, and what light there was scattered about the halls was dim and only giving off a glimmer of its surroundings.

The last action on his mind at the time was to yell, so he crouched, getting as close as his conscience was comfortable to the figure wielding the pipe. He peeled around for a glance, his throat clogging but body refusing to swallow in fear of exposure. His eyes were bloodshot to the sight, and the terror nearly sent him tumbling from his cover, but he was able to catch himself. Even from what he had seen, he knew it to be real. It was no costume—the figure before him. No fake. The body, at a quick glance, had looked shriveled and worn. The man, or girl, could not seem to get a solid grip on the pipe (which was why it kept dropping). Its entire body seemed trembling as though possessed, but not.

Carls tried stabilizing his breath but couldn't. The figure had looked almost inhuman, and he had a hard time believing that. *What's going on? Where am I? What's happening? Where's Joan? What ARE these things? What were they?*

"Where am I?"

It was too late. Before he could stop the words, he'd realized his cover had been blown. *I actually said that?!* A shrill echoed off the walls as the figure jabbed its pipe against the floor. He was up and running the best he could, the creature screaming behind him. He caught wind of the pipe as it flung past him and clattered through an overlook and to the main floor. Both his hands were to his ears to stop the screeching as he simply ran, eyes practically shut to the dimness.

His panic led him down the opposite end and into a clothes shop. He remained huddled beneath a clothes rack, rocking back and forth in childlike fear. Reverberating throughout the halls were shrill cries—at least five more he could count (if at all his mind were keeping track). What were those things? Who? Why? Where?

He hid there for some time, trying in every way to calm himself and slow his breathing. *Ok, so maybe this IS real, and I'm not dreaming.* Whatever was happening, he HAD to find his daughter. He prayed they hadn't taken her too. It was all he could hope for that to her everything was alright. *I pray she is safe. God, I hope she is safe.*

He lifted his head, a hand barely nudging aside a jacket so he could see into the hall. Nothing—just as he had first awakened—*nothing.*

Now what? He tensed his body muscle by muscle to help ease his nerves. *It's all in your head, Locke; it's all in your head.* And he just kept telling himself that, quietly emerging from the clothes rack. *I can do this. I can find Joanna.* His throat was still clogging up, but he refused to succumb to its' plea. Instead, he eased forward, watching his every step as he progressed towards the front.

Still no noise.

His feet stopped. Something didn't feel right. It was almost *too* quiet. He took a steady step backward, mind suddenly uncomfortable with the thought of leaving his safety. He felt a tingling on his neck. *It's all in your head; it's all in your head.*

It feels... moist?

Carls flung his body around, wrists clipping some dank clothes as he turned. Something clenched his left foot, and he shouted, kicking into the fury of whatever it was attacking him. Racks suddenly toppled over, and noise erupted from the now shattered silence. Locke lunged himself across the floor and to the glass door. He had enough sense in him to grab hold of the handle as he exited and to pull it shut, causing whatever it was chasing him to crash into the glass separating them. It was way too close for his personal liking, and he, tripping over, tumbled back down. His shoes seemed to be sweating themselves as he frantically struggled to gain traction—once again fleeing for his life. Only this time he had control of his breathing.

Isn't It About That Time?

But that in of itself didn't mean he knew where his legs were taking him. All he knew was the sudden jerk back to reality and present as he rolled down the escalator, banged up and bruised, his head bleeding again. *Oh, God, please...please help me!* He couldn't help the influx of disbelief. Why was all this happening? *What* was exactly going on? Where was his daughter? Where was *everybody*?

He looked up. *Where is my wife?* Blood covered his sleeves as he coughed into his hands, picking himself up but failing just as quickly. Before him, the sound of water was somewhat comforting. He had almost reached the fountain. He was where they were supposed to meet. *Where are you, babe?*

Since his legs were still aching, he forced himself to crawl—the pressure of trauma and adrenaline beginning to wear on his body's ability to function. *I can do this. It's almost over.* He'd reached the midway mark before his fall began to get to him. Everything was spinning. He tried checking what time it was but his watch was no longer there. It had been ripped off during his last confrontation. *How can I fight this?* he asked himself, lying exposed on the floor between the escalator and fountain. *How can I fight when I'm... when I'm scared?*

And so he waited. Patiently (if one could say). Time seemed to stretch forward and backward. He remained there for a while. For more than an hour, though to him, he could not tell the difference. To him, one minute without the one he loved was a lifetime too many. The tiny hole of doubt in his soul grew deeper. And as time yet progressed, it grew wider. *Please come, Elairah, please*, he prayed. *I'm here waiting for you...*

It was almost too long for him. He approached the fountain and rinsed his face in its cold, dead waters. The only peace he felt was in the memory of his daughter clinging to it so as to jump in. "No," he had said, "we are not allowed to play in *that* water, Joan." And here he was splashing it over his forehead.

What is happening to me?

Nothing, it's just all in your head...

Then why does it feel so real to me? And where are my sweethearts?

Don't worry, it's just all in your head...

Was that really the best he could answer?

It's all you need for now.

But he wasn't satisfied with it. Where was Elairah? "Elairah," he mumbled, waiting for a soft whisper to answer him. "Elairah," he repeated, heart growing more anxious. "Elairah!" His hands were to his head again as he cried in the deadness of silence of company. "Elairah!"

A baby was what he felt like. And to outside ears, what he sounded like. Disregarding any sense of pride, he continued calling out for her, only the echoes of loneliness coming back to him, and his emotions could not take any more of it. Though he was a man, he was also human. He had a heart, a soul, and a mind. Sadly, his heart seemed torn right out from within him, his soul scathed with doubt, and his mind stripped of reality. Truth. He wanted answers.

Why is she not coming? he cried to himself. *Why is she not here? Is it not about that time?*

For once, he cleared his throat, swallowing his brokenness to attempt making sense of everything. This place was supposed to be all that it now was not. What had happened to the peace? The joy of it all as a time to never forget?

Well, now I definitely won't forget it, he scoffed. What had happened to the lady at the front desk? The Paradise Suites—he had a doubt for that name now. This wasn't paradise. There was no such thing as "paradise" on earth. There was no "utopia" or "safe haven". There was nothing man-made that could obtain God-like essence. *"You should take your family to that place,"* so Bill had said. *"And while you're there, say hi to my fam!"*

The words were sweet. *And while you're there, say hi.* Did he really have family here? Were they now a part of the same condemned nightmare?

"It's beautiful," his wife had said. *It's beautiful.* How could this place

be so beautifully terrorizing? How could this be happening to him? *What happened?*

A shrill in the distance caught his attention. He recognized that sound.

Once again, his heart quaked, his pulse jumped, and his eyes shot open to his surroundings. *Yes, the sound.* They were not creatures out there. What he'd first glanced at around that corner, what had hit him, and what he had seen hit against the glass—they were human. The one he'd encountered in the shop had been brutally depicted. Human but deprived of sanity, frail but overpowering, unstable yet driven to act. He could not yet understand what had come of them, only that they were terrifying. So un-kept and wasted. So worn and malnourished.

A second shrill joined in with the first, and that's when he remembered his position—as prey. *I have GOT to get out of here—before this all gets to my head!*

Paradise Really Is Here? (No Escape)

Somehow his body was able to keep going. He reckoned he had God to thank for that. No human invention could adapt as fluidly as the human body. No human invention could react as knowledgeably in any given circumstance. Especially as such the one he was in. He was fleeing for his life, though this time able to think of where he was going on top of maintaining his breathing (regardless of how out-of-control it was). His memory suffered the flashbacks as he revisited the earlier experiences. He caught a whiff of the place to which he had taken his family out to eat.

But it was only a whiff of momentary setback that his body came to a halt. He recognized that hall. Before him, not but a hundred meters away, lay the towering entrance now colder than ever, and as he relieved his lungs, his nausea began to return. He glanced to his left—to that which had caught his attention.

The Paradise Suites.

Another glance at the glass panes and his decision was made: he had to check the suites. Maybe his wife had ran and hid in there! He couldn't risk the slightest chance of not saving her before freeing himself from the madness.

The same spinning doors awaited him as he stepped through. The whole interior of the building was just as dimly lit as everywhere else. The desk remained empty to him as he cautiously crawled over to scan the files. None of the monitors were on nor seemed to be turning on (and that didn't make him feel any more comfortable). He scanned the desk for papers and sticky notes.

He found one. Not the one he was looking for, but one of interest. On it was written the number 317. It was circled one too many times. *317,* he repeated to himself. That meant the top floor. He hated the top floor given the events he had been through, but he progressed nonetheless. *Please, oh please! Just be in there!*

There was no wood to creak beneath his every step, being as they were made of stone. The elevator wouldn't work either, though he would have never chosen it, even if it had been a choice. Thus, he climbed the stairs.

Slowly. Carefully. Once again, his breathing began picking up. It seemed forever until finally he reached the second floor. Still nothing. The hallways were vacant and still. The lighting made them feel like a morgue. *Some paradise.* Confident to proceed, he put his first foot on the second flight of stairs. The lights flickered.

He swallowed the frog in his throat, biting his upper lip and tightening his jaws. *It's all in your head.*

Every other step was as swift as possible with stealth still in mind. He now stood atop the third floor, looking down the long, narrow, still hallway. Room 301 was to his right.

He stepped forward. *303.. 305..309...313...315.*

I definitely haven't lost my sense of manliness, he told himself, trying to ease the trembling building up inside of him. *I can do this.*

He had that kind of feeling where everything seemed so silent that he could hear the static in the air—a consist pick that is only *just* bearable. And when he reached out to grab hold of the door, he could hear the handle clink to the turning force.

The door of room 317 slid open across the carpet.

It was in his face before he could react otherwise, fingernails digging into his skin. He tumbled backward into the wall behind him, yelling to get it off. All he could do was slam himself to the ground in hopes it would loosen grip. And it did. Thrusting his arms between the breasts, he tore free of the merciless grip just long enough to regain footing and start down the hallway.

Then the shrills came. Not just from the one, but from ALL the rooms. Doors were bursting open right and left now as hands reached for his throat. He deflected what few he could before he was tackled from the side.

They were coming up from downstairs too.

He screamed to break free, his body raging in flight-and-flight. But he forced himself to do otherwise, knowing that the last thing he needed at the time was tunnel vision. And so he was up, slamming through opposing forces in a frantic counter-strike-while-fleeing move. *Window*! his mind yelled to him. Were there any windows in such a building?

There had to be.

He pried open one of the empty room doors, almost crashing through like bowling pins with so many others fighting to get to him. There had to be at least twenty already on the third floor and twenty more on their way! He spun around to slam the door shut, just managing to lock it while being hit by the ones who'd made it in. There were four inside and all as equally strengthened—that being more than he could handle. He couldn't take their jabbing blows and brutality. Colliding with a near dresser, he felt his way to a sturdy chunk of broken wood and dealt a swift blow to the head of one of the attackers. He saw the window and went for it—two others now reaching his already torn shirt. *What floor am I on?* he asked himself again, preparing for the worst (not that it could get any more so).

He was out. For a brief period of time, Carls felt free. He felt as though he'd just escaped a thousand demons only to soon face more. The figures had clung to him, making an ugly descent from the window above. Thus, flesh and stone hit—though his body had ended up atop theirs. The three that had fallen with him were dead, and the fourth bellowed from the third floor in anger.

Locke could hear the footsteps changing as they rushed back down to get him. His body ached in torture as his adrenaline forced him up. Screams roared from the Paradise Suites as he made that last turn the exit-way. *Give me strength*! Carls pleaded, giving it his all. For every drop of blood left in him, he poured out twice the amount in determination. He had *not* saved his wife; he had *not* found his daughter. No, he was fleeing them.

He was deserting them.

His stains smeared against the glass doors as he panicked for one of them to open. He couldn't tell if it was his lack of strength or lack of will that was failing him. His fists pounded against them, kicking them, punching them.

"Open up to me!" he yelled helplessly, the shouts of his pursuers coming in behind. He slipped from the slick glass and fell to his knees, head lifted upward, hands raised. "Why won't you open up to me?"

They were coming. He didn't have time to play the blaming game; thus, he tore himself away from the only hope of escape he had. He fled into one of the side stores and hid there, crouched in fear and covered in trembling. *God, how could You do this to me?*

The Illusion & The Illusionate

His shirt reeked of blood and sweat; his toes were still tingling from the fall. He had to stop the bleeding. But *they* were still scavaging out there. They probed like animals for their lost prey, who remained as still as possible behind the wooden counter of the potter's shop. His light breathing was about the only factor keeping him undetected. Whatever these *humans* were, they cared nothing for their own bodies. They felt pain, but it was not burdensome to their actions—it only changed the means by which they moved. And they were moving steadily towards his place of safety. He knew it was only a matter of short time till their fingernails would dig into his skin again. *What is wrong with them? Why do they act so demented?*

If there was one aspect about them that he did finally note, it was their fear. They seemed scared. Their eyes were always wide open and dry. Their breathing was heavy, as though in fight-or-flight mode, and their whole bodies shook feverishly. It was some physical state they had acquired or some mental depravity that made them what they were.

Regardless of them still being human, he praised God that he'd made it out of Paradise Suites alive. When he thought about it, it had to have been a right-sided door for him to have escaped. Not only that but if a few *hadn't* gotten in the room when he'd locked it, he would have had the three-story fall all to himself. He had God to thank for that, and yet he still felt anger that he was not let out. *Why, God, why trap me in here? Why keep me with these* things?

His body shook to the tears as his mind dove into sorrow and self-pity. Why had *he* been left with these possessed? He needed answers, but the only thing answering him was the heavy breathing of an entering figure.

He crouched low and on all fours. The illusionate (as that was what they were called) began studying the area, looking over, around, and under the displays. Carls took as many deep breaths as he could to calm down, scooting on his belly until he was flush with the counter's edge, just able to peer out. The figure jolted back cradling its head. *His* head. He could tell it was a male up this close. His clothes were withered and stank. His pants were held up only by belts about his waist and legs. A large gash covered his left shoulder as he crashed about in severe pain. He was suffering.

Stay focused, he told himself as he braced to make the swiftest move if necessary. The figure tumbled before him, their eyes meeting. They were bloodshot. Both wanted to escape, but only one acting on the desire. Carls propelled himself up and over the counter, making a break for the shop's entrance. A second illusionate entered the scene, quickly aiming its movements towards him. And then the scream.

Again, his ears hurt to the awakening masses, but he ignored them, trying hard enough to keep one foot in front of the other. He took the first possible left down the next hall. *Where am I going?* he asked himself, feeling his vision start to blur. In his current condition, he couldn't do anything as well as he'd hoped. Nonetheless, he slid his body across the stone flooring to clear another corner in hopes of losing sight of them. Now he just had to find a place to hide, preferably one that had a first aid kit.

He saw an escalator to the second floor. *I don't like floors*, he told himself as he recalled the fall, but he climbed regardless. Reaching the top, he rushed into the first shop to his left, slamming shut the glass door and frantically searching for something barricade it. *Where?*

It was too late. A single figure emerged from the first floor and came rushing at him. They both hit the glass at the same time, Carls giving it his all to keep the figure out. His strength just wasn't there, and the illusionate burst through the glass and into him. He hit the ground, throwing a fist to the figure's face. Once more did fingernails dig into his skin, but he refused to yell. He threw another fist, knocking the figure off him momentarily. He scrambled for anything near him to use as a weapon and grabbed hold of an action figure. *Batman?* his mind jabbed as he threw it, reaching for another. The figure screeched as the toy hit it. Not to the impact, rather to a surge inside its own mind. Locke just kept throwing whatever he could at it as it reeled backward and over the shattered glass. The thing was barefoot and yet seemingly didn't notice. The glass cut deep, and it fled back out.

Carls himself couldn't move an inch more, his body shutting down from loss of everything. His head slapped against the flooring, and he caught glimpse of a small kit. *A first aid? Thank you, Lord, thank you.*

The pills were the first to go down.

Trip & Bait

For the most part, he'd recovered. Not in the sense of strength and healing, but at least now he wasn't getting worse. His condition was steady, his mind now able to *think* while fighting these illusionate. He praised God that only one had followed him up to the second floor. Also, that it had retreated to its own pain and not to his. Though he wondered what could possess a man so much as to not care for bodily harm. What was in these things to make them so ruthless and yet hurt?

He'd exhausted all the supplies in the aid kit. It was only enough to tend to his throbbing forehead, but that was enough for him. Maybe if he wasn't so beat up and cold, he could handle himself better. For now, his emotions acted as nerves to his thoughts. His body still shook, hands still sweat. Once again, he found himself wishing he still had his watch. He hated the feeling of being trapped in a state outside of time and yet still bound by it.

Searching the back storage, he was able to salvage some pans and a jacket (for the place seemed so cold). A pellet gun was all he could find that could be used as a weapon. He *could* use the glass, some tape, and a bar, but he wasn't the type for gore. *No, they're still human*, he told himself. They're still *human*.

A sobbing not of his own reached his ears. He propped against an entrance toy rack, peering around the bend and into the hall. He could make out the faint form of a figure leaning against a corner shop across from him. In the sobbing came mumbled words sounding as one about to die if help was not assured. It was not an illusionate—at least that he could tell, but it was hard to see in the dim light.

"Help me, please..." the man's faint voice came. He had to be real.

God, please don't let me be alone, Carls prayed, taking one last look at his surroundings before sliding behind a rail overlooking the first floor. It was still just the man and no one else.

"Please!" the man cried out blindly. Carls' heart wrenched as he debated what to do. *Please be real,* he thought.

A second voice stopped him—that of a girl. He managed to peer far enough to see her crawling towards the man, body all-the-more beaten. "Dan? Is that you?" she yelled at the man. They *had* to be real.

"Help me! Please!"

"Dan? Is that really you? Dan!" the girl seemed overjoyed, but her body cringed at every movement. "Dan!" she yelled out to the man.

Carls couldn't take it anymore. "Sir!" he yelled, breaking his cover and running towards them. The man's eyes met with his own as he was tackled to the floor. *What?*

His head slammed to the floor, the bandages only just holding. He couldn't believe his eyes! Dan and the girl were still there, but neither reached out to help him. They but flickered and soon faded as he was left to face the illusionate.

He sent the hilt of his pellet gun into the temple of his opponent, knocking it to the side. It took a second too long for his shoes to make traction, and he was forced to grapple with the figure. With his bare hands, he slammed the illusionate's head to the floor, breaking free of its scathing grip. A shrill cry threw his balance off. *What on earth was that?* He dove for the pellet gun, spinning around in time to see another illusionate leap the corner. A whole clip was out before he realized it wasn't doing anything (not that he expected it too, but he had hoped for something). The illusionate simply charged at him, and he shuffled backward in terror.

The ground shook again.

Suddenly did the illusionate collapse. Something had crushed it from the third floor, and now the emerging figure arose. Carls didn't give himself time to notice what it was; he but turned and fled with every ounce of sanity still in him—the pellet gun left behind.

"Get away from me!" he yelled as a roar erupted from the new, much larger, figure. Lucky for him, he was not its first prey. He heard the screams of the illusionate as they cowered from the beast.

Carls just ran.

He was around the bend and down another hall before his feet puttered out. *What was that thing? What on earth is going on?* He was standing just outside a coffee shop, hands on his knees as he gasped for air. *Feet, don't fail me now!* At least he was able to stand. Whatever it was back there, it nearly caused all control of his senses to be lost. What horrendous beast was it now? How had it jumped a whole flight without hindrance? Where had it come from?

What's happening to me?

Locke stumbled across the empty halls and vacant shops. His mind was playing a deathly game with him. He was on the verge of insanity in his search for something real. The images weren't leaving him—the crippled man and the crawling girl. They had seemed so real, so true; he was sure of it! *How can I fight this?* he begged himself for an answer.

"I can't," he whispered, quickly deciding otherwise. But what did it matter anyway? *I am alone and depraved, and in only a matter of time, I also shall be diseased.* A plague it was. A demonic plague devouring *everyone* who thought the place as some "Grand Attraction". *Lies! It was all lies! How could ANYONE believe in lies?*

But he had, and he hated himself for it. *This was supposed to be perfect,* he reasoned to himself. It was supposed to make the perfect vacation from the world, not drive him deeper into it. Something was wrong with him. *This can't be real. It's all in your head.*

His body froze. At first glance, his heart had skipped a beat. Now it was rushing in anxiety. "Elairah?" he mumbled forward to the figure that strode before him. *Is that you?* Maybe she hadn't heard him. Or maybe his mind was playing tricks on him again. *What if it's another trap?*

"Elairah," he called out louder.

Her figure progressed away.

"Elairah?" he said again, more convinced. He rushed toward her, heart like a volcano, soul praying it was her. "Elairah!" He grabbed hold of her hand.

"Carls?" she replied, surprised to see him. *Thank God she's real!* Carls sprang for joy, embracing her fully and tightly.

"Carls, are you ok? Where have you been?"

A tear slipped his cheek. "Thank God you're real!" he praised, "Thank God you're safe!"

"What are you talking about, Carls?"

Something wasn't quite right. He held both her hands in his and looked her in the eyes. She was real. He could feel her, and he could sense her heart beating. But did she honestly not know what was going on?

"Carls, is everything alright?"

He didn't know where at all to start, mind frantically searching for someplace to begin. He stuttered. "I've been chased, hit, shoved out of a window, beaten..."

"Honey, what happened?" she said again, calming him with a gentle hand lifted to his cheek. For a moment, everything in his world ceased but her touch to his face. He didn't know how to respond to the crossbar that suddenly drilled her head to the wall beside them.

"Elairah!" he bellowed out, blood in his eyes and her hand slipping from his. A roar caught his rage to the left and across the hall. But the rage quickly shattered to terror as his jaws dropped open to the sight. A towering beast of a depraved figure stood not too distant. Carls crashed to the floor in bewilderment. It was coming after him.

He prayed to God for it all to end, but reality wasn't budging. He dove to his right as another projectile clanged across the floor where he just was. The beast let out another cry and swung both its massive arms. With the strength of an ape but the wit of a man, the beast flung Locke across the hall. His body broke glass as he then tumbled through clothes. Everything in him was screaming *"flight!"* but the trauma of losing his wife immobilized him from doing so.

No, his returning rage forced him otherwise. Every muscle tensed to the point of cramping, he yelled back, grabbing hold of the nearest weapon to him—a wooden clothes hanger. Back on his feet, he snapped the hanger in two, wielding it as a dagger and bracing for the second impact. Indeed, he could do nothing to stop it.

The wood was but a splinter to the creature's forearm, and he but a puppet being thrown across the floor. The adrenaline in his veins blotted out the pain momentarily. He forced himself to his feet and charged, realizing all too late the stupidity of his actions. A third hit knocked any fight left right out of him. He hit up against a pillar and dropped to the floor. His worst option was now the only one left.

To run.

He looked up from his feeble position and at the distant figure of his wife. *I can't do this*, he cried to himself, crawling to his feet and ducking behind the pillar as the beast pounded into it. Now wasn't the time to mourn. He *had* to flee. And so he did. Before he knew it, he was behind two glass doors of another shop and forcing a steel bar between the door handles to brace it shut. It was only seconds before his body collapsed and fell unconscious to tears and blood.

The Hologram Speaks

A soft whisper had awakened him to his numb pain. His vision came back to a light on above him (and by light, he meant a bright one). Locke stirred from his rest and looked about himself. Nothing had changed, only the light of the single store. The voice came again from across the counter. *Now what?* he asked himself, pulling his body next to the counter. The current store he was in seemed to be more of a help center than anything else. Instead of wood or glass, everything was supported by stainless steel inside.

He lifted his body so as to sit upright. He didn't know whether to treat the voice with curiosity or terror. The scenes with the monster were still in his mind, but he forced the thoughts away before they reached back enough to touch on his now deceased wife. *Why, God, did she have to die?* he pleaded, head raised.

But his attention returned to the voice. His whole body was numb and weary. Each muscle twitched independently of itself, and his skin could no longer break sweat to cool him down. Then his body began to shiver. Inside, he felt as though burning up; outside, he felt cold and dry. It was definitely playing with his head now—all these instances.

"Are you even still there?" the voice cut into his false security.

He didn't answer. *It's fake*, he told himself, recalling all too well the man and girl he'd first come across.

"Sir, are you hiding from me?" the man behind the counter asked.

Carls' mind neared breaking point with the disillusions of the Grand Attraction. He couldn't contain himself any longer, knees bent, back leaning, and head throbbing. *I really can't take this anymore! God, save me, please!*

"Sir, are you still there?"

His pain broke the silence as liquid streamed down his face once more. He looked up into the light—a brief flicker of hope in a dark place.

"Leave me," Carls' voice cracked, "Just leave me be!"

"Easy for you to say; I was here first. Now would you mind? I find it sort of lame that you're hiding from me. Or trying too, that is."

"Who are you? And why are you speaking to me?"

"I won't say a thing more till you get up!"

Locke hesitated. His body still trembled in not knowing whether he could trust the voice or not. *Is he real?*

Carls carefully lifted his body to the countertop, giving in to the stranger's demand.

"There now," the man said (his form flickered in attempts to sustain itself).

Initially, Locke was caught off guard, tripping back and against the empty display rack. He just stared, eyes not blinking once.

"Ah, am I still of a surprise to you? My apologies, but I thought you would have expected it."

"Expect what?" Locke asked.

"You can call me..uh...Xavier," he said with a smile. "And as you can probably tell, no, I am not real at the moment, sorry."

"What *are* you? And why did you trick me before?"

Xavier smiled. "I am a hologram. And though we are the same, we are not in the least bit related. What you saw out there, those were Trippers. Nasty little mind devils, I say."

"Then what, exactly, *are* you?" Carls asked again.

"I am... *not* a tripper. Only a hologram."

"Okay. Hologram, I get it...But these trippers, what do they do? Why were they there? Why are *you* here?"

"Ah, and so your troubled mind asks away. Ha, I find it fascinating the circumstance you're in—"

"My wife is DEAD because of you guys! And if you don't start answering me, I'll END you too!"

"My, my! Calm yourself down! I was but gesturing at your sanity, that was all. Sheesh, don't take a compliment so offensively next time, it really hurts."

Now he was getting weird. "A compliment?"

"Yes. You see, I can't have conversations with *them*, the other holograms, and the illusionate are so far lost that they don't even know *how* to converse! So really, I am quite alone in this place just like you."

"Wait," Carls raised a hand to his forehead. So many questions. "So, you're saying—what? I...I just want to know what's going on in this cursed place! *Why* are you different? *Who* are the illusionate? And *what* are these *trippers*? None of this is making any—"

"I say, please take a breath before you die," Xavier jumped in.

"Excuse me?" Carls inquired.

"You want to know the difference between you and *them*, it's your *head*. Seriously, just think about it since you still can. What do they look like?"

He thought a moment. "I've already been over that, that's not answering anything for me."

"Obviously, you haven't thought on it enough. I am just a hologram; I can't do the thinking for you. It's no fun!"

"Human," he said, "they looked human."

Xavier smiled yet again. "Ah, yes, but be more specific." *Be more specific? How?* "What did their bodies look like? Describe them for me."

"Bent, worn, I don't know. Exhausted? Scathed? Deprived—"

"Yes! Exactly! Keep following there."

"They looked hurt. They...they're numb to physical pain yet suffering all the more in their mind."

"Perfect!" Xavier exclaimed. "Minds, yes, and how about yours?"

"What?"

"Your mind—or scratch that—their mind. What do you think is going on in *their* minds?"

"You're not making any sense," he stated, mind of his own wandering.

"Well, fine then. But I'll have you know you've turned out to be quite the letdown for a conversationalist. I was hoping for more, but I guess it must wait. Like I said before, I cannot do all the thinking for you, but I can tell you that all of which you have undergone, they have as well. Your pain, your hurt, your doubt, your fear—they too had struggled with it all. As for the rest, you must find for yourself."

"Wait, if they are just like me, then how are we so different? What changed?"

"I cannot save you, sir. I cannot simply open for you every door. If you are so curious and anxiety-filled for an answer, why not ask them yourself?"

He wasn't quite expecting the last comment. "How?"

"I'm sure you'll found that out here shortly...."

Fists pounded against the glass. They were outside screeching to get in. "You tricked me!" Carls shouted at Xavier.

"I already told you; I and the others are not the same."

"You're lying to me!" he said, slamming his own fists on the countertop. "If you're not, then why are they here?"

"I am *still* a hologram, my ever so anxious acquaintance. It is only in my nature that interaction attracts. You're lucky I was able to misguide them even for this long..." and the man disappeared, leaving Carls to face the illusionate yet again. The light above him flickered and dimmed, the sounds from outside the doors now piercing in through the cracked glass. It was only moments till it shattered, and he was unprepared.

What They Really Are

With reality screaming back at him, he had no choice but to force his attention to the savages now bursting through the glass. He hadn't been blind the whole conversation with Xavier. He'd noticed to have woken in a security center of sorts, and behind the counter were locked casings of what he guessed to be weapons. However, they were locked, and he had not the time to open them himself.

He wasn't very knowledgeable in weapon types, nor their ammo. He stashed what he could into a bag and leaped the table—a single case in his right hand. *Please be a shotgun*, he whispered to himself, the initial remembrance of the illusionate pounding at him. *Am I really resorting to this?*

But it was already too late. The first figure crashed into him, knocking Locke from his holdings and against another empty rack. They tumbled to the floor as nails yet again dug into his skin. There were four illusionate.

Thinking on his wits, he quickly neck-handled the first, ignoring her hands as they flung violently about to stop him. He needed farther back—just a little more—and he got that request as the rest tackled into him. He let go of the first illusionate and hit the floor rolling, his reach just near enough to grab a re-bar and wield it to another's face. Now he used his surroundings to his advantage, dodging them from side to side as they collided into the racks.

First mistake: there were six. Second: he was farther from the weapon's case than he'd anticipated. He had to lunge for it.

And lunge he did—his body screeching across the cold tile flooring—his injuries more than just crying out in pain. They had reached his feet before he had the chance to pry at the seal, leaving his tool with the case. *I can't multi-task like this. I can't face them all at once.*

Bearing his teeth, he drove a fist at one of them, loosening their grip. But just as two more nearly jumped him, they suddenly stopped, hands to their ears, voices cracking under the pressure that they seemed to be experiencing. *Thank you, God*, he praised, crawling back over to the case and prying it open. He hadn't the time or pleasure of knowing which gun fate had given him. He simply unlocked and loaded the ammo casing beside it, spun around, and froze.

He didn't know what to think of the dismembered bench flying over him—only that it collided mercilessly into two of the illusionate, instantly putting them out of the picture. He needn't even to have turned around to hear the trembling voice of a Fallen One (as he recalled what had happened to his wife). Pain erupted in his head to the remorseful thoughts and the agony that came with them. He was on his feet and to the side as yet another object, a large vase, flung through the air. *What on earth* are *those things?* He couldn't say it hadn't crossed his mind to ask Xavier of them while he had the chance, but Xavier was gone, leaving him to face the demons of corrupted madness. *If you are so curious, why not ask them yourself?* Or so Xavier had told him.

Ask them yourself, what a strange thought to *actually* have running through one's head while fighting for one's life. He pulled the gun to his chest and fired.

His body shook as a blanket of bullets tore past the distance between them and into the enlarged figure of a physically altered being. He forgot to take into account he was still fighting the illusionate, for he was hit from the side and against the counter. *Both?* His mind was yelling at him. *I'm fighting both?*

The beast charged toward him, ignoring the bullets it had taken (yet somehow still feeling them all the same). Carls and the illusionate could not escape the Fallen One's thrust and were sent crashing out of the shop and into one of the hall's pillars. Carls had just managed to get behind the illusionate before impact—saving him from the brunt of it. He slid to the floor, the gun skidding away from him. More illusionate were arriving at the scene, but he noticed it wasn't just him they were fighting now. They almost seemed team-focused as they half-heartedly coordinated their attacks on the creature—all of which had grotesque results. But they did do one thing: *they bought him time.* Time to drag himself toward his gun, time to realize a couple stray had noticed him and changed direction. *God help me now,* he said, forcing his feet to catch grip and put him in motion.

He dove for the gun, sliding (as if to say) behind one of the nearer pillars, placing his last cartridge into its chambers. They emerged around his cover. The first was easy. It took the hilt of his gun to its gut and bellowed over. The second, he'd bent low as a fulcrum to propel the figure over him—knocking out both its knees. And the third, he knelt and in a single fluid action, sent four bullets flying into its chest.

The chest of a male.

Before the illusionate could drop, he slammed it with the hilt yet again, quickly turning his attention to the fifth figure coming toward him. *This is the one,* he said, taking a breath and step back. *I have to keep this one alive.*

He barely cleared the path as a rack from the store was sent crashing into and through the figure. The beast had redirected its rage at him, ignoring completely the last few illusionate tackling it (as it was ten times their size in body mass). One by one, they lost grip as it charged at Carls.

He lifted his gun yet again and unloaded all that he could at the creature's legs—but it didn't need them anyway, its massive forearms making up for the loss as they bore its entire body across the distance.

Bitter remorse, he noted. The creature seemed raged with hate for its actions yet carried them out nonetheless. Locke dove for more cover while he had the chance.

The hallway exploded. Or rather, not the hallway itself but the storefront from which he had come. The blast ignited Carls' eardrums, and he covered them a moment too late, the force only but knocking the creature off balance and against the opposing wall—the action of which angered it as it roared at the cracked glass, running its fists violently through them and into the room. It re-emerged even more so outraged to confront Locke's still numb body. He'd lost his opportunity to escape— ears still pounding.

Carls was scared. And in that fear, he fled as swift as his body could in the opposite direction. He could only make it to the other side before the creature caught up to him and lunged both its fists through the air. He ducked, and the power collided with the near pillar, now fragile from the explosion. It broke, and the whole section above, which had held the second floor, showered down upon the Fallen One in pieces.

He praised the Lord in one breath and caught eye of a wounded illusionate with the other. He'd barely escaped the rubble and already had a new threat the worry about. But this illusionate was weeping at the far side, hands to its head and shaking from right to left. He limped toward it, picking up the gun from where it had lain. Reaching out, he grabbed the figure and thrust it against the wall opposing.

"Why are you after me? Why are you so different?"

There was only more weeping.

"Answer me!" he shouted, leaning all his weight into the interrogation—also keeping his own body from falling.

The figure's hands were at her side, her face tilted to the side and up as if crying for release. Tears. He could see her tears and the blood that stained her face. His aggression deflated, and he lowered her to the floor; he himself dropped to his knees beside her.

"Why are you so different?" he asked in a change of tone.

She looked at him, and for the first time he could see her aching inside and felt pity. How could he feel pity for such a creature? *She's not a creature; she's human. They're all human.*

"What happened to you to make you like this?"

The girl but wept. She must have only been in her early twenties. She was scathed—scrapes and bruises were all over her face and body. *How can they be so inhumane? How can they act so ruthless yet be in pain?* Then the answer came to him: they were doubtful of their actions but convinced they were necessary. How this answer came to him, he did not know, but it burdened him all the more for their condition. The words of Xavier came to his mind: *"...all of which you have undergone, they have as well. Your pain, your hurt, your doubt, your fear. They too had struggled with it all."*

They were just like him. Their sanity had once been there, but they too had been exposed to the condition of the place. They had been drawn in, misled, and ravaged by the Grand Attraction—just as he had. Only they had fallen for its trick and stumbled to its bait. They were illusioned to what it was haunting them, acting as if it had overtaken them with no choice to resist or fight it back. He remembered how he had felt, how he'd been weakened, how he'd nearly given in to the madness and insecurity. In fact, even now he was not much different. Who was to say he didn't look like them? For all he knew, the only difference was that he was still fighting it.

He had resisted the plagued mindset. He had chosen to *not* be defeated by it.

He'd chosen to *hope* for something beyond the suffering and illusion that there was no hope at all. And he had God to thank for that.

To Speak & Be Spoken To

Carls Locke stood as the illusionate's limp form collapsed cold to the floor. Xavier had meant something in that conversation—something that he only wanted Locke to realize on his own. He'd hinted at it, but now Locke knew what it was.

Conversation. Xavier wanted him to converse with the illusionate, to speak and be spoken to. Somehow, he was supposed to save them, or at least open their eyes. Saving them against their will was pointless and impossible. *Thank God I'm not alone,* he reassured himself as he turned to face the wreckage that had been caused. *What had caused that explosion?*

So, I'm supposed to reach out to them, is that why you locked the doors shut? Why you took from me the love of my life that I would feel the need for theirs. But how? How am I to save them less they choose? Is it my place to act outside their will for what's better? Or am I to only speak when spoken to? Please, God, help me.

He looked down at the rubble where the Fallen One had been slain. On his own, he had done nothing. Something of fate was consistently favoring him. He knew it was only a matter of time before his favor ran out—and by then, he'd better know how to fight himself. But he was no fighter.

Just a thirty-three-year-old and stuck inside a supercenter of mankind's fatal attractions, fighting off demons and illusions and just hoping for peace of heart and desiring rest. *And a bath.* His body reeked of blood and sweat. His skin was dry from a fear-shot nervous system. He knew it would take time before he could calm himself before every confrontation. As for now, he was glad to just be alive, but he needed to rejuvenate less his body drop from the physical stress that was demanded of it.

I need a place to gather myself—a safe haven. But he knew they'd manage to find him regardless of where he was. At the time, to keep moving was the best idea. Thus, he moved. Onward down the hall and past several blocks. Since he'd awaken from that pipe to the face, everything seemed so abandoned. He knew there were people all over the halls—but where were they? Why had it all changed *so* much after that moment?

He remembered his daughter. *Joanna,* he whispered to himself, *where did you go?* He could only pray that she wasn't seeing all of this. That she was still seeing everything as they had at first. As his wife had. *"Honey, what happened?"* she had asked him. The words hurt. She hadn't seen *them* or the world she was really in. But he'd been able to hold her hands...he'd been able to see her smile one last time...to call his name.

Why, God? Why did she have to go? The doubt still filled him as his nerves began to tingle yet again to the thought. She'd also died in his hands—her body so savagely pinned up against that wall. Anger was now infiltrating him, his lungs and heart now pounding. *Why did* she *have to go?*

He had to find little Joan. He had to see if she was alive and oblivious or not to what surrounded them. *She had better be here...somewhere, but here.* He heard their growling in the distance—the tension breaking to an uneasy feeling. He didn't know where from, but he knew he had better find refuge quickly before they found him. *I have to find ammo,* he told himself. *I need another gun.*

Breaking The Typical Regime

He'd turned the corner to catch sight of a white-clothed table. It was off in the distance and the obstacles in-between made it impossible to see but the edges. At first, he'd crouched low and crept slowly toward it, but upon further revealing, he could see a rounded figure of a man in a blue tux seated behind it. Another tripper was the first thing to come to mind. *It's all in your head,* he repeated, easing even closer to get a better look. He knew not the full extent of trippers except that they distracted from the real threat. He remembered the girl and man at that corner. He recalled their pain and pleas. He could feel the chill that vibrated in the atmosphere—

His body jerked to the left from a sliding sound. *It was just in your head,* he said to the overreaction of his senses. *I cannot be so easily distracted.* He drew near to the figure at the randomly placed table. *Who would station themselves in the middle of a hall and right behind a center display?*

There was more growling in the distance. He could only pray it wasn't another horde of illusionate or, worse yet, a Fallen One. The man seemed distracted by the cards he dealt with. Locke stood slowly from behind the center display, gun held forward. It was empty of bullets, but the presence was all he was using at the moment. Another illusion of sound sent his nerves jumping, but he remained steady, peeling (as if to say) from behind the display.

The figure seemed to not notice him.

"Who are you?" he asked, taking one more step.

No response. The man but played his cards and reshuffled them.

Locke took yet another step—the howling suddenly stopped. Everything was silent but the figure before him. He could hear the cards now as they were being shuffled and stacked. Carls' heart began racing as he came up to the table's front. *What trick is this now?*

The man looked up, but not at him. To his right. Carls followed his gaze, eyes widening. He could see it, but there was no sound emanating from it at all. No sound but the dealer and his cards. There, not but twenty paces from where he stood, was a Fallen One—pounding an illusionate against a pillar supporting the overhang of the second floor. The expressions and the actions were all real, just absent of noise. The illusionate dropped, mouth gaping open, but was picked up again and tossed in their direction.

A shrill cry filled Carls' ears as it flew past his perimeter. And then silence as it hit the opposing wall. The Fallen One was quickly after it— Carls' body cringing but not knowing what to do. It was almost as if he wasn't there. And for a brief moment, the beast's stench filled his nostrils as it raced toward its prey. It seemed to recognize something too and spun around. Locke was ready to break off in a run, but the man before him motioned otherwise. He remained still, the smell no longer there, the beast's breathing past. It was staring right at him, but soon quickly lost interest in whatever it saw and returned to the crippled illusionate. Were they in some cloak of protection?

"If you haven't noticed yet," the dealer spoke, "we're in a bubble that prohibits ANYTHING inside to be seen, smelt, or noticed from the outside, and vice versa for the most part."

"What? Who are you? And what did you say this was again? A bubble?" Carls was astounded at the statement, and at a loss for grasping it as the norm.

"Yes, a bubble. You're safe as long as you're in here, so long as you don't decide to lure it inside too. I don't think it can hold one of those things, and I don't want it damaging my table."

"Wait, then how did I see you? Who are you? *What* are you?"

"I am Serve Per Card!" he announced proudly, obviously a card dealer who knew the business (and was obsessed with it, seeing as his body had grown big from sitting so long). "And I am so glad to have met you, Carls!"

"How do you know my name?" Locke asked.

"Ah, I'd be a fool not to with a character so familiar to one I've known before."

"You're not making any sense."

46

"And rightly so! Here, I have a little gift for you as we embark on this new business relationship!"

"A gift? I don't need a gift—I want answers."

"Oh, hush. You don't have to be so excited all the time! Here, watch." The man dropped the deck to the table and spread his hands over it. Cards flowed flawlessly where his hands went, and soon the whole surface was covered. Carls' mind was boggled at the sight of them as they began moving apart from the dealer's immediate cause—and they began interacting (so to say) with each other. Before he knew it, he was staring at a single card held before his very eyes.

"Take it, my friend. It is a gift that we may continue business together."

He shook his head, not knowing whether to believe it or take it as the work of a tripper. Despite the confusion, he took the card, turning it over and reading its name. "The Inquisitor?"

The man laughed. "You don't say! Let me see!" he said, taking it back and chuckling some more. "Oh, the memories! You're just like him! Here, let me get you another."

"Just like who?" Locke asked.

"Here, try this one." The dealer handed him a second card, his expression obviously anxious with joy to see Carls' response.

"The Seal of Bondage?"

"The Trust Seal of Bondage," the man quickly corrected, body shaking in his chair from the excitement. "What luck you have struck! I wouldn't have guessed one in a million for that to be your first."

Locke was utterly lost. "This isn't making any sense. Sorry, but here's your card back."

"No, no, no, no. It's yours to keep! That's the whole point of a gift: you're given it, and then you decide whether or not to use it."

"You mean it's my choice to receive it, and I'm handing it back."

"But you can't, see? You've already taken it. It's yours to keep. And I highly suggest you do. That is no easy come-by card. It may be just what you need in times not too distant."

"What is the whole point to these cards?" Carls asked, shaking his fist about the air.

The fat man smiled. "They can only be used once. That particular card, the Trust Seal of Bondage, creates an indestructible (yet destructible) bond between the wielder and whatever he casts it on. It is a bond of trust—and it makes you responsible for the protection of the other, for its safekeeping. In return, well, like the card hints, you have its complete trust."

"You mean this is magic?"

"By no means!" the man laughed. "Yes, it is *like* magic, except it is the card that does the casting, not you. You simply tell it when and how. And by '*how*', I mean more so like in what direction. They are called *Hensers*. This here is a Deck of Hensers." The man gestured at his stack of accumulated cards. "Here, I will also give you this since you are still doubtful."

He handed Locke yet another.

"Chamber of Fire?"

The man's tone hardened (surprisingly enough, considering his joking manner of business). "Use it well. Hensers are no joking matter. They do real things and have *real* consequences just like everything else. Simply draw, point, and release to call forth their power. Should you do so blindly, you too might be burned."

"Release? How do you release? How do I know you are not just playing tricks on me like everything else here?"

"Oh, hush. You are just like the other and so doubtful of the powers at work behind what meets the eye! Watch, oh ye doubtful, and learn." The man stood from his chair and drew a single card of which he held outstretched. *Vacancy*, it read at a glance. A stern look crossed the man's face as his muscles tensed, and he suddenly swung his arm to the side. In an instant, he and his table vanished, leaving nothing but a whiff of air.

Shedding Light

Carls Locke was left to the distancing movements of the Fallen One that had just previously crossed his path. He didn't believe in magic. His mind wouldn't let him. But that hadn't explained what just happened before him. The dealer had vanished!

He looked down upon the two cards he now held, not knowing what it was for sure he should do about them. For the time being, he stashed them into his pants pocket and shoved the confusing thoughts from his mind's reach. Instead, he focused upon the hallway still before him, Xavier's words echoing through his head: *ask them yourself.* His body shuddered to the thought as he reminisced his last encounter with them—the illusionate. They were still *human* and dying. He had to find out what had happened to them so as to save himself. But not just himself. Xavier wanted him to converse with the illusionate. To reach out to them and open their eyes. He'd had a chance, but it slipped. If he was going to find another one to break through, he would have to follow the Fallen One, despite how against the thought he was. *I need answers*, he told himself. *I need a second hand.*

The air was thickening as he pursued the beast. He hadn't yet fully grasped what had happened to them. All he knew at the time was to avoid them at all costs, and yet this cost was too high to avoid. It was a price he was willing to pay. He *had* to find answers. He *had* to secure his sanity lest it be founded upon a false belief. He slowed his breathing. The sight and sounds still haunted him, but at least now he was as prepared as could be for the unpredictable. If this thing were to turn on him, he knew but to only run.

Run or use the cards.

No, they are not real, he reassured himself. *You don't have to use them. You can do this without them. You can do this yourself.*

He came nearside a pillar adjacent to an herb center into which the Fallen One had disappeared. *Oh great, close quarters is* exactly *what I* don't *need.* Locke lifted the gun to his chest, calmly breathing out all the anxiety he could from his lungs. *All I need is one. Just one.*

He stepped into what was known as the Hanging Gardens, feet sliding across the floor from cover to cover. The place was moist. Very moist. The plants and herbs had overgrown their pots and divisions, some even climbing to the glowing ceiling for light. Artificial light—it wasn't the same by any means. Carls could feel that his body ached for the real deal. His bones cried out for the sun, his skin beckoning to be freed from the dampness of the gloomy atmosphere around him.

A sound came in the distance causing his breathing to influx and hold. He knelt ever so low to the ground, the hilt of his gun pressing against his chest. *It's empty,* he reluctantly recalled. He'd used it on his last confrontation. *I'll have to act close, without the aid of bullets.*

Carls Locke was unaware of the form lurking overhead, unaware of the unprecedented darkness creeping about him. His focus instead was upon a single figure that wept, dried of tears but drenched with moisture and pain. Slowly, he eased to the last corner's bend, not knowing for sure what he was to do. He wondered to the source of their pain—for they seemingly bore none physically. *What runs through their heads?*

His shoulder brushed against a pot, sending it crashing. The noise instantly gave lead to his presence. The illusionate scrambled to its feet—expression as though outraged at whatever had intruded upon its privacy.

And it was after him.

Locke had barely managed to respond in time. All while he ran, he beckoned the illusionate to stop. The only answers he was getting were screams and flying pots and shrubbery. *There has to be something I can do!*

He saw an overhang and went for it, but it was too late. The illusionate had somehow caught up (regardless of its poor condition, something drove it to react beyond the human standard, yet blindly). His body crashed over the ledge and down, water engulfing them both. He'd already dropped his gun and now thrust just enough distance between him and his attacker that he could crawl out of the cold water only to wrestle atop marble tile.

"Get off!" he yelled as teeth bore down upon his flesh. With his feet, he propelled the figure backward, crawling back to his own feet and bracing himself for its charge.

"Why won't you just listen?" his voice cracked, back hitting against another aisle as the figure toppled to the opposite side. Unlike his opponent, his body cringed in pain.

They locked fists—the illusionate trying to reach him yet again with its teeth. *An animal!* Locke couldn't stop thinking. *Their behavior is like some kind of animal!* He released a burst of oxygen from his lungs as he fought back the force of the male illusionate's attempts to overpower. *Conversate,* he told himself, *that's what Xavier hinted at. I have to conversate with them.*

"Can't you see what you're doing?!" he bellowed, finding his back against a pillar supporting a second floor. "Can't you stop this and see!"

The eyes before him glistened in an attempt to tear. *It's working.*

"Stop this foolishness and listen to me! I can help you... you don't have to be like this. You don't have to fight me."

He felt a temporary break in oppression. *I can help you*, he reiterated, eyes staring into the figure before him—a tear streaking down his cheeks. For a brief moment in time, he did not fear the life-strained, joy-abandoned figure that he struggled with. For a brief moment, his heart felt pity for them, and he felt an influx of strength pour into his veins. Not strength to overcome, but strength to be overcome by the desire to give hope. "I can save you," he said, the illusionate's attempts shattering as it suddenly collapsed to the floor, bent over its knees.

Carls but took in a deep breath, thanking God for whatever had just happened. He looked down at the broken form now weeping. *Weep with those who weep*—the saying came to him. The cause behind his was the memory of his wife. He knelt beside the hunched figure of a once hopeless man.

"I'm not here to fight you; I'm here to understand you and give you hope. Please, stop this foolishness. Fight back. Not against man, but whatever it is that you are warring with inside. Please, fight back!"

"I'm... trying..."

He couldn't believe his ears. Had the man just spoken? He rested his hand upon the shaking form, its weeping coarse and unchanged. *Can they truly be reached?* He began asking himself that. After all, they were *still* human. Just like him.

Screeching echoed to his attention. More were coming. They must have heard the noise from earlier and now were beginning to answer. He looked and saw the figure on bended knee exposed and weak—not about to move on its own strength. It wouldn't do to just leave him. *No, I shall not forsake him.*

Carls was forced to resort to lift the man himself and place him beneath one of the overgrown aisles. He then stood, knowing all too well what was to come next. *They will come for me. And as of now, he can do nothing on his own.*

He took in a deep breath. Not to run, but to distract—that was the thought behind his next step.

Fatal Mistakes Have Fatal Reactions

The damp center opened up to a vast display of extravagant plants hanging from the raised ceiling. Across from the opening was a small pond being fed by an overflow of waterfall between two staircases that led to the balcony. Granite tiles were placed like checkers on the floor, and light filtered through the smudges in the window panes above. He could see where he had broken through the railing moments before when the illusionate had been his pursuer. And here again, he stood, the voices closing in the background. The ground as his confidence suddenly faltered.

It was more than just illusionate coming.

His nerves were at their ends again in search of a spot to hide. A pillar was all he could reach before the Fallen One leaped from the top floor down to his—the same one he'd followed into the place. Its roar of disgust vibrated the pillar to which Carls clung for shelter. His hiding was not good enough.

Giant arms swung around the pillar's side and down to where his body once lay. Carls ducked, rolled, and was now fully exposed in the clearing. *God, I need your help right now*, he pleaded, limbs shaking to the emerging beast. *I'm hopeless.*

The Fallen One had grappled with one of the gondola shelves, tearing a section off. It was sent ripping through the air as roots and dirt and shattered pots blanketed its shadow.

It wasn't directed at Carls Locke, though he did all he could to cover his face from the shrapnel. He turned on his heels—the beast roaring in despicable hate towards a new foe.

Carls tumbled backward. There, above the balcony, was an emanating darkness. Its appearance was void of solidification, but all the more defined by a black shroud of... something. No arms, no legs, no eyes—and yet it retained a sense of source (or head, as one should put it) from which the rest of it acted. It took no notice of the Fallen One's attempt to devastate. Instead, its form overcame its surroundings, bending them to its will. Any and everything was sent the creature's way (and yes, that meant at Carls' as well). He took a large vase to the gut, crashing him back underneath the second floor, terrified.

What on earth!

His mind was yelling at him to stop the pain, but he no longer had control over his shock-frozen body. He watched as the Fallen One bore the onslaught of inanimate objects, trying to counter with what it could. In a matter of seconds had the dark form (a Possessioner, as they were called) descended upon it, and the beast violently flung its body in all directions. The futile attacks showed its lack of full comprehension that it could not strike its opponent. It seemed to rage against the dark presence's representation, as though angered by its daring presence.

But all that was changed as the Possessioner lured the beast into the water—drowning it by its own attempts at wrestling the possessed liquid. It soon fell lifeless and face-submerged. The Possessioner was then left to Carls, who still remained motionless.

God, help me move!

It was all he could do to avoid direct confrontation with the blast of cold water sent at him. The touch felt as though being drilled by a fire hose—his skin cracked. *I can't win this*, he mourned as another shelf was torn from behind and sent knocking him into the open. *I can do nothing!*

But then he saw her—in the distance, just past the right-side staircase. His daughter.

"Joan!" he shouted out, a desire to protect suddenly sweeping through him. She could not hear him in the least, nor did she seem to notice. Her small, little form but skipped across the tiles—completely oblivious to that which surrounded her.

"Joan!"

The Possessioner noticed her too. And as if to gloat of its evil intent, it turned toward her, Carls still pinned to the floor by the torn-up shelf structure.

"NO!" he bellowed out, squirming to get his arms free. *God give me strength!*

His hands were free before he knew it, and not even knowing what he had drawn, he held, outstretched, a single card. "Dare you touch her!" his lungs cried. The card sparked and quickly caught ablaze, soon scorching the air above and then everything around it—including the figure of a man attempting to free him of the weight bearing down upon him.

It was too late to stop his actions.

The same man whom he had saved not but moments before now tumbled backward, body in flames. Carls' fleeting efforts to reach the man were helpless and exhausting. He could do nothing, for the weight of the shelf still held him. He could only watch as everything around him burned—even his eyes drying up, the moisture on his skin instantly evaporating. He looked to where his daughter was, just hoping it hadn't reached her too...

She was no longer there, and neither was the Possessioner. "Joanna!" he wept aloud. *Joanna... where are you?*

PART II

DESPERATION

"We are simple-minded, our race, and will fall for anything so long as it fits our vision. And that vision can be ever so manipulated and controlled that, without a growing conscience or pursuit of understanding and purpose, we become a slave to it."
-Mike Dyrdrik, In Search of Life's Mysteries

To Hear Her Sing And Feel Her Breathe

His body could barely move, but he crawled from beneath the gondola shelving nonetheless. He pulled himself up against the small ledge of the outlining pond from which steam still arose and filled the air. What had happened, what he'd done, and where he was were all but a blur to him as his eyes strained to see around the curve of the stairs to where his daughter had been. Had he acted foolishly for her: taking another life that he might secure hers? He looked back to the smoldered remnants of a man that had once been—who had tried to save him, and yet his rescue had brought death. Hands still burning, Carls dared to venture his palms to the water's surface.

He jerked away. He cared not to wash his stains in the blood of his foe—for there still lay the Fallen One, its body seeping of strange liquid (resembling that of tar). The rough skin had melted into streams, revealing the flesh of the prey buried deep within. It too had once held a separate entity. For some reason, he felt pity for the destructed life. And he felt remorseful for the life he had taken of one just saved from illusion. That and he felt bade to the pursuit of his daughter. *She is* still *alive, and I must find her.*

To his feet his body rose. Every muscle twitched from exertion, but his mind was too occupied to tend to his body's plea for rest. Joanna was his first concern. But where? *She could be anywhere in this place*, he told himself. He came, with feet that staggered in pain, to stand before the staircase leading up the balcony. Before him, ash-like stains spread across the flooring. Or rather not as much as stains but steps. *Steps? Had someone carried her?*

Had someone stolen her?

His mind pelted him with a million questions. First and foremost being if his daughter was even aware of the nightmare.

He still thought of his wife. How she had failed to realize until it was too late. How the bar had pinned her head of innocence just in front of him. How he'd been helpless to avenge her against the monster. How he'd ran.

And yet how he lived. How he breathed.

He closed the thought—a tear streaking his face. *I will find you, Joan. I will find you, and I will never let you go.*

His hands felt down to the remaining card he had still in his pocket. *Trust Seal of Bondage.* Just the idea of using it stirred nausea from within him. Instead, he focused his attention on the clearing just beyond the eastern entrance to the Hanging Gardens. The steps were fading even more, but he at least knew them to leave the gloomy atmosphere of his more recent tragedies.

Carls Locke stumbled across the vast space of two halls as he passed from the Hanging Gardens onward to the large poster plastered atop the opposing wall. He felt nimble and exposed; tired and alone; worn but cold. Throughout the distance, he could feel no breeze and hear no sound. His legs but dragged. He longed for her—his family. It couldn't be helped that a man be broken when his heart is ripped away from him and put on a chain. Only, he had not the slightest idea as to where the chain led. For some reason, he felt tugged to simply press forward.

The poster hung loose above him now, his eyes straining to read: *Life can only be lived once, so you might as well live it UP.* He could tell by the signs and displays afterward that he had entered another district of the grand mall. Deserted but packed in likeness of a city market, only with bars and gambling holes. He knew not the name of the place, only that there, off in the distance, was a small shape moving toward him.

And then the sound. *The soft, gentle ring of melody*—a faint strain of momentary hope. He stopped, heart pounding, eyes wetting, mind trying to put it all together. The voice came closer as he began to notice the form running towards him. Not in panic, but joy. His fingers sweat, knees dropped steadily.

It was his daughter. Or at least the flicker of light to her child-like eyes made it seem so; her hair waving in the motion.

Breathless. The singing penetrated deep into his swollen ears. *Joan*, he called to himself, then in a whisper—his life on hold. And as she came within his breast, he reached out to embrace, eyes springing open, breath exhaling in a deathly plea. Her figure fell through his, his embrace empty to the hallucination his mind had fooled him with. The hope was shattered—

And he screamed. Thoughts of doubt and grief flooding him.

He had given everything, but what for? What ends did he have to strive for? How was he to know any hope still remained? What was he even fighting for? Himself? Survival? Or his family?

The small halls and hidden passageways of the district echoing with his pain soon fell silent. *I am alone and forsaken in this place. And why so, oh God? Why all this pain? For what purpose am I supposed to struggle toward? Is there even hope for me at this misery's end?*

Something flashed past the corner of his eye, and he turned, catching a glimpse. It was a cart (and not just any, but one resembling that which he and his daughter had seen). Carls felt a sense of calmness sweep through him. Was he to follow? Was it a pursuit that had answered him or to simply leave him stranded? His mind lay broken, but his will drove him again to his feet. What *was* he fighting for? Answers? At the time, the only thing he desired over his life was that of his family's.

I can't do this on my own strength, he told himself. *So give me something worth fighting for. Give me hope and lead me to her.*

Is She Truly There? (The Tapes)

The cart had disappeared behind the bend before Carls could reach it. Bodies lay limp in the corner, almost unnoticeable in the darkness. They were deceased but still warm. He hesitated, making sure it was clear elsewise. Slowly, his footing made the curve and he knelt beside the forms. There were four of them: three men and a lady. Two lay folded at the end, the girl lying on her back, the single man bent over his own body—a tape nearside his hand. Carls withdrew it and examined.

It was not typical. Though a tape, it seemed it could play itself. *A tape recorder of sorts?* Atop it were switches to which he could maneuver its content.

The tape reeled. *"Is she okay?* (a man's hurried voice came) *Praise God we found her before they did! Her innocence is still trickling; thus, it is safe to conclude her eyes have not yet opened. We're in time...*

(A feminine voice interjected) *"Chase, I think I heard something! I think it's them!*

"I can hear them too, they're getting closer. Let's get going to Revail Flats. Fidious, you carry the girl. Mark, help him keep straight. Trena and I will pull up the rear, quick!

"Revail Flats? (a second man inquired) *Isn't that a bit close to* them?

"We have no time! That's the last place... (the record buzzed) *... should be there, I hope.*

"Isn't it a little late to be 'hoping', Chase? (another in the squad asked) *"There's no time to squabble, we have to—"*

The tape clicked—Carls gazing at the wall. *Her... was it his daughter?* He studied the tape once again. Along the back was etched the company's name, *Mx3*, and faintly beneath it, their motto: *"Putting to memory what matters most"*.

Revail Flats. He was determined to find the place. Whatever had happened, whomever they had found, was now in different hands, and all he could speculate was that they were in the hands of a greater evil. And for now, daughter or not, it was his only lead. *Please, God, let this be her and keep her safe.*

He pushed through the narrow walkways and crevices of the district. In the pockets of one of the bodies had he found an overly detailed map with markings too numerous to make efficient use of. Nonetheless, he pursued what he presumed to be in the northwest direction.

Revail Flats seemed to be crammed in the middle of a puzzle of winding passages and interconnected rooms. One thing was sure: the theme of old-town multipurpose use of space was evident. No life, but proof of existence was everywhere—from food stands to cold drinks and open bars. Glasses left half drunk, plates unfinished and molding. Guitars and instruments alike were still lying where they'd last been played as though waiting for return.

He had no time to ask all the questions, he only proceeded as best he could through the once busy display of a care-free existence. For some reason, no illusionate walked these parts, and he took it as something to be thankful for. *But why not?*

A lamp flickered against the sheet of an outstretched tent. It hadn't taken him long to notice he was completely lost. In fact, he'd begun to take notice by the fourth right turn. By all accounts, he should have been going in circles, but nothing was familiar, and he had no sense of the poles. Instead, he stared into the flickering light which cast a shadow over a limp form. At first glimpse, he'd thought it an illusionate, but no breath emanated from the man's lungs. At his feet lay an overturned table, a drawing flung from its holding and items scattered over the floor. Papers were piled—a burn mark at their center as though in attempt to erase. He bent over to retrieve them, noticing the man's fingers unravel.

He froze, heart pounding.

The man pointed to the far end of an adjacent division from which a veil overhung the entry. Carls couldn't believe his eyes, let alone his ears, as the man's breathing hoarsely cut in and out and then stopped. The hand pulled in and shriveled up with the rest of the body. Just the fact that he hadn't been dead put an even deeper fear into Carls. Were they some kind of living dead? He looked back in the direction that had been pointed to, weary to follow through.

But he wasn't left with much more choice. A stool firm in his grip, he penetrated the veil. A cassette lay atop a centered table, bookshelves outlining the rest of the room. Beside the cassette was an old-fashioned block TV. It had obviously been hit and battered but held together nonetheless. Carls watched as the screen flickered as the cassette slid in, displaying a desperate man, his voice cutting in and out due to the damaged cassette:

"Time is /short. TAP can no longer help us /they're getting too mischievous. /must do it. Fr/lock .... /have to stop. As for these kidnappings, we can no longer /leave that to TAP. Andy Friedel is stepping up his game /have to as well."

The cassette ejected to even more curiosity. *Andy who? Andy Friedelock? Who was he? Who was anyone?* He looked to the wreckage about him. The man in the footage had resembled much of the man now shriveled up as though fighting the cold touch of death. As Carls reemerged from the tent, he tore off the veil and wrapped it about the shriveled form. He had no idea the shoes he was stepping into, but he now at least had a name. And the case seemed fresh enough to suppose the man, this *Friedelock*, still alive. But where?

With the veil down, he could see the entrance marked with words of comfort to his conscience—a location. Unfolding the map, he scanned frantically, finally finding himself.

He wasn't that far from Revail Flats after all.

It was less of a word and more of a symbol of where he'd last been. It was a 'z' with a circle around the top corner. What it meant, he had not the slightest clue. But he thanked God for the clue regardless.

Revail Flats looked as though someone had stolen an old-fashioned motel or apartment complex and simply placed it in the middle of a maze. A building within a building simply put. It had its own roof, walls, windows, and curtains. It was even stranger for him to enter into it and see the whole building hollow (of what should have been two floors above the entry level). Inside, his sight was limited to the orange rays of light that pierced through the ceiling. A dining hall of sorts; tables and chairs everywhere—all seemingly in order but the far corner table, which was turned slightly and had its metal chairs folded. For such a high-end "grand attraction", this place sure seemed to be the low-end hoods of the place. He maneuvered his way toward the corner, cautious to not make unnecessary noise.

In that corner, a small tile lay tilted as though removable. And he did just that: lifting it to uncover a small flashlight and a collection of broken cassettes and torn files (also having burn marks through their centers). But he noticed at the bottom there was a loose cloth hiding another compartment seemingly left untouched from the previous finder. Reaching in, he withdrew a small device bearing the signature of Mx3. It played a recording to his touch, the small screen displaying its previous owner, Echon Pfeifer: *"I can't believe he caught on so fast. It seems our insider has found second motives. Regardless, he'll be here soon, that Andy Friedelock. I gotta find a way into Friedelock Industries before he finds me. I heard that TAP was able to enter through the sewers. Too bad our communication with them went black. Oh well, I guess I'll try there next. ... In case I don't return, I'm leaving this for anyone who follows... hopefully not him."*

Friedelock Industries—that was where he had to go. Whether the tapes were linked at all or not, that was the only place he had to go by with hopes of finding his daughter. From his pocket, he pulled out the tape he'd first stumbled upon and found a slot for it to fit into. Instantly the tape reeled and the device played, recording it to its memory. Once again, he heard the conversation. *"Joan, I hope it's you,"* he whispered, pulling out the tape and shoving the new device, the Hand-Pal, into his pocket along with the flashlight.

Friedelock Industries

The sewer gate was not a preferable entrance. Even as he loosened the man-hole, he could smell the stench and flow of thick waste below him. Wielding a single flashlight, he dropped down, barely holding his ground in the fast-moving current. Had it been any higher than his knees, it would have knocked him right over; instead, he braced against one side and held the light to the other, pushing through the tunnel.

As he got deeper and deeper, he began to notice the scale to which such a place had been constructed. To be just a mall, such a sewage system seemed unprecedented. Why build a place so big and have it so twisted? Who had even built this place? What had happened? And what in the world was TAP? He shone his light along the side of the passage, seeing the three letters etched into the sludge. *TAP... why do they keep coming up? What exactly is going on?* The mystery of such a once-crowded attraction astounded him.

Carls Locke came to a dead halt. His passageway was met with another straight on, only the second seeming to be extensively deeper. He tip-toed to the edge to scout any means of crossing. There were none, but above him was a glimpse of a small chamber room. It was just high enough that he could not reach it by jumping. Two large pipes stretched across the wall in front of him, and a smaller pipe clinging above him with wedges and joints disappearing into the passageway beyond. It was impossible to even think of climbing such slippery walls to reach the chamber. There had to be another way.

And it came to him.

Wrapping his fingers around the thin pipe overhead, he wrestled to twist a section loose from its joints. He paid the repercussion but ignored the spew of stench. Taking the pipe, he wedged it between the two larger ones and pressed down. Using the fulcrum, he was able to get a footing on one of the loose ends he had undone and propel his way onto the next chamber. The clanging of his pipe trailed his success, and he observed the room in which he stood. Sure enough, an ascending ladder scaled the wall to another man-hole. He could only pray it was the right one.

The hole lifted to a lit hallway. The walls were white brick and the flooring concrete. Obviously not a tourist attraction, at least at this point. Carls climbed from the sewer and hesitated at replacing the lid. If he did, how was he to recognize it should there be more? He saw fit to leave it ajar.

It took his eyes a moment to adjust to the filled lighting of the place. It felt cool—not some damp chill as he had felt in the Hanging Gardens, but as though the air were actually being regulated. Vents steamed along the hall as it wound to the left and back to the right. Carls stepped cautiously but eager enough to know what such a place was. It wasn't far till he reached an open room and entered to see the likeness of science. Vials and tubes gathered dust from abandonment. Not as much from time, but the unregulated exhaust from the ceiling vents. Locke had to cover his face as he scavenged the room.

To his favor, a filing cabinet under lock and key remained cracked. He was able to pry it open despite the rust of the elements. Inside, papers of a language he cared not to decipher lay, and with them, a tape. Inserting it into his Hand-Pal, he listened as it recorded:

"Strange, is it? That a man could know so much yet be content with so little. The Big Man himself said that our research was sufficient, yet he always asks for more. Could it be he has something else in mind? I came here to admire a great work, not further it."

The voice trailed off in a murmur and ended. Carls pulled the tape back out and placed it into the filer. As if just Friedelock weren't enough, now this *Big Man*? His breathing was beginning to huff and he decided best to clear the room. Back in the hall, he was able to think over the tapes he'd uncovered. Up to this point, Friedelock was the focal point. But now... now it seemed as though a simple task of reconnaissance was turned into a scientific anomaly. He was no scientist, but he had a feeling that before this was over, he would have at least tasted its role in the bigger scheme of things. After all, such a turn in events *always* had a tie to madness, and who better to ruin than a man who thinks too much of his work—a scientist.

The sudden spurt of sound sent a pulse throughout his body as he spun on his heels. It came from every which direction. The laughter, the voice.

"Ha ha ha, welcome Stranger... or are you?"

He saw the COMM system on the walls (their white blending in but shapes protruding).

"Yes, I saw you peek your little head through that sewage hole and sneak your way in here! Did you really think it'd go unnoticed? The question is: why have *you* come here? It seems you act off ignorance, not some cult. If that the case, then I welcome you as a guest! But if not, then there's use of you yet..."

Carls felt exposed as an ant atop a table of mazes and mystery. How was he to react in such a situation? Run? Demand? Harsh judgments lead to insecurity, and he couldn't afford to be acting outside of confidence. But how was he to find confidence when nothing he'd done yet had been of success? *God, help me*, he pleaded to himself.

"Come," the COMM interrupted again, "I have much to show you, Stranger." The place momentarily went dark before flickering on. Now, only a single path was lit, and he was inclined to follow it. *Now I'll never be able to find where I got into this place*, he noted to himself. *I just hope he's not someone I'll have to deal with for long.*

Two large doors poised at the end of the hallway with lights beyond them. Shaking in his shoes, he pressed through them, one hand over his face in case of toxic air (after all, what was he to expect?).

A Strange Stranger

Cylinders stretched across a vast open room. Not just any ordinary cylinders either. They bore a resemblance to tiny chambers into which a single body could be contained. Their shells were of steel, doors barred shut, so Carls had no way of knowing for certain what they held. Unlike the vast dark halls he'd at first roamed helpless and alone, this place cast no shadows, and yet he sensed every bit of it as being shady.

"You see?" the voice stretched once again over the COMM, "Feast your eyes upon the birthplace of success and be proud! No Stranger has ever before stepped past these doors and lived! Not to give cause for alarm.... Go ahead, feast upon the greatest achievements of man to ever be beheld! I give you... Friedelock Industries!

"Ha ha, but you can have none of it yet, nor shall I simply hand it over! There used to be days when man could walk my halls in awe and not detest to the atoms of which they breathed. But what of it now? Why only those who despise? Who's to say you are not the same as them—all here only to ruin my home? Let's test to see who you *really* are, Stranger. Prove to me your purpose!"

Everything flashed red. Buzzers were going off, and Carls found himself pressed hard to the cover of a near cylinder. He could hear humming from within it, suddenly fueled with second thoughts of coming to this place. Sure enough, he recalled nothing of warning to the force that pounded into his ribs, sending him toppling over concrete. His eyes shuddered. How was he to fight when he could not hear?

He couldn't move either. He was encumbered with fear. *God help me, please!* He screamed but with no sound; he kicked but with no movement.

Slow down, Carls. Breathe.

But, how could he? He had no time to slow down!

Just do it. Breathe. Concentrate on what's before you and take note of your surroundings.

Cover. Where was cover?

No, no time.

He flung his body to the left of a pulverizing fist (or the likeness thereof).

Counter. I need to counter.

He shoved an elbow beneath him and propelled to his toes in time to lunge above another attack.

Now.

His shoe dug into the hindquarters of whatever it was fighting him. He felt the resistance as the enemy braced and turned to grab his heel. Obviously, he hadn't been quick enough.

To say the liquid leaving his mouth wasn't blood would have been swiftly doubted—it being just as red as the lights that flashed about him. He'd caught glimpse of the creature he fought (that brief moment in which his back struck the steel of a cylinder, body then collapsing). It was smaller than the others, and yet still much larger than himself. It bore long, massive limbs in comparison to the rest of its thin body. And yet it stood firm, back hunched over, eyes shut tight to a reverberating roar.

A Fallen One.

He had no time to think of a plan as his shoulders were grabbed by a single hand and his eyes gazed into by dried out sockets and hoarse breath. He could lift nary a finger against it, so fragile in the arms of a foe so terrifying. The monster held him there, lungs choking for air, nostrils taking in every scent of blood.

He was running out of breath, and as his world seemed to be fading out, so did the creature before him. In but a drop of sweat mingled with the blood of his desperate position, he felt a sense of hesitation. The glimpse was so brief that in any other predicament he would not have noticed. It was in the same drop of blood that he tumbled. Not in attempt to hurt or kill, but as a result of being let go. And so he fell—his hands, face, and chest collided with the floor.

The creature reared in outrage as Carls barely clung to consciousness. It was at war within itself, raging over whose possession its body was. Not just that, but the entire being seemed repulsed of its actions yet forced to watch them. Had this too once been a man? What had overcome him? What had overcome this whole place?

It bellowed in pain and ripped through everything it thought standing against it (vials flying everywhere from overturned tabletops and shattered cabinets). And then it vanished—in its trace, sparks of electricity and fuming wire.

The sirens stopped. With the flicker of light, Carls could see the reflection of glass all around him. In particular, needle-point vials from a spilled kit. He managed to slug his arm to one of them, slowly propping his limp form against the steel he'd been forced upon. With vision a blur, he could make for certain none of its labels. But who cared? *I'm near death,* he thought; although it would have been better put scientifically: "Nothing ventured, nothing gained."

The needle penetrated his skin.

I can remember the last time I had a shot. My wife gave it to me. Being a nurse, I couldn't have asked for anyone better to do it. And so he dazed in memory, for a moment even forgetting his existence in the now. No weeping, just joy. He savored every bit of it.

His beautiful wife and adorable child.

His only child.

His angel.

"Little Joan," he whispered.

"Well, well..." the voice seized his thoughts. His eyes shot open, and mind made swift back to reality—to the white brick walls surrounding him and to the trickles of blood down his chest. It was the COMM. "Isn't it wonderful? How man has created such a euphoria so as to have means of stimulating the mind. Really, it's quite fascinating. Not only that, but look! It works, and you're a living testament to it!"

Carls Locke fought the desire to suddenly jump to his feet. His heart raced, fueled by some unknown force. He looked down. Sight restored, he could now read the vial. It was an e-Link, or rather a rehabilitation boost, not like anything found in a typical first aid kit. *Thank you,* he relieved, head resting upward against the steel.

The COMM hissed with momentary static. "Now, now, you seemed to have proved yourself. Not only that, but you're still conscious. So, rise, it is time I welcome you, strange Stranger.

Yet again, the lights on the ceiling blacked out except those leading to a single door on the far end.

The COMM came again: "I have to admit, I am looking forward to meeting you...."

Chambers Abroad

The door slid open.

Carls felt as though at a skit and he were the puppet being manipulated. His head was spinning from adrenaline waste. The injection he had taken proved to be substantial. What was it? Some sort of drug? *A stimulation*, the man had called it. *Stimulation of what? The body? The brain?* All he seemed to be doing was going with the flow of things and he detested it. However, it was all he could do. As for the e-Link, it was at least working. He could move when otherwise he'd be lying senseless. But was it a good thing? Stimulation or not, the body has its limits, and he knew he'd passed those an hour into this whole mess.

It seemed he was in an observational room. A large glass panel expanded the area to his right. Just beyond, a door hid entry to a second room looking adjacently into the glass. A figure stood there, hands behind his back, a gray tux and white shades. His hair was gelled (obviously making up for his aging complexion). To see so clearly, Locke was astounded to not have noticed the scene unfolding within the glass chamber.

The man without name seemed a bit surprised at his entry. "Oh, you're not who I expected at all. Regardless, welcome to my greatest accomplishment: The Age Capsule!"

He motioned toward the scene that had already consumed Locke's attention. A girl, no longer three, held the hands of a young man whom she loved. A teenage girl nearing twenty. His girl. *Joan...*

"Amazing, isn't it?" the man said to him. "She has matured astoundingly! Look at her! It seemed not but hours ago she was only three. Look at her smiling—"

Her smile, Carls wondered off. Obviously, she had found love in a stranger. But how? How was she so unaware of her surroundings? How was she so satisfied in a love disillusioned? Carls' hands reached out to the glass, eyes pitying his beautiful daughter—so deceived.

"You know her, do you not?" the man said. "Well, quite honestly, she's been difficult. Most would be swayed and laughing and dancing. Something seems to be binding her. It's prohibiting me from seeing the full results! Here she is—a testament to man's ability to manipulate the cell infrastructure itself! But she is unyielding of much else to me but age—oh, what's this?"

A third figure entered the scene, drawing up a gun and firing at the man near his daughter and then proceeded with suicide as poisonous fumes burst throughout the room. Carls' eyes shot wide open in disbelief and he pounded against the glass already too late. "No!" he yelled, the holographic bodies intoxicating his daughter. "Let her out!"

"Just watch," the man replied, "She cannot be harmed in this way." But Carls didn't have to wait in order to act. Even before the man could raise a finger, Locke had penetrated the glass in an outburst of desire to protect. The fumes entered him just as quickly. He managed to catch his little Joan as she fell—feeling, for once, something real.

The escaping air sounded the alarm. "Fool! Your act of ignorance will kill her!"

He ignored the remark. His skin was burning from the toxins and he knew hers to be as well. Shielding her head against his shoulder, he stumbled back out of the chamber and looked for the exit, but the place was in lockdown.

"Ignorant fool!" the man scoffed. "Come quickly before the gas kills you both!"

Carls looked to where the man had been—he was no longer there. His voice played over the COMM, "Quick! Through that door!"

A single green light directed him as he fled through it and into another chamber hall.

"Dad..." came the voice so tender (a calming breeze to his troubled mind).

"Hold on to me, Joan, I'm getting us out of here."

He found the next door to be locked. Spinning on his heels, he searched for another. "Friedelock! Let us out of here!" he yelled, not knowing who else to blame. It *had* to be him. This was *his* industry.

"Now, now, whoever you are, being as you've put the whole place on quarantine, this happens to be a lot harder than you suspect! I suggest you take this time to gather yourself and think over what you've done. At least until the quarantine lifts." The vents steamed. "Don't worry, this exhaust is not toxic, though it may taste weird. Just hold tight."

His breathing wasn't slowing down. All he cared about was keeping her safe. He found a corner and laid her against it, gently pressing the hair from her pale, dripping face. Her eyelids shook and heart trembled. "Hold in there, Joan!" he pleaded. But who could blame her for feeling so weak? For all he knew, her eyes were open and she now took in everything he had once panicked about as well. Her hands felt for his, palms soaking his dry skin. *God, please help her through this. Don't let her die. Not now, not here. Not like this.*

Carls held her close, not knowing what better to do than wait for the quarantine to be lifted. Something strange was occurring with his daughter. Her skin, covered in sweat, was shriveling. Why? He had not the slightest idea. Only that it was not ordinary. Then again, in a place like this, what was?

"So, you've noticed," the COMM spoke softly (at this point Carls had concluded it to be Friedelock). "It's only expected, you know. She *was* in an Age Capsule. What you're seeing now is the repercussion of your wild act to save her. See, in there, her every cell was being manipulated and tweaked. Inside the Age Capsule, one's body begins to rapidly adapt to an unprecedented pressure of pure science. The young grow old; the immature: mature; the defected: perfected—man is no longer bound by time and environmental consequences. Reality becomes only what the mind *needs* in order to live. Naturally, this allows for the injections of chemicals and currents that take hold over and motivate the body of an individual to process reality faster and differently. A desire becomes action. But not of the individual, rather their surroundings. This allows the mind to remain in a satisfactory state while the body progresses, rapidly, and the changes go unnoticed. *You*, however, completely obstructed that. I do not know how or why the scene that took place unraveled as it did, but she would have been fine if left in that mental state.

"But she no longer is in that state, is she? Now her body is fighting the reverse effect. Since being in that chamber, her body was forced to grow and mature (and she did that well). Outside, she has to fight herself as her body slowly begins to revert *back* to its last known state. All her memories lived inside her mind are discarded as simply a dream. Now she's waking up. And let me tell you, it sure isn't joyful.

"I don't know who you are or why you're really here. I only know that unless you do as I ask now, she will die."

Trust... after all this? "What makes you think I could trust you? You were only using her!" Carls remarked.

"Well, look at her. Is this something you could handle alone?"

He looked down at her. Her body was paler than moonlight, her face drawn out. She looked younger. Despite how slow the change, she looked younger.

His fists clenched and back hunched over in a surge of pain. *What's this? Am I also dying?* "Did the toxins affect me as well?" he asked, loosening his grip on the frail hands he held.

"I do not know why you suffer. It would be highly unlikely. But there seems to be quite a bond between you two..."

He could only bite his lips to contain himself from bursting. His body ached. "What must be done to fix this?"

"That's the spirit. Sadly, time is not a luxury for you right now. In brief, there is a serum that one of mine had been working on. It works, granted, but I only have enough for one—which makes it all the more valuable. I *would* just give it to you, but that's not fair at all, is it? In return, I need something. I would say a replacement, but that doesn't seem like an option for your type.

"Now, this same man also did research on another specimen, but it seems someone stole away with it before its completion. Bring it to me, and I will have for you the serum. To prove my honesty, you will find a vial at the far door. Take it and inject it into her. It is the same I promise to you that will save her, but only a small dosage that you may take me seriously about my request."

Carls heard a latch across from him as a slot ejected from the walls.

Inside was a vial, and he brought it to Joan's weakening body. In just moments he could see it at work—her face relaxing just slightly.

"I would get going if I were you. The serum you gave her won't last long. However, it is best you leave her here. I promise not to touch her in any way. In fact, I will keep her there until your return."

"I'm not leaving her in your custody," Carls responded.

"Oh, but you must. You wouldn't want her in even more danger, now would you? We have not the time to debate. Get going."

He was caught between two paths. *Joan, please keep fighting this*—his back hit the wall behind in response to a pinched nerve. He knew he was in no condition to bring her, but no mindset to just leave her behind. *I will be back*, he knelt down, kissing her forehead. "I don't want you to die," he whispered, tucking her into the corner of the only safety he could find her.

"Now hurry!" Friedelock ordered.

The quarantine was lifted.

Outside Friedelock Industries he could no longer hear the voice of Friedelock on the COMM. Instead, he felt the buzzing of his Hand-Pal as it picked up Friedelock's final words of advice:

"Good, you have a radio device, though I don't know how well nor for how long it will hold up, so let me inform you as best I can. The man you seek used to work under my name, but through many corrupted intentions, he was removed. Not by me, mind you. I was but attempting to counsel him in his misguided ways. He left in a fury, taking all his work with him—though it wasn't even his to begin with! Ah, and so he fled. I want back what he stole, it's as simple as that. What you do to obtain it is of no concern to me, just get it. The man goes by the name of Shaw Norwick. Find him and return to me what is mine. I will have the serum ready by then that your daughter might be saved. Last I heard, Philis Antoinette may know something of his whereabouts. You may find him at the e-Company—less he's started his own cult by now."

The signal dropped, leaving Carls to wonder whether trusting Friedelock was worth it or not. The man seemed twisted and yet also held the only key to his daughter's life. He hated the thought of serving his enemy; thus, he shoved the thought past him. For now, he had a job. For now, he was on a mission. *Find e-Company and find Philis Antoinette.*

But he couldn't help feeling he was only getting one side of the story.

Who was this Norwick? What had he taken? What exactly had he done? *A scientist gone crazy*, he guessed. Then again, Friedelock didn't seem too far off either. He didn't even know what Norwick had stolen. *Find Antoinette*, Carls reminded himself, hearing a faint clanging of metal off in the distance, a small reminder of the corrupted world he was in. *Some grand attraction—this place seems more like the end-line.*

He still had the map he'd found earlier and was able to locate the e-Company. It was all the way back across and beyond the Hanging Gardens (his last encounter there still fresh in his mind).

A second clanging reminded him to keep low. He hugged near the support beams of the second floor, running (as if to say) from cover to cover. He had no means of fighting. No weapons, no defense. He had to find something in case he encountered what he could not avoid. But where in such a massive place was he to even *start* looking for arms?

What was *that sound he kept hearing?* Whatever it was, it was lurking closer and closer to him, never losing scent.

Other Souls To Be Met

"I can't believe this place, my dear! It's like everything the world outside is crying to become! Oh, how I wish you could be here to witness the splendor of a true wonder!"
-Terrance Wilford, A Tourist of the Grand Mall

White lampposts scattered themselves amidst the vast hall stretching from side to side. Carls had once again found himself puzzled as to direction. One thing was certain: this place was to a scale he had once thought immeasurable by man. Across from him and to the right, an enormous pavilion extended from which hung diverse advertisements from food products to things strange as e-Links. What had happened to his place? Where was everyone?

Where was he?

A clatter beckoned his attention once more. *What IS that noise?* It was definitely from the hall to his left. *An illusionate?* It didn't matter to him so much as it was someone—something—that could help him find Antoinette. He stayed close to the walls and proceeded toward the distant clatter.

Stores were once again aligning everything. Stores, shops, restaurants, businesses—they all seemed once thriving with interest but now left to hum their attracting tunes without any listeners. Or at least ones that cared. He knew his wife would be entering every one of them, scavenging their shelves for antiques and watches. She loved watches.

The sign above read: *Peter's Wine and Soul,* and it was obvious this place had been once filled with drunkards. The place stuck out from everything surrounding it by its cabin-styled architecture and wood design. Classic wooden stumps were used at the efficiently placed tables. Sure enough, in the far corner next to the bar, a figure sat crouched over and grasping a beer with both hands. The old, rag-covered man moaned to himself, bottles spread across the floor beneath him. The clatter came once more. Carls saw that the man had been attempting to refill his cup.

His body was still shaken, but he realized this man to at least be sober of illusion (but at what cost he was soon to find out). He stepped inside.

"Are you... alright, sir?" he stuttered. What kind of question *was* a man to ask in such circumstances?

He wasn't heard.

"Excuse me," Carls said, cautiously venturing forward. The man seemed to catch a glimpse over his shoulder.

"One more step and that'll be it, boy," he said (his words suddenly backed up by the sight of a double-barreled shotgun propped against his chair.

Carls held his hands up to show no threat, but asked, "How are you not like the rest?"

"I was gonna ask the same to you," the old man coughed. "It was all because of young fellers like you anyways that things got like this, so scram!"

The cause? Did this man know?

The man was mumbling to himself again. At this point, Carls had lowered his hands. "Could I at least ask for a name? You wouldn't happen to be Antoinette, would you?"

"Psch. Name. You can't even respect a man's privacy having barged into here as if you owned the place! And you're asking for a name? Ha..."

His words trailed off. It was obvious his drinking was getting to him, but he ignored the fact and kept on, saying, "If you want to find someone with a name, then go look'n for Sherlin. He'll talk to ya, heh, he'll talk."

Locke could tell that was all he was getting from the man. He didn't even care to ask who Sherlin was or even if Sherlin was real. Something didn't feel right about the guy. He seemed burdened. Not by pain or suffering—nothing of the like.

The man's cup over-spilled as yet again he was left to himself.

Worn and desperate, Carls pressed tightly to the wall of a corner outlet.

He'd seen a figure around the bend. Coarse and frantic, an illusionate struggled to pry into a wall device, its limbs shaking in hunger. Carls couldn't blame it. Even in the condition it was in, was his much different? He had questions to ask, as did the illusionate have intentions to be fulfilled. Its head jolted up as in awareness of another presence.

But not his.

A scoff of air and it backed away, taking a second gander at the machine before tearing itself away and fleeing. Carls, of course, waited. He had not the strength to pursue, nor did he think it safe. Something had scared it off, and he'd do best to be wary himself. Instead, he inched closer to that which the illusionate had been fiddling with. The protruding device bore resemblance to an ATM, only advertising something more bizarre: e-Links. It had seen better days, being as its contents were valuably desirable. Upon further notice, he saw an object drop loose from its hold.

He took the vial from the slot on the side of the device. The illusionate had shown so much interest in such a simple object as the e-Link he now held, hands of his own shaking around it. *Is this some kind of addiction? Am I to become the same as well?* he asked himself, recalling his first experience with e-Links. *But why had the illusionate fled?* He'd seen its face, *his* face. So eager. So driven.

The company title stretched across the length of the glass. Beneath it were faded words obviously smudged from the damage dealt to the machine. He held it in his hands, sweating and in pain. *A stimulation*, he reminded himself. *Nothing permanent, but something out-of-the-ordinary.*

An addictive substance. That would explain the expression of desperacy. But why then had it fled? Whatever it was, he could feel his body trembling from all the trauma. He'd never been put through so much before. Never forced to function whilst everything else cried otherwise.

He injected the serum.

The initial sting was nothing in comparison to the nausea that infiltrated his veins thereafter. He stumbled backward, head throbbing. *What's... happening?*

Then it began to clear in a queer manner. He felt a subtle flow of energy through his bones and flesh. His eyes widened despite being burdened for rest; he saw more clearly but lost peripheral. He now faced the adjacent wall, heart adjusting to the sudden influx—the vial clinking to the floor.

In silence, the illusionate stood. The same that had attempted retrieving the vial earlier. It looked depleted as though its entire life had now been emptied with the substance that now resided within Carls. He looked up at the figure, palms low so as to not startle the illusioned man.

The figure but stared.

Locke eased a foot forward the best he could to adapt to the adrenaline rush. *Now what?* he asked himself.

All it took was the span of two heartbeats and the figure was gone—a shade of black rushing toward him in its place. The cold substance clashed against his lower abdomen. It was fortune he had missed the support beam and instead skidded across the hard tiles. His mind was still trying to convince himself of what was attacking him when he took the second hit. Only adrenaline kept him conscious as he collided into the concrete block. It definitely was not what he had faced in the gardens.

Nor was it a Fallen One.

Its breathing was harsh, skin blacker than ebony, face void of identity. That, and the form itself seemed to be constantly shifting according to its momentum. The basic figure of a man, but it was not defined by such. Its head seemed to lash out at him from the distant stance. Carls thrust his body to the left, feeling the impact to his side—cold, sharp, and crushing. No bone, all muscle (or whatever the substance was).

He found himself breaking for cover behind the pillar he had at first missed. The gun was useless. He could only evade this desperate creature as it ravaged against him. Xavier's words were of no comfort to him either, and they echoed deeply. Once again had he fallen to a *tripper*—a holographic trap. But this was no previously faced foe. Indeed, the head of the creature cleared the curve of his cover screaming at him in war. The thud hit directly above him—black dripping everywhere. Carls looked up to see an arrow pinning the form to the pillar but only for a moment as it rearranged itself and peeled away, form now resembling a four-legged hunter.

To Carls' left stood another figure—this one sane. The man held a crossbow in his arms and a smile across his face. "I said scat!" he yelled, tossing a canister at the foe which resonated as lightning through the open halls. A shrill and the form dissipated from sight. The man but smiled, his eyes tight but somehow aware. "Stealing from my machines, are you?"

Carls looked to the puddle a black where the shade had once stood.

"Don't do it again," the mystery man said.

"Wait," Carls pleaded, still struggling with controlling his attention. *The drug, the tripper, the demon*—what was he thinking? "I need to find someone. Norwick, do you know of him?"

"That, my friend, is no friend of man or beast," he said, pointing to where the hunter had last been. "A Shem is what they are, and you do best to not play chicken with 'em next time, you hear? As for the man of whom you speak, I know not his whereabouts."

"Wait, please!" Carls said again. "I can pay if you want. I didn't steal it; it simply dropped into my hands, and I was desperate—"

"They, too, are desperate. There is no cost to you, just don't do it again. You'll just be look'n for trouble. Later."

"Sherlin," Carls cut in. "You wouldn't happen to know someone by the name?"

The man looked over his shoulder. "As I said, you're just look'n for trouble." And he left.

Carls Locke had thought it best to avoid another confrontation in the Hanging Gardens; thus, he had taken to the second floor. For the most part, it was silent. He tried focusing on the way things had been—seeing a faint illusion of his wife still wandering from store to store. He wondered if she had noticed it at all or had been just as blind as he was before the illusionate had struck him. Perhaps, in another's eyes, it looked all the same. Had he but crossed into a nightmare? If so, was his reality even real?

He stopped before a shattered display. The mannequins still bore smiles in their eloquent poses. Their clothes seemed stripped of the vibrant life they once held. Was he but seeing an illusion of what was? Was his reality still in beat with the one he had thought to be real? Was he a ghost?

Looking down at his hands, it was hard to doubt their substance. They felt dry and worn and even a little stained with the blood from his confrontations. His clothes suffered the wear and tear of countless poundings. The buttons of his shirt had ripped from their holdings— having once bound his movements. It was no longer white as he had once recalled. The jacket that he had shown with pride was no longer on him. He missed the warmth of it already and that of his wife's embrace. So smoothly had she brushed his face with her palms. So tender her voice had been, even amidst his trembling. So innocent her eyes to his battered form.

No, she had not seemed to recognize him for the state he was in. She had not seen the nightmare he had been awakened to; for that, he was grateful. *Her last memory was not tainted by fear or illusion. And nor shall mine.*

A faint tone emanated from his Hand-Pal. He adjusted its volume and signal.

"I hear you are quite the venturous fellow," came the voice of an old man. *"And that you seek a man by the name Shaw M. E. Norwick. I am Philis Antoinette. It seems you seek something the Big Man himself has desired for quite some time now. I may be able to help you there, but only for something in exchange. What knowledge I have gained was nothing easy to come across. I only hope you have what it takes to succeed where I did not.*

"As for Friedelock and me, we used to share many ideas—though I doubt you truly know anything about the man you are entwined with. He is more than Friedelock Industries, and Friedelock Industries is a whole lot bigger than you think. Regardless, I care not to reminisce over such pointless recollections. If you desire my help, there must be something in return. Do me a favor and swing through the Euphora Gateway and pick up some tarsh lilies before you come to me. Then we shall talk more. Face to face, man to man, eye to eye."

Something In Exchange (A Mystery)

Carls Locke had yet to convince himself he was capable. His feet barely managed to clear each step as they pattered across the stone tiles. He was being chased and had been since he turned off the last hall. The Euphora Gateway wasn't too far off now, but he doubted being able to reach there in time. He couldn't run forever, and he certainly was no coward when presented with ordinary situations. This, however, was different. What part of *ordinary* was a rampaging man withered and beaten, already having a chair to the back of his head, chasing after another human as for food? A mutant, one could say. Or simply a bold-tempered illusionate.

As bold as those he had encountered at Paradise Suites.

Carls felt the hands reach at his feet as the figure dove, yet again, at him. His face hit the floor, waist twisting so as to confront the pursuer. He freed a leg and sent a heel digging into the illusionate's face. For the third time, he broke its hold; for the third time, he escaped its rage just barely, and for the third time, he scrambled to his feet and ran.

The illusionate seemed four times stronger than he, but it balanced out in a loss of communication and understanding. Carls found his way through some shattered glass and into a woodwork store—the illusionate closing behind.

His hands grabbed hold of one of the displays, flinging it at the man. Simply enough, it was taken to the head, and the figure momentarily stumbled. This time, however, Locke decided not to run. He grabbed hold of another display and lunged it at his oppressor. It hit hard, and the figure dropped to knee.

But that didn't immobilize it.

For carelessness, Carls took a fist to his knee and before regaining balance he found another palm digging into his falling chest. He bore the impact as he hit nearside the wounded illusionate. *Wounded? He'd already taken a chair to the back of the neck! Nothing seemed to be slowing it!*

Carls reached for a near nightstand and flung it at his opponent's exposed abdomen. The illusionate guttered in pain, seizing the object and throwing it back. But Carls had already made it to his feet and leaped to the side, barely dodging the projectile as it crashed through yet another display rack. The figure neither wasted time in recovering itself nor in standing. It simply propelled its body as though a lion lurking for prey.

Carls Locke had found hold of a stool and also charged, pounding his every intent into the illusionate.

Glass shattered as the illusionate tumbled backward. Carls had met with more than enough force (having not only met, but overpowered his foe, stool locking its shoulders and now holding it against the broken display). Still conscious, the illusionate struggled to break free, but Carls held it there trapped beneath the weight of his stool. Its hands could not reach him, and its body could not twist from the wreckage.

It was helplessly pinned down.

He didn't have the luxury of taking an extra breath. He did notice, however, that this illusionate was different. The eyes were not bloodshot, skin not as frail. It did not bear the irregular heartbeats. Instead, its chest pounded with a sense of rage. External rage. The source of everything he saw seemed to be anger, hate—much more so than the confusion and madness of the illusionate. *Was it another stage? Were they all stages?*

His eyes penetrated into those of the ones before him. They were dark and cold, no longer wavering in doubt. It seemed forced to act. And though its actions could not be disregarded nor justified, Carls felt pity for it. His fight had not been with a man, but the demon that possessed him (or whatever it was that he had yet to find out).

"You are no illusionate, are you?" Carls asked the still raging figure which bellowed back at him. "No, you are not. You are something else. But what? What are you? Why are you like this?"

The sudden jolt in force had been unexpected. Carls' body was flung into the air as the beast roared below him, palms outstretched as though its inside were boiling and body being manipulated. And it was. A dark substance tore through the man's shirt as he gained another twenty pounds in muscle. Carls hit the floor still amazed at the transforming.

Of the soon-to-be *Fallen One*.

"You don't have to be this!" he yelled, hands sprawling to keep distance. The beast ravaged *everything* around it, its body untainted by the force that steadily overtook it. Its chest grew to three times what it had been (a miniature hulk).

Carls could not get through to it, and so he fled, feet once again skidding across shattered glass and into the open hall. In only a matter of seconds, the Fallen One had emerged and regained pursuit.

God, I don't know what these things are, but please save them.

He was relieved to see unfold before him the Euphora Gateway. He now had but to cross the vast open space in order to reach the only hope of escape he had. As if the mall weren't already big enough, the entrance of the Euphora Gateway was massive. It held the entire opposing wall in hard plaster. The letters were enormously lit and lampposts lined in front of it. *What was this place?*

He'd only the time to clear the revolving doors as he found himself freefalling—the Fallen One but a few steps behind, pulverizing its way through as though the doors had not existed.

What Are Tarsh Lilies?

His palms bled into the dirt in an attempt to raise his chest. Oxygen was dire. He could not feel his feet. Something about the air was burdening him—weakening his mind. Maybe it was from the sorrow he felt for coming short of expectation. He had let her down... again. Only this time it was on the last thread of her life. He *had* to find the samples. He had to finish Antoinette's work.

Carls Locke inhaled yet again as he thrust an elbow beneath himself for support. He would have to watch his step next time. To shake hands with a rival of his enemy secured no position as a friend—an acquaintance has no loyalty beyond the appointed task. It just so happened that Philis Antoinette was as twisted as Friedelock. They balanced each other out yet were never even.

One thing was sure, he was not in the least bit prepared for what his eyes were to behold. *There is no way this is real,* he told himself, gazing endlessly at the vast expanse of foreign land and mountains and waterfalls (even more astounding as they flowed upward). *Was this some kind of illusion or trick?* He didn't know what to think, only that the Fallen One had taken a fall to the bottom—a landing he was grateful to have not undertaken. Only a small ledge held him from certain death. But how had he fallen here?

He looked to his left and saw a massive plant scaling the cliff seemingly to its top. However, at the last minute it branched above and away (as though a bridge once led to it). *What sort of plant grows to such height?*

"Hi there," came soft words from behind, nearly jumping him off the ledge. He turned to see a girl in blue robes bearing extravagant yellow designs across her coat and blue markings on her bright face. Long, fine-lined hair hung across her back and she folded her hands before her. "I should welcome you to this place and apologize for such a forceful entry. So many things have been changing that not even I have had time to repair the bridge-once-golden."

"Who... are you?" Carls asked, quick to grip his side in agonizing pain. Nausea also had infiltrated him.

"Oh, pardon me for my rudeness! You're badly hurt—I can help." She smiled at him, kneeling to his level and touching his forehead with her palms.

For the strangest reason, he felt a wave of relief swell over him. Petals as bright as her eyes flew everywhere but he took no notice. He but inhaled the air that was oh so sweet to him.

"Do you feel better?" she asked.

He looked at her, scarred and clothes dirty but body healed. *Had magic taken place?* "Who are you?" he asked in return.

"I am Pamella," she answered with a smile and outstretched hand. "Come, let us get you off this cliff. The view is much more enjoyed when experienced."

"Wait, how—who—where... tarsh lilies."

"Haha, you must have so many questions! You look perplexed!"

"I happen to be. Nothing, and I mean *nothing*, has made any sense since... I can't even recall."

"Why are you here, Carls?" she asked.

Carls? "How do you know my name?"

She seemed to laugh. "Because there are only two of you who have entered as thus before."

"What do you mean? You look human to me *and* just as bizarre as everything else I've been encountering lately."

"Well, here I am known differently, and you are easily recognized as different yourself."

"Then what are you? A fairy? A witch?"

"Haha, quite the jump there! I am neither. My people are known proudly as Calnor."

"Well, you are the first to heal and not wound, and I thank you for that, uh—"

"Pamella. Now, shall we?" She held out her hand yet again, eyes focused deep into the valley below.

He stood, for the moment without burden, and hesitated. "For my wife's sake, I shall not," he said, mind still at peace to the thoughts.

"Oh, by all means, I respect you." And they were off (strangely enough). It felt nothing like flying nor falling. Blue rings lit about them as they passed through some vortex of... something. Before he knew it, he was on two feet again, she before him looking down upon a small town.

The structures themselves were simplistic but resembled extravagant huts united by pathways and wood fencing.

"What is this place?"

"This, Carls Locke, is Littlerut—the town below Waterrise."

"Waterrise? I take it that is where the waterfalls fell upward?"

"Yes," she smiled, "that is where. All our fields are blanketed by its clouds, and we are grateful."

Half of it hadn't even registered—the skies were filled with colors and streaks of vivid hues, and streams of silky wateriness flowed freely and independently high above him. Plants, shrubs, and trees alike were of quite overly-peculiar shapes and disproportional sizes. A fairyland never before imaginable.

"You said *tarsh lilies* when we first met. Indeed, they are beautiful remedies but hard to come across. If you wish to find some, the people here will be of help. But there is one you must first meet if you are to be welcomed here. Shall we go?"

"Go where?"

"To the Hall, where you shall be welcomed."

Even despite his confusion, they were off yet again—the world around him passing in wonder and attraction. *What is this place that everything is so unexpected?*

A City Within A Mall

He was led into the most magnificent hall he had ever seen (unlike those of man). The palace structure itself towered above the proud city of marble and marvel, but it compared nothing so spectacular as the Hall which led to it. Massive pillars arched overhead, and extravagant stones formed the walls between them. Streaks of green and yellow flowed across the floor and ceiling like veins giving life, warmth, and peace. A deep velvet carpet held the middle, running from door to door (that is, from where they stood all the way to a glorious throne of indescribable petrified wood, behind which lay the entrance to the palace itself).

"What is the meaning of this?" a deep tone reverberated from the man seated before him known as Keyno.

"The golden bridge lay broken upon his entry. It is only sensible we welcome him personally, my lord," Pamella answered him.

The man of great power pondered. "And who might this be to enter at such a critical time? We neither called him nor prepared."

"He—"

"Speak for yourself, sir," Keyno gently interrupted as Pamella spoke. She calmly smiled and looked to Carls (who, oddly enough, was on bent knee before their leader). *What feeling was this that resonated through his being?*

"I am here that I might save the life of my daughter. I seek a man that I know nothing about and was told to first come here before receiving further information of his whereabouts. Please, I was told to gather up some tarsh lilies in return for this necessary information. Her life depends upon it, though I would rather another way."

"You speak as the man before you, and I trust you to your word. We are at war here in this world, but I shall make one exception under *one* promise: that you return whence you came when your task here is done."

"I promise, my lord," Carls answered without even a thought. For some reason, he felt as though compelled to act on anything Keyno asked of him. *What is this power such a man wields so as to make one desire to serve?*

"Then give him his coat," Keyno commanded.

Carls saw, from the corner of his eye, a chamber rise, bearing the shimmering reflection of an ocean blue. Pamella drew it forth and stepped near him, placing it over his withered shirt (which he just noticed to be whiter than snow). As it touched him, he sensed a wave of unprecedented comfort and protection—as though he could jump into flames and not be hurt. This feeling, not in the slightest, faded, nor would it so long he wore it. In it, he found confidence; in it, he felt revival; in it, he had strength.

"I welcome you, sir Carls Locke, temporarily to our world that you might, in turn, save the life of your daughter and many more. Go now, take this coat and return to Littlerut. The people there shall welcome you with haste and aid you in your search. Go now, Pamella, and ensure he does nothing more until in their hands."

Thus, they left the presence of Keyno and stood outside the palace overlooking the expansion of land toward Littlerut. Carls had yet to accept it all. He but stared into the openness and into the light that shone off in the distance.

"Come," Pamella said to him with joy, "we shall not linger here any longer than necessary for many things have yet to unravel and your journey to begin. I shall take you to Littlerut."

"What is that off in the distance?" he asked, looking into the light radiating past Littlerut and beyond Waterrise.

"That is our light," she said simply (as though there was nothing else to it). To Carls, it seemed to be a lighthouse on land, steadily beaming across the entire landscape. They took off through the blue rings yet again.

The people of Littlerut were very well collected and simple-minded, yet aware of much more than they let on. A man wearing clothes of earth tones and a staff across his back came to greet Carls.

"Welcome!" he said with outstretched arms, embracing Carls with confidence. "We have been waiting for you."

Pamella calmly interjected, "He is not here as Karier, Topi. He seeks the tarsh lilies to save the one he loves. Do you have any with you?"

"Tarsh lilies? Ah! Yes, we have but two..." Topi seemed hesitant upon the words, though not showing it for long. He added, "If it is of utmost importance to you, you may have them and be on your way."

The words drew the attention of nearby townsfolk. They seemed surprised and spoke to their leader, "Topi, is it wise to give them to—"

"Hush," Topi assured, looking back at Locke and explaining, "He is with Pamella and a welcomed guest. However, if you would so desire, we could seek to find some of your own."

Carls knew nothing of what to say, simply turning to Pamella for an answer. She but stood there gazing back at him. "It is your call, Mr. Locke. What shall it be then? I could return you to your entrance rather quickly or later, but choose now."

They needed it, and he did not know why, only that it was of concern. But he needed it also. "Time is not something I have much of. Even as we speak, she grows weaker and more in danger. If it is at all possible, I would prefer to take them and be on my way."

A stillness held the air.

Topi took in a deep breath, "Then we will give you what we have."

"Sir—"

"Hush, Copi, I am aware. But we must help him. Now please, would you so kindly retrieve them for him."

"Yes, sir," the town's troop said, momentarily disappearing.

"Thank you, Topi," Pamella said.

"I wish these were different conditions, but we are honored to help you, Mr. Locke. Here," Topi said, handing him a folded cloth Copi had just delivered him. "Use them wisely. And you are welcome here anytime. The people of Littlerut wish you well."

Carls took them cautiously—absolutely unaware of the full repercussions.

He felt a tug on his hand and both he and Pamella vanished, just as quickly reappearing atop the large plant scaling the mountain. The bridge lie broken to the gateway—the shattered doors. Pamella stood at the plant's edge, peering down the mountainside with worry.

"What is it?" he asked, nearing as close as he would dare.

"Do you see it?" she said, stretching her hands before her and forming a rectangle (just as children would play picture-taking, only hers seemed to magnify). From where he was, he could not see through the haze of imagery she cradled. But he didn't have to. She smiled at his incompetence and expanded the rectangle that he might peer through it also.

And he saw.

"Did that happen to come through with you?" she asked.

"Yes, it is what chased me here. I was lucky enough to find that ledge—and you. I am sorry if this brings trouble to you. I did not mean it to."

"I only pray that it does not." The rectangle dissipated, and she walked to the fallen bridge. Holding out her arm, it began moving. Not just that, but the entire platform on which they stood rattled under her force. The blue lines across her face glowed, and her robes twisted and turned. He was breathless as the bridge steadily reconstructed itself.

"Tell me, Mr. Locke," her voice carried, "Who gave you that card?"

Card? His hand reached into his pocket, the memory flooding him. *The Trust Seal of Bondage.* She smiled at him—the bridge finished.

"Do you know of its power?" she asked.

"I know of their terrifying potential and fear using them," he answered her.

"Indeed, they hold great power. But if need be, you should use it and her pain be shared with you. It will not save her, but it may just buy you time. But it could very much as well mean the death of you."

"These *Hensers*—what are they?"

"They are gifts to not be wasted—as are many things in life. Was it a dealer that gave them to you?"

"If that is what you call a man with a white table, then yes."

His answer relieved her. "I cannot imagine what it is like for you to be experiencing all of this. It seems everything once known is changing and realities are colliding. However, they led you here, and from here you must return. Please, when your task is complete, return to us. I trust you, Mr. Locke, to the end. We all do."

He withdrew the single card that he had been given ever so long ago, its weight burdening his heart and mind. *Such power; such effect.* He looked up and she was gone, his world returned to that of which he feared. His spine shivered to the oppression of it all. Now what was he to do? It didn't seem that there would be a quick-fix to anything.

Holding the card before him, Carls began to utter its words in accordance with what the dealer had said to him. *It makes you responsible for the protection of the other, for its safekeeping. In return... you have its complete trust.* He only did it in hopes of sharing her burdens and lightening her pain. The card suddenly lit with colorful rays. Slowly, the warmth of its burning sparked, and it broke into a thousand pieces (each one forming, as if to say, a string that entwined itself and shot off into the distance). Instantly, his own body gained weight and collapsed to its knees. His lungs gasped for air and mind took the impact as nausea flooded in. *Is this what she felt like? Is this how she is suffering?*

He began to shake, the pulse of what had just happened still settling in. *I pray this helps, Joan. Stay strong. I'm coming back for you.* His sight started spinning, and his face hit the floor.

The Delivery (Gaining Leads)

A single candle lit the small room in which he stood. Red cloth draped over the walls and furniture. A leather couch to his left lay in silence near empty shelving. Both were wrapped in thick plastic.

The candlelight flickered.

To his right posed a door leading to another room—the door being locked. Beside it, another bookcase bearing miscellaneous books and pictures. *Yes, lots of pictures.* Portraits of various depictions held to the four walls. Most were blotted in cold red (as were the stains alongside the couch). His body drew closer to them, eyes peering around the curves of furniture to get a better look.

No corpse lay in its wake, only an overturned table stand. Not far from it was a shattered picture frame of a man. Beneath the smudge of neglect were a young woman and their daughter. Four letters etched across the child's innocence: *Dead.*

Dead? He left the picture there and walked to the shelves. A single portrait had caught his attention. One of a man holding a plaque. Beneath which were the words: *By what means does man strive to succeed from loss when all hope seems out of his reach? With this small step, I plan on crossing that bridge into blissfulness.*

The candlelight flickered once more. *Dying. Fading.*

He began observing the abandoned content on the shelves. He saw a single key nudged beneath a book entitled *In Search of Life's Mysteries* by Mike Dyrdrik, a philosopher. A note lay beside it: *"I am sorry, dear, but whatever has overcome him, trust me in that this work must remain out of his reach. I cannot express the sorrow I feel, but this message* must *be delivered to him clearly."* It was signed by *Andy D. Friedelock.* He pressed onward, reaching the door that yet remained unabridged. He stood there, raising the key he had found to the lock (a soft tone began playing in the background). *What could all this mean? Where was this? What was this? Who was he?*

What had actually happened?

The door unlocked and the candlelight died.

Carls awoke from the vision to a white-filled room with a sense of illusion and in desperate search for understanding.

A man spoke to him: "I have bestowed upon you all that I know of this so-called Shaw M. E. Norwick. You should know that this process was only possible while you were unconscious, so I apologize for the unfamiliarity of surroundings. You were, however, already unconscious when my... watcher... found you. Do not be alarmed, I did not drug you in any demeaning way. You retain full ability to act as an independent." Antoinette was in the opposing room, separated by thick glass. Carls himself lay bound to a cross-shaped restriction that supported him at every joint. Though his eyes still adjusted from a blur, he could see the mechanisms from which he had been injected and performed upon. Across all the machines he could make out the faint imprint of *TAP* products.

"Who are you?" his voice slurred at the man whose back was turned to him.

"I am Philis Antoinette as you already know. I am but an old, dying man bound to a wheelchair and lingering only to finish a very important research. *You* brought me the specimens I needed to continue, and I thank you for that. As for your coat, I have not taken it. It awaits you once our conversation is done. But for now, we talk. Man to man; face to face." At this, the man spun his wheelchair towards Locke, revealing the age that had betrayed him. His arms, however, remained functional, though thick they may be—the rest of his body being bound to his chair due to an inability to act alone. Large glasses shone through the barrier between them. "I only hope you are ready for what is yet to unveil, my friend."

"What have you done to me, exactly?" Carls reiterated, his bare chest pounding to refill his body with depraved oxygen.

"My apologies. To keep you in stasis I had to manipulate the oxygen intake of your cell. Don't worry, it will pay off. You'll understand."

But he didn't. All he could think about was the vision he had experienced—the room and portraits. *The blood...*

"You said your *watcher* brought me to you. Where is he now? And why not send him into the Euphora Gateway? Why did you need to use me?"

The man coughed his laughter. "Such desire. You only ask in fear of a cult you were falsely worried about, am I not right? Friedelock wanted you to think I posed a threat, ha! I tell you the truth: I am no threat to those I trust, but you break that trust and I shall break you." He wheeled his chair back to his observation desk.

"So, you are an enemy of Friedelock?" Carls inquired.

"Friedelock... no. But his industry, yes. His research astounds me, and I, in fact, desire his remedy. But with that I would have to accept his means, and that I shall not partake in. He remains only as a tool. Not of mine, but one of darker intent than he. There is something you should know before getting into this. It is no coincidence that none have yet recovered Friedelock's stolen work, as you shall soon find out. And there is also much more to this reconnaissance than you could have ever imagined. Take caution in your steps, my friend, and heed my words. Your eyes are still but opening to what lies beneath. Do not overstep yourself else you be swallowed up like the rest. The illusions are powerful. Do not think you are yet free of them."

"You understand what is going on here?" Carls asked.

"I only wish to. But no, I know nothing of the big picture. I only care to finish my own work before my time ends. When our relation began, I told you I would need something in return, but I have found out we desired the same thing: Norwick's serum. Although, you could have done differently. I have to admit, I am surprised that you brought *them* to me when they could have just as easily healed your daughter."

What? I held the cure all this time? I was tricked? "Why did you use me?" Carls suddenly demanded, and sense of abuse infiltrating him. He still felt her suffering in the distance of his mind. He still felt her need.

"As I said, we seek the same serum, only for a different purpose. And I have chosen to give you the serum fully in exchange for the plants."

"She could be better now, and I'd have avoided all your politics!" *How could he have been so foolish?*

"Now you listen to me, young man. More is happening here than you, your daughter, or *me*. And if you could only care about one thing: *do NOT make it a possession*! She is ill, I understand that. But I also take it that you have already bettered her chance of living, am I not right?"

The card.

"So please, don't go hating me when you do not understand the full repercussions of it. I know you love her. But for now, she is safe. Friedelock can do nothing to her so long as the watcher is looking over her. You have already left her once, so it would be best you not return to her empty-handed. There is much work to be done. As for the whereabouts of Norwick, I have sealed them within you already. All you must do is seek them out as they come and gain an understanding as to where they lead. Remember my words and heed them well. I cannot afford to lose you. No one can."

The bindings let loose and Carls' bare feet slid onto the floor. The oxygen had returned to him and the door opened. He reached out for the coat and felt its warmth about his body—mind questioning Antoinette's true motives. Of anyone's true motives.

Even his own. *If you could only care about one thing, do not make it a possession*, Antoinette had said. To him, his daughter was no possession. She was only the *only* thing he had left worth fighting for. *I am coming for you*, he said to himself as he followed the lights out from deep within the e-Company. *I will yet get you that serum.*

Just A Little Deeper

He remembered the room in which he had been. The candlelight still flickered in his mind; his body poised before the opening door. *But where? Where had it been?* He reached deeper. It was there. He knew it. A name, or location, grained upon the wall or an overlooked portrait. *It was near the sciences; it was near Friedelock.*

Mike Dyrdrik. A philosopher and writer. He *had* to have answers or at least another clue. But where? If only he had looked into the book! It would have a location or something of more use. *I have sealed them within you already... you must seek them out...* His eyes closed; his lungs began to calm as he steadied the thoughts and relieved the scene.

The portraits, the red, the flickering, the plaque, and, finally, the shelf.

He moved toward the shelf, observing its abandoned contents. Beneath one of the books, he had found the key. The book had been entitled *In Search of Life's Mysteries*—a work by a man known as Mike Dyrdrik, a philosopher. He grabbed hold of its withered binding and sifted through the dirtied pages (all of them wrinkled and worn). A smudge of ink caught his attention mid-way and he shuffled back. Chapter eight was entitled "The Luxury of Not Knowing, and Dreading It".

"We are simple-minded, our race, and will fall for anything so long as it fits our vision. And that vision can be ever so manipulated and controlled that, without a growing conscience or pursuit of understanding and purpose, we become a slave to it. Indeed, it would only take a fool of convincing measurements to distract us. So long as we are in terms of agreeing upon the facts, we tend to become blind as to their potential...."

He turned to the book's front, its title and author all passing in vision and he focused in on the small imprint at the bottom—everything around him blacking out and words quickly fading.

Mx3.

His eyes opened. What did Mx3 have to do with philosophy? They were a technological branch, weren't they? The same ones that did his Hand-Pal. But there was no such place labeled on his map. Without it, he had no idea where to start. He needed answers. He needed to talk.

He needed an *illusionate.*

Boulevards, posters, and shops lay in wreck down each hall he wandered. If he was to get any answers, he needed persuasion. Running wasn't doing him any good, and he felt a sense of calling to bear such a heavy burden. He was determined to do everything in his power to save her. Wandering the vast emptiness, he stumbled across a woodworks store. He couldn't help the recollections. He saw the craftsmanship and he saw *her.* The thoughts fueled his veins, and his fists clenched. *No more running, Locke. Your cowardice ends here. It ends now.*

He stepped inside. Not to delve deeper into memory, not to trace her every predicted step, but he moved toward the back where a door resided. Something was drawing him in. More than instinct; stronger than intuition. His feet moved across the splinters and shattered glass of abandonment. Carls pressed against the rear door and slid in. A fluorescent bulb lit the room brightly (an odd trait for what he was accustomed to). All along the four walls were shelves and shelves of merchandise—and by no means woodwork. It was bits and pieces of tech and machine parts to which all once had purpose.

Someone's obsession.

Someone had sought refuge and accumulated an arsenal.

A custom-made, single barrel gun lay between two racks. As though all its pieces had been thrown together in a post-apocalyptic manner, a gun nonetheless. Its barrel extended just shy of two feet. Its handle was of antique bronze. Four adjustable nods followed the length of the barrel and a single insertion chamber held to one of the sides and a latch to the other. Dark gray. He reached down and picked it up, fumbling to its weight and proportions. A strap was also attached to it for carry. Small enough to manage with one hand but big enough to maintain a force worth reckoning. *So, he'd found a gun, but where was the ammo?*

A small letterbox rest upon the top shelf of one of the storage racks. It was clunky to his touch, but the lid slid upward in relief.

Six shells, a small sack, and small book. The shells, thankfully, were indeed meant for his earlier find. The sack contained a vial of black. No label. No description. The small book weighed at least ten pounds and neither opened nor held any words. *Almost as though it had petrified.*

Leaving it, he stashed away the vial and ammo and emerged from the room, the loaded gun slung across his back.

"Look at you now," said a figure before him. *It was Xavier.*

"I still remember what happened last time," Carls replied, implying on the illusionate lured in.

"Don't worry, I'm not here to waste your time, only offer you a bit of help."

"But they're still coming, aren't they?"

"And isn't that what you want? Regardless, I thought it necessary to inform you of the task you are undertaking. You spoke with Antoinette, didn't you?"

"You either know or you don't. Why are you really here, Xavier?"

"If you plan on saving lives, a bullet to their chest won't do anything; but if you plan on escaping death, just talking won't get you anywhere. It is no coincidence you were led into that room. That gun that you hold is no typical arms. It belonged to a man by the name Isaac Clenneton, and he died to keep it hidden."

"You're telling me to leave it?"

"No, but be wary of its significance. It was made for a specific purpose—one closely related to what you soon shall meet."

A distant patter was heard.

"They come for you, Carls. Prepare yourself and remember your true intentions for fighting. Remember the reason you *can*."

Can? What did he mean?

"Go now," Xavier said to him, "And find the man you are looking for."

"Wait... where can I—"

It was too late. Xavier had vanished, and the illusionate were only getting closer. Carls had cleared the shop and started in their direction.

The Run

He didn't know the whereabouts of Mx3, but he knew BrainWare and maybe it would be there as a branch corp. Either way, he at least needed a direction to start towards. Xavier's words still welded into his mind of the illusionate pursuing him. *I can't take them all on anyway. I need to find a way to separate them. I need a trap.* But what kind of trap could he use while on the run? All in all, things weren't panning out in his favor. But still, he ran. *I'm ahead of them, and that's all that counts for now.*

He reached the foot of an escalator, deciding quickly to take it and claim the second floor. Directionally, he knew only to hold to the main hall he was already on. He hadn't the time to look too intently over his course of procedure. The BrainWare Corp was just beyond the bend and the last extent of the hall—or so he hoped. His feet moved briskly and heart pounded in his chest. He could feel the added weight of his weapon but chose to endure it. It was for the better. He wouldn't let himself face another Fallen One without it.

But there was another burden he felt. One deeper than anything he had known before. Faint, but ever so persistent in its growing. At first, he was not certain of its source (for it was so queer an emotion), but then he remembered. He'd used that card and supposedly it had worked. Whatever it did, he could only pray it was lightening her load. He couldn't bear the thought of her suffering steadily bringing her to death.

No. He could not live with that thought. He wouldn't live with it. So long as he had lungs to breathe, he would do anything and everything to keep her safe.

His foot caught the rise of his energy dropping. He momentarily staggered in movement before regaining speed. *Where am I going? I can't keep this up forever and I sure as well don't know where I am going. Left. When in doubt, always left.* The last thing he wanted was to be running in circles.

I can hear them, they're getting closer. So, what now?

He looked to either side of him for options. He needed a count. Too many and it wouldn't be worth it. He was no superhuman, and they were no dummies. If anything, their chemical imbalances made them stronger. But in all sense of the word, they were overcome by the illusion, he was not. And that gave him just enough of an upper hand so as to have hope.

But he had to lose them. All of them but one. Fighting the lack of fitness, Carls spun hard on his heels and into a bookshop—where it was cold and dark. Either a smart or terribly bad idea.

Taking cover behind one of the shelves, he waited for one to pass, quickly shoving the hilt of his gun to the back of its head. The young figure of a man slumped to the ground. So much for stealth, now the rest knew where he was. The cries pierced his ears as he tore from his position and at another wandering illusionate. The two met head-on and sent books crashing. Carls fumbled for his gun as it had been knocked away, his eyes still adjusting to the shadows of his residence. His palms felt the grip as his foe met the metal—tumbling backward into the dark. Were there still just two? Had he lost the rest?

He regretted asking. For as he did, the conscious illusionate let out a bellowing cry of outrage. It began slamming into the aisles of books on either side, hands held tight to its forehead. He'd seen this before. He remembered the last one that had screamed from some pain within its mind. Only this time, cries called back to it. More were coming. *I have to get out of here!*

Shuffling to his feet, Carls' made a break for it. Illusionate or not, he didn't have time to sit around and wait. But as he broke the cover of shadows, he came to a halt—at least six more appeared in the distance. His mind yelled *"Shoot!"* but his heart spoke otherwise. He couldn't in good conscience kill another human being. Not unless it was justifiable. Then again, his life depended upon it. Xavier's words repeated like strikes of lightning as two more fell to the pull of his trigger. *I'm sorry,* he said to them. More so to himself, for he didn't know if they'd understand.

I'm just trying to save my daughter, then I will come for you.

The rest seemed to scatter, and he took the chance to make a run for it. Sure enough, he was relieved to see the BrainWare Corp just around the bend. *Thank you, Lord.* Now, to find where exactly Mx3 was. If even in this building at all. Or if the place even had any connections whatsoever to Shaw M. E. Norwick.

He was in before they had noticed, his heavy breathing filling the vacant room. Bent and gasping, he collected himself and took in all that lay inside. The place seemed still in use but void of staff. There had to be someone. It didn't seem right for everyone to just vanish into thin air. There were the illusionate, but not everyone had ended up as them. The group he'd found way back was testament that he was not alone. *What made them different?*

His hand slid across the smooth countertop of the front desk. Still clean; still used. *But where is everyone? Why only a few? And why only the acclaimed?*

He pressed against the counter. It was as real as anything. He definitely wasn't living in some fantasy. He could smell; he could see and touch and hear.

A faint melody played in the crevice of his mind. Someone was here, and he was determined to find that person. He found it queer that there were no computers or phones. Not but a single pad held the counter's surface (an obvious product of BrainWare). It was open to a spreadsheet which displayed names and appointments.

Mike Dyrdrik. His name took the bottom of the list. He slid his fingers to the second page. The name appeared again midway through. The appointee of both was anonymous, labeled only as Mister. It appeared again on the third, fourth, and fifth pages—all to the same room, the same man, each about two weeks spread. Maybe it was Norwick, he could not tell.

Behind The Curtain, Another Layer

Third floor.
Second right.
Fourth door on the right.

He stood before it as though some detective in pursuit of a mysterious victim. Or as prey. It was altogether unknown. He reached out to the handle, eyes blinking back to where his vision had last left off:

The door opened up to a balcony centered around a magnificent chandelier. Pews, all emptied and bound in plastic, lined the bottom. His attention turned left and down a narrow stairway where he was led to the open chapel. A podium held the front stage which was elevated by two steps. A church? A small one perhaps, but it resembled more of a banquet hall. Flowers, all dried up and shriveled, still clung to their dusty pots. He moved on up to the podium. A book lay open upon it. It was the beginning of a new chapter, but even as he tried to read, his surroundings suddenly came to life—a man standing where he stood, looking out over the filled pews. The faces gazed blankly at him, and instantly he noticed the single figure approaching the back and taking his seat.

The man at the front was none other than Mike Dyrdrik, his enthusiasm radiating to each and every ear. His words were music and yet a blur. The crowd dispersed, and soon the two stood alone in conversation.

Dyrdrik and Norwick.

Carls caught himself in the nick of time (having nearly fallen through the open door). His face lifted as he beheld the small office room and realigned himself with reality. He hadn't been able to make out their conversation. Only the expression of a matter being urgent. A philosopher, yes, but also a counselor. That, or a trusted friend. But what would Norwick have with a philosophic writer?

The nerves in his spine pinched to the scene unveiled before him. Behind the single office desk slumped a figure in his chair, long since moved and with two bullets to his chest. The blood stained the man's formal clothes. His name tag was barely readable, and the title upon his desk scratched over in red. The two names conflicted, but the red claimed Shaw Norwick.

Carls took in a deep breath, the level of threat increasing in his mind. *Norwick? Wasn't this the philosopher's office? Wasn't Norwick the one meeting with him?*

The door closed shut behind him. Now his mind was playing tricks on him. He did everything he could to fight the panic, his body dropping low to the floor. *If this indeed was Norwick, then where's the evidence? Or did Norwick do this?*

Too many thoughts, Carls. Focus on the task.

He could see the shadows of two figures beneath the door's crevice.

Better yet, think of how you are going to get out of here.

The figures moved. Not in, but away. Carls wasn't going to take any chances. He held close to the cover of the desk and waited.

Then the lights went.

In the moments it took to adjust, he had already heard the breathing. Not of his own, but something else. But it was too dark—everything was dark. He could only make out sounds and tension as he was forced to cling to any bit of human sense he had. His breathing was also escalating. *Was this some sort of trap?* He heard feet shuffling down the hall. In a flash the lights came back on as a figure burst through the room door, eyes bloodshot. A young, terrorized lady. She was surprised at the sight of Carls and yet reached out to him as though for some pleading escape. *Escape from what?*

Black, silhouetted hands blotted out the light behind the woman and took vicious hold. She screamed in desperate attempts to grab hold of Locke. And for some reason he did not know, he wanted to help. Just as quickly as it had appeared, the hands had vanished—taking the lady with them. Carls only knew of one thing able to make such a powerful move and sudden appearance. It was no Fallen One, nor a Possessioner, rather a *Shem*—just like his encounter before near the e-Link machine.

But it was gone. He heard the distancing pleas as it fled the building. Carls leaned back against the desk, every inch of skin breaking sweat from nervousness. *I can't take much more of this*, he moaned to the ceiling. *But I will, if only to save her.*

He stood from the corner where he'd taken refuge. It was then that a small object lying on the floor beside him caught his eye. There, below the supposed *Shaw Norwick* lay a tape. He picked it up and withdrew his Hand-Pal, hoping for the best. With the click of a button, the tape unwound and his mind reeled and eyes closed—his mind once again escaping into the vision:

"It's too dangerous!" the man said, slamming shut the door behind him. "I can take it no more!" The individual's nametag read *Mister* (as from the records). Across from him was Shaw M. E. Norwick.

"Calm down!" Norwick replied to the man.

"That's easy for you to say! You didn't mention *they* would be after you as well. I grow weary and the Big Man is growing impatient!"

"If you break from the deal now, we *both* will die. Now, sit. Let us converse calmly so as to not raise suspicion."

The man took his seat and a second breath. He and Norwick looked much alike, both with a typical build of high-held shoulders and a raised chin. But the Mister wore a thick leather coat as though acting as some agent. His hair bore a darker tint; whereas, Norwick's shone orange in a lathered gel.

"What has changed?" Norwick asked of the man.

"Don't go all *counselor* on me! I'm the one who has the degree, remember that. You are in *my* chair because I *let* you."

An eerie silence befell the room. The two stared at each other until, finally, Norwick stood and paced the room. "*Growing impatient*, you say? Has he noticed? Has he sent them after you?" The man fumbled with a lighter between his fingers, withdrawing a cigarette from his back pocket.

"Yes, *impatient*. I just don't see how me being there is helping anything! He's a demon for all I care! Have you not seen what he's done to find *it*?"

"Indeed, I have seen. That is why you are there." Norwick lit the cigarette and turned to offer his guest one. "I need to predict the pattern of movements so as to ensure *its* hiding."

"You don't understand, do you?" the Mister refused. "With him, this affirmed he will stop at nothing. His circle is growing tighter, and he is beginning to notice those who are truly under his control. And there are now *others*..."

"Is that a problem for you, Dyrdrik? You used to be so determined..."

"You watch your words, Norwick. You may be playing as me, but they're getting smarter. My tail is about to get scorched, and it'll burn through your end too. His men won't be coming after my blood, it'll be yours that they'll savor."

"Threatening me won't help any," Norwick replied, a puff of smoke leaving his mouth.

"You just sit here atop all my domain and do nothing? I'm beginning to question whether our bargain is being held out on both ends. This isn't worth my life!"

"And I apologize that it has come to that, but we both are in too deep to start doubting each other. I'll tell you what. Go and lead them here. Give yourself the time to escape, and I shall end it with *me*."

Dyrdrik stood from his chair also. "Sorry, old friend, but I can't leave my family like this. They still wait for me."

"I understand," Norwick said, face downcast and shrouded in smoke. "But realize that this will ruin any chance you had recovering your business. And I apologize for that."

"I am aware."

"Just one more favor. When you leave, instruct my shareholder on what to do. They are not to have *it*, not even over my dead body."

As Far As The Blood Trails

"Anywhere businesses are thriving, conflict is always around the bend. Why is man so easily tangled is motives against one another? Why is it so hard for us not to find something wrong with the other? What ever happened to satisfaction of all and not simply admiration of self?"
-Shaw M. E. Norwick

The carpet beneath his feet hid each step—both his and his enemy's. He strode cautiously down the hall, his eyes more focused on memorizing the doors and turns in case the lights went out again. Despite having had the door closed on him, he wondered as to whether they had been trippers or actually real men. Be they real, they could be anywhere and capable of lunging out at him from any corner. Be they trippers, then he had all the more reason to fear. The place was tormented by a dark creature—a Shem. He recalled the face of the terrorized girl. Where had she come from? Who was she? Why was she there?

And was she just a trap?

Either way, he couldn't focus on her. He had to concentrate on his surroundings and the keeping of his body under check. He was ready to react at the slightest sign of danger. For one, the melody still played in the background. Or was it a melody? As he wound his way back to the staircases, the sound steadily grew. It was a repetition of words, simple but dark, and was sung oddly. Almost as though by a child. He couldn't bear the thought of a child living in such darkness, eyes open, alone and on the run. He wondered if his daughter knew. If she had been exposed to this new reality at all or not. He prayed she hadn't. Not yet, not now. Her suffering from the reverse effect of Friedelock's dirty work was enough for him. He could feel a rise of tension as he began to doubt if the man even carried the cure or was to be trusted.

But now wasn't the time to doubt. Regardless if he wanted it or not, Friedelock's serum was the only thing left that could save his daughter. It had to be, for he'd been given a small dose already. But even that had worn off. Now all he had was what the dealer had given him. And he definitely didn't trust the use of the Hensers. They were black magic in his eyes. Sorcery. And yet they weren't. He still couldn't grasp them or the man who'd given them to him. "*A gift,*" he'd said. One that had simply burned through life as though it were not. One that had killed. Carls despised them, for he knew nothing about their source or reason. They'd only brought pain thus far, so who was to say they'd bring anything else?

Definitely pain though. But if it was giving her a chance, he was willing.

He could hear the singing around the bend. Someone or something was there, and he eased near to the corner's edge, peering with all intent to avoid confrontation. What his eyes beheld caused him to stumble. It was a child, a boy, crouched by shattered crates and black walls and toying with something that was obstructed from his view. He fought every urge to call out to the boy, not knowing if it was true or simply an illusion. But what was a child doing here? And why *right* where Carls needed to be. The staircase was just past the boy and the crates. Carls had to decide whether to break for it or find another way.

A sound crackled behind him, and the boy jumped to his feet, gazing in Carls' direction. The singing stopped, and the boy just starred for a moment, tears in his eyes. Carls, exposed and speechless, stood staring right back. The boy then took off down the stairs in a fury, too quick for Locke to pursue him. What had caused him to flee?

He came to observe what the boy had been meddling with. Behind the crate lay the imprints of a dead man. Next to one hand, a battered revolver resided, cold and chambers empty. His other hand cradled a Hand-Pal tightly. His hands were raw and burnt—as were the walls about him. Remnants of ash lay to his side (Carls guessed it to be where the ashes of the Henser fell). From the looks of it, the man had attempted blasting his enemy with flames. Carls knew too well the results of such action.

Prying a little, he was able to free the Hand-Pal from the man's grip.

He held it loosely so as to not damage it any more. He was just glad it still worked, though barely.

"Well, we tracked down the man as instructed, but when we got there, he was already dead. It was enough trouble finding him and now this? Friedelock isn't going to be happy. But just to assure no mess-up, we put two bullets to his chest. He shouldn't be waking from that..." the tape began buzzing and skipped ahead.

"...I still don't know where the research was hidden or if even in this wretched building. All I know is that this place is possessed. *Ever since we got here, my men and I have been getting weird vibes... I think it's/ ...I doubt we'll be getting out of here alive. I should've known better. It's not like Friedelock to tell the whole story. And now we're paying for it. We've already lost two/ ...wait, it's here again/ We need help!! ...must reach/ ...."*

The tape blared in static and skipped ahead again, the soft singing of a child filling its chaos. *What?* And then it stopped. *The kid? The Shem?* What had they been talking about? Why had they stayed in the building?

His memory flashed back to the vision:

A dark place—water trickling down the walls of moss and overgrowth. A man sat in the corner, a cigarette to his mouth and a pad of sorts in his hand. Before anything could be made of detail, the man in coat stood and began walking away. Locke followed. Down the tunnel they went—the faint outlining of the inhabitants that had once opposed the man. He caught a glimpse of writing on the walls, familiar yet vague, retaining no pattern whatsoever. *The Big Man, TAP, Holstein is in the Dark...* Some even extending into small, pleading phrases such as *"The rain is falling, it's the Dark calling"* and *"The light has long since dawned."*

The man stopped, lifting from his coat a massive shotgun. "Where is he?" the deep voice resonated into the chamber before him.

"Long since gone," a figure shrouded in hood and mist answered. "Less you wish the same fate, you'll leave this place."

The man raised his gun, scoffing, "It's a little too late for that."

"Then I guess you'll have to prove yourself worthy of my knowledge—"

The vision blasted off and Carls plumped to the floor in heavy breathing. He thought he'd recognized the man but nothing came. No confirmation, no assurance. And to whom had he been speaking? Where? Why? It *had* to be something important. Friedelock wanted what Norwick had stolen from him. And whatever it had been, Norwick no longer had it. *Had what? What is Friedelock wanting so badly that Norwick hid so well? I have to find it! But how? How can I find what so many others seemed to have failed at? Even Antoinette...*

He pulled himself up against the wall, senses returning. *Think, Carls. Norwick was here under a deal with the philosopher. But why? They had switched places for what reason? For what would Dyrdrik do such a favor?* They had obviously been meeting each other often, and most likely for updates on Friedelock's search. *"Instruct my shareholder on what to do,"* Norwick had told his friend. *Who was this shareholder, and what was the instruction?* And what was the meaning of this new hindsight? A man asking for another and shots sounding? *"Long since gone..."* But who?

Carls was finding more questions than answers now, and it worried him. He made his way down the stairs and to the exit doors. Either way, he needed to find the place he last saw. It would hold the next clue. *"Holstein is in the Dark,"* he quoted from one of the markings on the tunnel's wall. He knew there to be a Holstein Sector on the map, though a ways off. He would have to go there next. Hopefully, more answers would arise when he got there. And more leads.

The Holstein Sector

The open streets and reinforced structures spoke of safety and comfort, but the abandonment and upheaval cried desolation. It seemed looted of all it had once been. Stripped of security; stripped of hope. Along the sides of the many structures were words of chaos etched in chalk and paint. Remnants of struggle still seen where a man once opposed an official, or where another who prophesied of death and destruction lay bound. He saw the warnings, the pleas. *"Hide while you can." "Don't sleep, it is their poison!"* The people seemed stricken by panic and desperation as order tried to be maintained. Buildings lay blown out and homes turned to rubble from resistance. Scattered about were bunkers of all sorts for protection from crossfire. He could only wonder as to the cause of such uprising—such fear and illusion. The residents seemed desperate and confused, all emphasizing upon the necessity of avoiding sleep, thus becoming deprived of it. But what for?

"Turn from the Resolute!" still more read. The whole place seemed to utter it. *How would sleep be their poison?* Thus far it was the opposite that had proved so. They had gone mad over the conviction of remaining awake. Small machines and outlets were smashed in, broken, and stolen of their goods. Carls found them all to be products of e-Company. More specifically: their caffeine and adrenaline shots.

Had they drugged themselves to ruin?

He came near a crumbled wall—a waving of a hand catching his sight. It was the boy again. "Hey!" Carls called out. Too late. The boy disappeared down a large hole in the floor ahead. Carls didn't like the thought of following after what just as well may have been an illusion, but he had nothing better to go by. Perhaps this child was an illusion, and perhaps not. Either way, he wasn't getting anywhere just standing. Thus, he made his way towards the hole.

His feet splashed as his shoes found grip. Thankfully the coat he wore was water resistant (being the chills that the cold flow sent shivering through him). He heard the boy off in the distance and quickening darkness. *"Don't sleep, can't eat"* he read on the opposing wall. A man lay beneath the white chalk no longer breathing. He'd given way to the sleep and hunger he had fought so hard to resist. A tramp. All of them seemed to be. Homeless in their own homes, how was this possible? Were they that afraid? He continued forward, eyes straining to bend the light before him. He clung to the side in hope that more would pass through and light his way—and avoid sloshing in the depths of the overflow. The boy's footsteps had vanished into the shadows, and Carls pressed after in blindness.

The passageway took a hard turn, and he saw a glimmer of faded light in the distance. Also, at the turn, he could see the lifeless bodies from his vision. It made sense now. Holstein had fallen into darkness and the people feared it. So much so that they had despised anything thereof. The white chalk, the blown-out corners, the power lights and lampposts—all were their attempts at fighting it. *"Don't sleep"* was their constant reminder. But why had such darkness befallen the place? Why the revolt? Why did they not run?

The small passage opened up to a larger chamber shrouded in mist. Power lights took up all four corners in an attempt to expose it. They flickered and fluttered, resolving no true redemption. However, Carls could see in the center the figure of a man strapped to a pole, head downcast and dripping with sweat.

"Who are you?" Carls asked hesitantly, "And are you alright?"

The figure neither replied nor lifted his head, but he was conscious. Carls stepped closer, a hand daring to pry at the ropes that bound the man. He made no motion of recognition but was aware all the same.

"What happened to—" the lights surged and mist swirled, a hand to his own that had touched the man's body.

"Do not tempt me!" the man bellowed, head raised and hair cutting sideways and up. With the single grip he had, he flung Carls back against the wall. The man's eyes were now glowing a deep green and his skin began to peel away to a darker scale—his clothes re-materializing. In an instant, the once weak and bound helpless man was now overflowing with power and awe.

Locke scrambled to his knees, pulling his gun from its latch and sending a bullet slapping empty into the brick ahead. The man was gone. The lights blacked out and ceiling broke away. He had just lifted his gun to deflect the crashing rubble. *What on Earth was that—if even of Earth to begin with?*

He heard laughter. From above, light filtered down through the rocks to where he cradled close to a corner. He emerged unscathed but desperate for any source of security. What nightmare had befallen his ideals of reality as it should be? Why was all this happening to him? Where was the information he sought to save his daughter? Where was she still?

Pain emanated from his lower abdomen. He couldn't tell if it was the impact or sharing of his daughter's suffering.

It ached deeply regardless.

Desperation

There is a feeling one gets when their desperation has reached such a level so as to destroy their sense of independence. It seems as if their entire world has been forced into a tunnel mindset with only one direction, one goal, for which to exist. For most, it becomes a desperate and final act after which they lose all sense of individuality and, for some, purpose in life. For others, this tunnel leads to the extensive use of their being, ending in sacrifice or defeat. Regardless of the end, they all share an obsession to reach its closure. Their willingness to lay everything on the line can often ruin every aspect of their intent or final results.

For Carls, everything fringed upon his daughter—his experiences only fueling the desire. When reality began mixing with horror, an unforeseen emotion took root. Not of numbness or doubt, but of singularity. His interpretations and intents all funneled into a single capsule: his daughter. So much that trifled what he knew to be real was discarded as a secondary motive. He no longer cared that his knees were shaking or back hunching in tiredness. It no longer mattered if he bled or sweat—it all was the same to him. His suffering, his determination, his longing, his desperation— they all meant but one thing to him: an even more pressing reason to save his daughter. Death was no option for him.

And so he drove his legs into submission once more and climbed above the rubble. He abandoned any attempts to dissuade himself from continuing onward. He forced his eyelids to lift against such insurmountable odds so as to guide his each and every step out of defeat. He would not linger on the pain but pursue the goal. He was going to find what he'd come for, and he was going to save his daughter. *I will come back for you,* he said to himself. *I will get you that cure.*

His heart rose above the ruin—a man stood atop looking down upon him. He wore a hood baring many markings. In the shadow of mystery, his eyes shone a deep green. *Was this the same man as below?*

"Please, I only seek—" Carls' words were cut off.

"I know what it is you seek. I warned you not to intervene, but it seems you lost all discretion long ago. A fool you all are, meddling with what you cannot comprehend, stifling with what surpasses your understanding. Do you even know why you seek what I have?"

"To save my only daughter," Carls answered.

"And yet you did not make use of the cure whilst you had it? No, you are not here to save her. You are no different from the rest. No less selfish, no less corrupt."

"It is true: man, at heart, is selfish and corrupt. But do not label me by such low standing! For I come to you honest and with good intent. My act before you is, as I said, that my daughter's life be spared. Be it my way, I would have none of this! I am not here to prove to you anything but a desire to save a life!"

"You speak boldly for such a minute knowledge. Too many before you have claimed likewise, but in the end, it is all for their own comfort. Should you be willing to give yourself, however…."

"That is something I have done long before I came to this place. You are right, I know nothing. Not who you are, nor Friedelock nor Antoinette or Dyrdrik or Norwick. But I know I am here now and that my daughter needs a remedy and that I am willing to give my life to save her. And if that be to fight you, then it is your choice to accept or refuse. Either way, I am not walking away empty-handed."

"Ha, well choosing of words. However, I cannot simply hand it to you. I am the Nightingale—holder of Norwick's life's work. I was summoned for the sole purpose of keeping what was his from the hands of corrupted men. Prove to me you are as you say, that you are different, and I will grant you his work. But keep in mind, oh oblivious one, that I was to ensure Friedelock never caught hold. Though your motives move me, you seek to give to the man I swore to keep from. We shall fight as men, and I with all that is in me. Prepare yourself, for I come with no restraints."

The man, calling himself the Nightingale, unfolded a staff from within his cloak. A mysterious power like none other began emanating from one of its ends, forming a spear-like edge. Carls himself felt unsteady, but drew his gun, inserting bullets into its chamber till it could hold no more. And then he looked up at his foe for one last thought—but he wasn't there! Beside him and to the left appeared the Nightingale, swinging his spear down upon Locke. He had no time to react, taking the brunt of it to his shoulder but somehow managing to evade the point. His body bent beneath the pressure and he slid back down the rubble. Once again, the Nightingale was above him for another blow—Carls used his gun to deflect it just in time. *How was he supposed to stop this guy? Move, Carls, move!* He forced himself to roll from his indented position, but before he could reach a good footing, he felt a boot dig into his right jaw—he plummeted to the very bottom.

I need help, he called to himself, hoping for some inner strength to take grip and drive him upward. For now, all he could see was the slow and persistent appearance of the Nightingale before him ready to strike again. *I cannot fight him like this. I need to*—Carls' mind went ablur. Not to being struck, not from exhaustion, but it simply faded to a strange sight. To his right and left posed two new figures only visible to him. He recognized them as both real and not. The figure of a girl was to his left (too far and too faint to make out) and to his right, a familiar and confusing sight. *Xavier.* Both seemed to be holding out their hands to help him but he could only grab one—

His wet palms slipped through the hallucination of Xavier's hand but also had fallen a vial in the man's place. *What was this?* Carls reached for it.

It was real and within his fist before a kick to his gut sent him spiraling sideways.

"Fight me!" the Nightingale beckoned him, obviously energized to continue but disappointed in the resistance. "Do not make me finish you so easily!"

He was on bended knee, hands drooping at his side. His coat hung low to his wrists—the vial in his hand and bearing weight to his knuckles. As the Nightingale spoke, he had popped the top of the vial and raised it to his lips.

"So," the Nightingale noticed, "you too must use such methods... maybe you aren't so different after all...." He raised his staff, another blade appearing on the opposite end (this one bending back down as though a scythe). Carls felt a surge of... something. Whatever it was, the vial clang to the ground, and his veins pulsed as with new blood. Every fiber of his being rejuvenated, and he jolted to his feet—and at the Nightingale. But simply matching movements wasn't enough. Carls could only deflect the blows, and attempts he had at countering were easily met and beat. Their feet slid atop the flooring as though an act to be reckoned with. As the Nightingale stepped right, Carls would follow-up with a reverse. But he was no match in arms. None of his shots hit their target. Too close. Too quick. He needed a distraction.

He felt the edge of a blade clip his heel.

Carls took a fist to the face and three more knots to his now-exposed chest. The one mishap cost him a valuable position, and he stumbled backward. No time. The Nightingale was next to him, a scythe swinging his way. Carls forced every bit of him to the floor and drilled his blood-dripping heel against the Nightingale's footing. They came empty. But at least he'd redirected the Nightingale's blow.

With the same motion, he twisted to his feet—lifting himself before another blast of pain to his back hit him down. The blade stopped at his coat.

"Interesting," the Nightingale remarked, his agile body landing a few feet before Carls. "Where did you get such a garment?"

Carls didn't allow himself the time to converse. He couldn't. *I have to save her... no matter what...*

He was to the side and behind a near structure. *Good, he's following.* Carls crouched low in the dining suite.

A blade cut into the ground where he'd been. His body barely managed to clear the counter, his coat folding from the currents that bent around him. He found a roll of string along the floor and quickly wedged his gun between the counter and stove (barrel first and reaching out into the room beyond). But being this low had exposed him. The Nightingale swung downward, and Carls caught the hilt—but didn't stop it. The force dug into his left shoulder and, for a moment, he felt trapped and at a loss, and yet a sliver a hope forced a smile. He still had hold of the weapon, and he used it to his advantage, pulling his feet from beneath him and forcing the Nightingale to pull away. In that time, he was back over the counter and facing the empty tables and chairs of the dining suite. The Nightingale was up and over in no time, his speed racing towards Carls as he bent over a table and spun across it. He regretted the choice of using his wounded shoulder as a prop but sent the table launching to its side.

The Nightingale cut through with such ease, unphased. *It was now or never.* String still in hand, Carls pulled with all his might—and it triggered.

POW!

The Nightingale toppled in confusion, struggling to regain a stance. Carls picked himself from the floor and made no waste of time. His heel dug into his opponent's face. But that was all he could do before his own exhaustion flooded in. He toppled as well, crashing against one of the chairs.

"What... did you do?" the Nightingale scoffed, blood dripping from his waist and mouth. Smoke still rose from the shrouded gun barrel. *It had worked.* Carls had wedged it just upright enough so as to hit center mass. He'd also wrapped the string's end about the hilt and trigger and held it loosely till he'd needed it. And it hadn't fired just once. The whole chamber had released (for better or worse). He could see three or so had broken skin on the Nightingale—and one had struck Carls as well. He hadn't noticed till now, but his thigh bled a steady stream.

"Curse man's intent of power," the Nightingale coughed. "You see an invention and turn it sour; you claim greatness but bring ruin. You desire freedom but not its cost. How sick, how pitiful..." his words trailed off and he resolved to look up at Carls. "You... had better be different than they. I entrust you with what I guard, but only you. Your move to put yourself in the way that you might prove something better is capturing. Take heed to my words: choose carefully those you give authority to. They so often go bad...."

He reached into his cloak and withdrew a small fold of cloth. "Take this as well," he said, placing it between them. "As for my vow, I have served its call and now depart. Farewell, strange man. And I pray your words hold true." The Nightingale collapsed to but the cloths that had clothed it.

The Reward of Risk

The same pews stretched beneath the chandelier. Everyone had emptied. Everyone but Dyrdrik and Norwick. The light reflected upon the two as they confronted each other—both their faces downcast and tense.

"It's been a while... friend," Dyrdrik mumbled.

Norwick reached into his coat and withdrew a small envelope. It wrinkled open and fluttered to the floor. "They took her too," he said.

Dyrdrik looked at the fallen piece of paper and then back at Norwick. "You knew better, I thought. Is it really that important to you—"

Norwick's hand was already gripping Dyrdrik's vest as the philosopher was pressed against his stand. "Gone! She's gone...."

"Relieve your grip, friend. I will not harm you. Now tell me, was it really worth this much?"

"I almost had it... the cure. She would have been fine... but then..."

"What Norwick? Then what? You knew Friedelock despised your work in secrecy, so why did you continue?"

Norwick loosened his hands. "I had too," he said, stepping back and retrieving the paper. "And now, my wife is gone as well."

"So... they took her too?"

"No, not *they*. Not Friedelock."

The expression on Dyrdrik's face dropped. "Don't tell me..."

"I had to. Please, old friend, help me now. Don't let all I have done amount to nothing!"

"Fool, he will pursue you to the end, you know that! So why prolong it?"

"I must."

"You've crossed the line already. I told you not to."

"Please, Dyrdrik. I only ask this once. He plans on crippling me from his movements, and I *must* foresee his plans."

Norwick handed over the envelope.

Dyrdrik folded it up, raising his head to his long-separated friend. "Only because I consider you a friend. Remember this though: nothing material can remain hidden forever. Either your work will decay or be put to use."

"I only need more time. As you've said, '*To clear one's lungs, you need only to take a deep breath and let it out.*' Give me the time to find that breath, and this all shall clear."

"Then what do you insist on me doing?" the philosopher asked as Norwick took off his coat and held it before him.

"To become a friend of my enemy..."

Carls could barely make out the blur of objects as his eyes focused in on the mess. Slowly his senses returned to him as he woke. *Where? What? Who?* He had overcome the Nightingale. The blood on his leg had dried, and he saw the fold of clothes covering something. *But who was he, the Nightingale?* He remembered the card. The vision. *Had Norwick summoned him? Was that even possible?* If Norwick had access to them then did that mean Hensers were nothing new to this place? That dealer... who was he? Pamella had asked of him... he had come from nowhere... Carls felt in his pocket, palms brushing against the Hand-Pal. *Of course, he'd already used his Hensers.* The first against the... dark. The second to his daughter.

Joanna, he recalled. Yes, he was getting closer. But now ran the question as to what he should do with Friedelock's demands. He reached out and pulled the clothes from their resting. There lie a brown folder and two tapes. He withdrew the first and played it into his Hand-Pal:

"*I am at a loss for words. I know now what Dyrdrik had been fearing. Somehow, he knew of the consequences and yet went with it. I should have known. A philosopher always knows more than he will speak. A good one at least. And Dyrdrik was just that sort of man. I cannot believe my most securing measure will also be my undoing. They come for me. I can only hope they get to me before Friedelock... that I might avoid the prolonged death and interrogation. Only God can save us now...*"

(The second tape played) "*Have we truly come to this? Is man's striving for accomplishment really what brings his ruin? My daughter was all I cared about. My daughter. But she is no more. Friedelock, in his obsession, forced me into my tombstone, and I am not responsible for her death! Indeed, he seeks the peak of humanity, but he shall have none of it! I have personally seen the forces at work here... there is much more than meets the eyes. There is more to our slumber than any could have guessed. If only we had stayed awake. Had actually suffered through and through... maybe then we could have seen better the rifts opening to us. They come, and because we brought them..."*

Who were the others Norwick spoke of? The ones that brought his death... Carls knew that Friedelock's men hadn't reached him first. The room, the body, the blood—Norwick had taken a risk to protect his work that exceeded anything Friedelock could have foreseen. *It's the Hensers, it has to be,* Carls thought. He knew there was something wrong with them. They were sorcery. Black magic.

They were man's undoing.

But how? How had they been used? Was the dealer behind it all? Was he responsible?

Carls' eyes lifted to a figure before him. He was still numb on the dining suite floor, but he was not alone. Xavier resided behind the counter where he had placed his gun.

"It's been a while," he said with a smirk.

"Enough games, why did you appear to me before?" Carls asked. "Not in the shop, but while fighting the Nightingale. I saw you standing there, and you gave a vial."

"Are you sure that was me? Illusions can be quite convincing you know..."

"I need answers, Xavier."

"Need? Are you sure? Wouldn't it be more correct in saying you *want* answers? I admire your curiosity, Locke. Conversate with me. What have you found?"

"Is this some sort of game to you?" Carls lashed. "I don't have time to fulfill your need of company! My daughter is still dying!"

A flicker of appearance and Xavier now posed beside Locke, kneeling low. "Trust me, young sleeper, you are still just awakening. As for your daughter, you are right. I shall not keep you. But know this: your actions as to *how* you save her will affect *everything*. Be careful."

"What do you mean?"

"You know what I speak of. You know that a man desperately wants what you have uncovered, and yet so desperately has it been kept from him. Is it truly wise to unite the two? Do you *really* want to know what happened and what *is* to happen?"

"I don't—"

Xavier was gone. He looked down at the folder before him, hands shaking. Was he to return it? Was he to actually hand it over?

"Carls," his Hand-Pal buzzed. It was Antoinette. "Listen to me. I have the cure. DO NOT return to Friedelock *that* folder. Your daughter is safe with me... at least for now. If you have it, come find me, and I will give the cure to you. Hurry, time is running short."

A prayer answered or a nightmare sprung.

Saving Joan

He was on his feet and running. So much going through his head. Friedelock, Norwick, Antoinette, Dyrdrik, the Nightingale—they all had ties somehow. They all fit into a much bigger picture, and Carls just *wasn't* seeing it. What had happened to this place? What *was* this place? Who were these people? These *things*? The group he'd found dead with leads to his daughter, who were they? They had obviously been against Friedelock, but were they with Antoinette? And TAP... what was TAP's connection to everything? Why did they keep showing up?

It was assured that Norwick had once worked for Friedelock. He recalled the tape he'd stumbled upon when he first went to the place: *"Strange, is it, that a man could know so much yet be content with so little. The Big Man himself said that our research was sufficient, yet he always asks for more. Could it be he has something else in mind? I came here to take part in a great work, not further it."* The Big Man. He'd been on the walls in the Holstein Sector as well.

Altogether, it was nearly too much. All Carls could think about for now was saving his daughter. But even then, the plan had changed. He was no longer to deliver the folder to Friedelock, but to Antoinette. And who, exactly, was Antoinette? Did he even have Locke's daughter? Was he any better than Friedelock? From his current standing: yes. Friedelock had been the one responsible for this to begin with. He was the one who had stolen his daughter and brought her this suffering. *Friedelock*—he hated the name, yet knew nothing really of it. *I will save you, Joan, I am coming for you, and we will leave this place.* But was that possible? He had tried... The doors, the screams, the stairs, the room, the fall—it all flooded him instantly. No, he was not used to any of it yet, but he carried on. He still forced one foot in front of the other. He still held the custom gun with no more shots in it. He still held the folder.

And the cloth. *Take this as well,* the Nightingale had told him, giving him a small fold of cloth. He'd opened it but found nothing surprising. Only a stick about a foot long with one end bent slightly. What it did, what it was, he did not know. All he did know was that if the Nightingale had made an effort to give it to him, it had value. Even if he didn't know how to use it, he would keep it.

Carls Locke made his way around the curve leading down the hall of the e-Company's expanse. *Antoinette, I have come for you. You had better still have my daughter. And you had better not abuse what I bring in exchange. "Choose carefully those you give authority to,"* the Nightingale had warned. *I am giving you this; I can only hope for my daughter's life in return. Please, do not lie to me. Do not be as Friedelock. Do not tangle me in this mess.*

The large, steel doors lifted, and Locke entered as a single figure to the towering skyscraper of industry within the mall of mystery. Antoinette's voice came over the COMM, "Good, you have come. Make your way to the Observatory Chambers where we first met, and we shall converse man to man, face to face, once again. Do not be alarmed, your daughter will be near there as well. You two shall yet be reunited."

He stood before the glass, a chill through his veins as he held the folder before him. The mechanism that had once bound him lay vacant as he stared through the glass and upon the figure of an old man. Philis Antoinette—an enemy of his enemy.

"So," the man began, turning his wheelchair to face Locke, "you have indeed found it. I am sorry it had to be this way—that your daughter had been used by Friedelock. Rest assured, she is here." He played with a switch on his armchair, and a door slid open to Carls' right. It led into Antoinette's room. "Come in," he said, "I trust you enough."

Carls stepped into the room, the air seemingly flowing between the crevices of his coat. Antoinette was an old, frail man, head strapped upright, legs shriveled but arms steady at his side. Steady and firm. "Your daughter, as promised."

The door behind him opened to a small table on which a girl rested.

Not just any girl—not just any five-year-old—but "Joan..." Carls called out, hesitant to believe his eyes.

"Go to her," Antoinette reassured. "I have already treated her injuries."

And he ran to her. His heart beat with an insurmountable sense of joy. "Joan!"

Her body was still. So innocent. So unaware. So tired.

"Will she make it?" Carls pleaded a glance at the old man.

He nodded.

Her eyes peeled open—her dark hair sliding from her forehead as she made her first breaths. "Daddy?"

Carls embraced her. He held her tight in his arms, his chest weeping, his mind easing, his muscles relaxing. "Joan."

She was crying. But who could blame her? She had been through so much. Too much. Was Antoinette to really be considered a friend? Was he to be trusted? *Choose carefully those you give authority to.*

He could have stayed there forever with her in his arms. His only care in the world had finally been met. She was safe. She was alive.

And she was two years older. He recalled the chambers, the flashing lights and toxic gas—but now he at least held her as *his*. But Antoinette still waited for the folder. Carls gave it to the man, however unknown the results would be. Antoinette had kept his daughter safe. And healed her. Or at least that's what he was seeing.

"You wanted the folder," Carls said, tossing it across the floor to Antoinette's feet. The man directed a robotic arm from his side and withdrew it, confident.

"My work with you is done," Carls added. "I wish to leave this place."

The man smiled bitterly. "Don't we all? I understand if you desire no longer to help, but leaving *this* place is not currently possible."

Not possible?

"However, you should seek out Sherlin if you want a place to stay *within* here."

"I have had enough, why can't I leave?"

"I myself ask the same question. Do not lose yourself, Carls. Find Sherlin and he will most certainly talk. As for me, I am running too short on time to answer all your questions. Giving up the tarsh lilies has not furthered my project by any means."

128

What? He'd used the tarsh lilies on his daughter? "Why?" Carls asked.

"Because we are not all that different. And I owe it to—well, never mind. Go now, my watcher will lead you to him."

Another man rounded the bend into the room. Carls was surprised he recognized the face. "He's the watcher?"

PART III

PURPOSE

*"Fear is a fickle thing. In some cases, it drives us to improve. To break down
barriers we once thought insurmountable. Other times, it erects walls of its
own, isolating us and creating for itself an endless cycle of detachment."*
-Andy Friedelock, Founder and President of Friedelock Industries

In Need Of A Place To Stay

Antoinette slid his wrist and arm so as to turn his wheelchair. "Ah, you're acquainted? Yes, Kit works for me."

He still didn't know how the man had warded off the Shem.

How he'd come from nowhere.

How he safeguarded the e-Links.

Kit still wielded proudly the bow that had shot *it*. "Haven't been getting into more trouble have you?" the man smirked.

"Those vials, what are they? How do they work? What are they for?"

"You may ask him on your way," Antoinette spoke, ushering them on their way. Carls held his daughter atop his shoulders (as she was still weak) and followed Kit down and out of the e-Company's lair. *Kit, the watcher.* What all did that mean? He remembered his first encounter with the drugs—the illusionate that had misled him. *The tripper.* Yes, it had been a tripper. And he'd completely fallen for it. He'd taken the *drug*. He'd felt its liquid course through him, fill him, tunnel him. But not the same as when he'd fought the Nightingale...

Kit hadn't said a thing. The man stood tall and fluid in steps. His tennis shoes made no sound as they slid across the tiles of the grand mall. *That's right, I'm trapped in this place.* But was there really no hope? He still ached from the thoughts of his helpless pleas—of when he had needed rescue the most. *But you kept me here*, he murmured to himself. He would have left his daughter and wife; he would have deserted every bit of dignity he had in fear and disbelief. What had happened here to these people? To *him*?

He felt a soft pressure against his neck as Joan fell asleep. *Did she know?* He couldn't imagine how a child would react to such terror. He knew her body couldn't handle it. It hadn't—Friedelock was proof of that. But he cut the thought off. No need to meditate on hating a man. He was done with Friedelock and with Antoinette. He prayed this *Sherlin* would give him an escape from it all. Or, in the least, a place to stay.

I need to gather myself, he said silently. *I am human after all. I haven't slept or eaten in a long time... I need the rest, and so does little Joan...*

He couldn't help smiling at the memories of his past joys. With her in his arms, he sensed hope for once. He could almost see Elairah walking beside him holding his hand. Her smooth touch would calm any storm of incompetence or pain. Her heart was a spring of comfort; her breath a breeze in a desert plain; her hair a fragrance of serenity. He missed her. He hurt for her. "Elairah..." he let slip out.

"You seem mesmerized," Kit cut in. "You know, I'd never expect a man of your likes to still be moving. I hope you haven't been stealing, have you? This place may have gone to pot, but I ain't going to let the business just rot. Even in times of trouble, stealing is stealing."

"What are those e-Links?" Carls asked.

"You've used them, you know."

"Why in the world would they be on the market if they're so dangerous?"

He could hear Kit laugh. "It is not my place to judge their unstable tendencies. I am only their watcher. Believe it or not, my job used to be much lighter."

"Then what happened?"

Kit had hoped to avoid conversation, but he knew Carls' interest had already been sparked as though a child's imagination. The creases of his eyes seemed set from his steady smile. So comfortable. So mysterious. So simple, yet so dangerous.

"Just know this: 'Where there is an attraction of groups, a business is sure to rise.' T.J. Lawrence himself said that. Sure enough, this place was quite the attraction. But I do not care to bore myself with already passed circumstances. The only thing that matters now is that the business is kept secure from tricks, lies, and thieves—I'll get 'em."

"The business, what is it exactly? Why are they so bizarre? Friedelock Industries, e-Company, Mx3, BrainWare... why haven't I heard of them before? What are they?"

"Simply put: you don't know anything. That is why Antoinette is handing you over to Sherlin. But even then, if you want solid answers, you got to find 'em yourself. Speaking of which, here we are..."

Carls hadn't noticed the time till now, nor did he recognize the scene before them. They stood at a junction of three halls and in front of them were two men ravaged through the overturned crates of an abandoned supply store.

Carls couldn't believe his eyes. In fact, at first, he didn't. "...Dyrdrik?"

The man looked up, his comrade noticing them as well, surprised at Carls' remark "Dyrdrik?" he inquired confusingly. "I thought you were—"

"Yes," Dyrdrik budded the man off, "that was my name. *Is* my name, but not what I go by anymore. It's been a long time; who might you be, Stranger?"

"I am Carls. Carls Locke. You knew Norwick, didn't you?"

The man's face turned stern. "Indeed, but don't think that gives you any right to burst into my past life. I escaped it, or so I had thought. Until they stole my wife."

"What happened to her?"

"She... wandered off. I tried to find her, to stop her, but before I could they had taken her away. And now she is gone—I no longer recognize her."

"Why did she wander?"

"It was her mind. She was... ill. And it got the better of her."

"Of a lot of us," his comrade included.

"I lost sight of her, and in that brief moment, I fear to have lost her altogether." The men suddenly were at unease. Something was coming. Kit was no longer there either. Carls hadn't noticed him leave, but now it was just him and a man he would have never thought to be alive.

"Come," Dyrdrik spoke, "it is not safe here."

"We can't just take him," his comrade, Jailer, added.

"Have you not noticed the child with him? I shall not desert such a man!"

The sound came again, this time Carls could make it out. *A Fallen One*. "Please, I need a place to rest."

"Who brought you here?"

"I was sent by Antoinette."

They both looked surprised but discarded any further questions they had. "Follow us, and we will talk where it is safer."

135

Who Is Sherlin?

Jailer did not approve of the action—that much was obvious. The man was a fighter at heart with the hands of a blacksmith and body of a sailor. Surprisingly enough, it was Dyrdrik who always had a pack of cigarettes on hand. They were quick through the halls and narrow alleys of shortcuts and bi-ways leading to their small encampment deep within the ever so vast mall. The place was located in the Upper Alleys just above Hanging Gardens. The structures themselves seemed under lockdown, and thus tents and tarps extended from them in odd angles so as to form shelters for privacy and segregation. And for once, there were *people*. At least two dozen or so too—women and children. The camp had two fires burning on the tiles of the mall operating as ovens. The lampposts glowed dimly about the circumference. But they didn't need it right now. For the first time in a long while, Carls saw what he thought to be a glimmer of sunlight glaring over the place. It shone vibrantly from high above as it penetrated the glass ceiling. *The sun, Joan, you get to feel the sun.*

Little Joan had lifted her head by now as Dyrdrik and Jailer strode on ahead to greet their friends with the recovered goods. *A scouting party,* Carls concluded. It made sense. They had to get supplies somehow. Joan leaned tightly against him as she dropped to the floor and stretched her arms. Her cheer of awakening had caught the attention of several other children, and they came running to see the newcomers. *Should I trust them?* Carls was wary to let her go. Especially considering he had just fought so hard for her—he didn't like the risk of losing her again.

"What's her name?" a voice carried from his left, a lady in her mid-thirties greeting him.

"Joanna," Carls answered her. Her hair was wrapped in a scarf and her tall body covered in ragged clothes. Her cheeks were stained with a dirty past but clean from recent pain.

She looked back at him, almost as though able to sense the suffering he had buried beneath. "That's a beautiful name," she said. "Don't worry, she is safe here. Sherlin has kept us safe thus far, I'm sure two more won't be a problem for him."

"Carls," Dyrdrik spoke, brushing his palms on his legs only to notice the splinters in his hands. "Let's talk," he said, motioning to the side but catching himself, "She's our caretaker. You can trust her to tend justly to your girl."

With his eye still on Joan, Carls reluctantly followed Dyrdrik, watching as his daughter steadily and shyly warmed up to the caretaker and kids.

"She seems happy here," the man said, also noticing.

"Indeed," Carls said, brushing his tired arm against his damp forehead. His body was beginning to take its toll. "Might we stay here for a little while?" he asked. "I don't know how I would repay you, but my mind and body are weak, and there are just too many doubts, questions, and fears on my mind."

The man looked wearily at him. Mike Dyrdrik—the man he'd heard so much about while pursuing Norwick. *Dyrdrik the philosopher.* So many questions, but for now all that mattered was for him to find a place for his daughter to sleep.

"There is worry spreading here, especially since you say Antoinette sent you. You know it's a thin line when keeping the hearts here sane and orderly. You've practically sent the whole place spiraling just by calling me by that name."

"But you are Dyrdrik, aren't you?"

"Not here. Not now. Here I am known as Sherlin, and I ask you learn it the same. Worry spreading like wildfire is the last thing we need. As for your stay, you must understand that there is more to it than simply giving you a tent. Our food is short and space tight. Here, if you have something to hide, then you leave. We aren't fans of secrets, nor can we afford to be. I don't know who you are or where you came from, only that you are here and that you have a little girl with you. *If* indeed she is yours?"

"Yes, she is."

Dyrdrik glanced back over the encampment. Not Dyrdrik, but Sherlin.

He was the people's leader. And rightly so. He seemed to be a man of high standings and solid ideals. He also looked burdened—as though accepting Carls and Joan was far more burdensome than first thought. Carls didn't like the thought of intruding on them, but he had nowhere else to go. He'd feel responsible for bringing any harm to them as an outsider. A stranger.

The man bit his lower lip to a nervous decision. "Fine, you can stay. But under one condition." The man seemed lenient to state his demand. Almost as though he carried it upon himself to ask no favors of anyone, if it was a favor at all. Surely, he had undergone so much since the events dealing with Norwick. His reputation, his past, his friends, his family—his wife, an all-too-relate-able loss.

"My wife," he mumbled, a hand through his gray, withered hair. "She's... missing... but she's not dead. At least that I know. Please, I just need to know where she went. Bring her back to me, if only her body, in exchange for portions to remain and to prove you are trustworthy. If you do, then the people here will like you a lot more also. Maybe then they'll welcome you without my convincing."

Carls fought his mind's every attempt to play the scene of his wife's abrupt end. He clung deeply to the hope that this was all still but a nightmare and he would soon wake to her. Yet, part of him doubted... part of him feared... part of him questioned. "Where is she?" he asked.

"I don't know, that is why I'm asking for your help. When she... *went*, I could always find her, always hear her, by her clanging. For some reason, she clings to the same pipe—" Carls' mind went a wander. *The pipe.* He could feel his frantic breathing yet again and the desperate panic for the sight of his daughter. He felt again the corner as he peered around it, the sudden flash of steel to his face—the blacking out of his conscience.

"You okay?" Sherlin asked.

She was still there. His breathing slowed, eyes blinking off the recollection. Yes, he knew of *her*, the illusionate. "I am fine," he said.

"I hope it is not too much to ask of you, but this is one way I am sure you will be welcomed with open arms."

Carls was still staring at his daughter—her laughter filling his scope of attention. If that had been Dyrdrik's wife all along then... the blood, the panic, the lights going out and his shoulders pressing against the desk. Her face... her screams...

BrainWare—that was where he had last seen her. It had been her following him. *Her* that he kept hearing off in the distance. *Her* that he had seen snatched by some darkness.

A Shem.

A lump of saliva slid down his esophagus as he put the memories aside. *Yes, her.* "I recall who she is," he said solemnly.

"You do? You have seen her before?"

"She is just like *them*, isn't she?" he implied at the illusionate.

Sherlin didn't seem pleased with the relation. Especially in labeling his wife as such. Carls wanted to ask of what *illness* the man spoke of, but he refused to intrude any further.

"I know it will not be easy for you, but please, at least try. That is all for now. You may leave first thing in the morning if you wish to help your daughter feel at home here. The people will not have a problem with her being here."

"I don't plan on leaving her," Carls said, his fists clenching at the thought of deserting her again.

"You must. I know my wife to have fallen deep, and your daughter has no place in witnessing such things. She is not ready. You have my word: she is safer here."

"Can she see?" Carls asked. "I mean, does she know what it's like?"

"I doubt she does. You can't hide it from her forever, but for now, she is simply *too* young. I will have Linda, the caretaker, look after her. She seems good with the children. Especially the girls. That is all I have to say for now. Go, spend time with your little girl. For now, the people will just have to deal with your presence, like it or not. Just don't cause trouble."

At that, Sherlin departed from the conversation and Carls returned to his daughter as she played tag with her new friends. *Five years old,* he told himself, shaking his head. *She was three last time I knew her. To think she has spanned so many years against her will—how could she* not *know of her surroundings. But at least she is happy. At least she does not have to face those... monsters. At least, for now, she can be at peace as Elairah was... so innocent, so unaware... God, help me understand and keep her safe.*

And help me to keep my feet aground.

A Good Man's Promise

Time seemed to have gone by far too swiftly for him to now be leaving her again. But he trusted her to be in good hands. He prayed she was. Sherlin was right that such a journey would be too much for her. Maybe, if he moved fast enough, it could all be over with before she could even start missing him. His palm felt to his heartbeat. The link was still there; he could sense it. *The bond.* He closed his eyes and inhaled a deep breath. Finding the missing person would mean returning to BrainWare Corp. Even despite how much he wished not to.

They had fed him well and sent him on his way. Sherlin had even given him an e-Link in case the need arose. He didn't savor the thought of using it but knew its value. This particular e-Link accelerated the white blood cells within the body. It was meant more for Sherlin's wife than him. She would definitely need it more. And perhaps he wouldn't have to use it before then.

His feet stepped yet again into the unexpected. His coat had been rinsed of its dirt, and he'd been given new pants and undershirt. Still the same worn-out shoes though. Same Hand-Pal and same sash in which still rested the armament given him by the Nightingale. What it all did and how it was to be used still surpassed him. He didn't know if it even amounted to anything; he only hoped he wouldn't have to find out.

Most of the shops were vacant, if not stripped of anything valuable. Sherlin's encampment had been making quick use of any and all goods near them. He saw the battered windows and wreckage in their wake. *Must have been others as well,* he thought. Sherlin didn't seem like the type to take unnecessary steps in acquiring supplies. But there were still the illusionate... the Fallen Ones... the Shem... Any one of them could have done the same things. But why? Why were they different? The Shem... it was nothing like he had seen before or could have even imagined. Its body was unexplainable. Its behavior was unpredictable. And then the Fallen Ones... their brute power and sense of rage.

Having confronted those two, the illusionate would seem to be a walk in the park. But they weren't. Their state didn't make them any weaker, only more unstable. He could see their blood across the floor and glass where one had tried fleeing a store. *So confused*, he remarked. They seemed to have lost their minds. If an illness it was, then a steady descent into madness seemed to fit. The Holstein Sector proved to support him. Though he hadn't met any illusionate there, it was plausible. Had that been the start? *"Don't sleep,"* they'd said, *"it is their poison."*

Poison? They? Who were they? A cult? A business? Or actually, something *darker* than anything man could do alone? Could this *they* be like the Shem? Was it the substance that possessed when its victims became weak enough? Was it the difference between an illusionate and a Fallen One?

He shuddered at the thought. He'd seen it firsthand—the desperate mutant of hunger and rage chasing after him.

"Still curious, are you?" Xavier asked.

What? Xavier?

Carls noticed he had wandered into the shop and now stood to face the flickering figure of a man as mysterious as the place he was in. "Why do you keep appearing to me?" Carls inquired back.

"Like I said the first time: I have no one to converse with and that leaves me quite alone in this place... just like you."

Carls knew what was coming. Xavier was a tripper no matter how much he refused. He claimed to just be a hologram, but *they* still came whenever the two spoke.

"Have you found some answers to your questions yet?" the man asked.

"No," Carls said, remembering his last attempt at reaching one of *them*. "It is not that easy—"

"But they need you, don't they? And you would do them wrong to just leave them. Tell me, what went wrong?"

"And why should I answer to you? Even as we speak more are on their way. I am tired of running and hiding, of hurting and losing. End this trickery now!"

"Oh, don't be so weak," Xavier scoffed, "you're the one who's been *choosing* to run and hide and *letting* yourself hurt and lose. If I am not mistaken, you actually had a recent victory..."

The Nightingale. Yes, he remembered. That man was not of here either. Norwick had summoned him—which brought even more questions.

"And I am implying on the young man you enlightened, not the Nightingale. You know, in the Hanging Gardens..."

"Stop," Carls said. His hands had finally healed from the flames; he didn't wish them reopened. "That was a failure if anything."

"But it showed it was possible," Xavier pressed. "It proved you *can* reach them, didn't it?"

"And how would you know? You weren't there!"

The man smiled. "There are many things I see that *you* don't. But I am not here to analyze your life for you, only to keep you thinking. You yourself said you wanted answers, and to get them, you must *ask*."

"It is impossible—"

Xavier laughed. "You truly are in denial still! Ha, if it were impossible, then why do you seek one now? If it were impossible, then explain what happened in the chambers! If it were impossible, then why do you keep trying? Truly, you need to decide within yourself where you *really* stand, because as of now, the only thing keeping you from finding answers is *you*. I can delay them no longer; thus, we shall part for a while. I suggest you use this moment to try expanding your little box of doubt. Goodbye, and we will speak again."

He was gone with the echoes bouncing through the halls. Carls looked up and saw that he was still too near to the encampment. *I cannot let them be exposed.* His teeth clamped down. *Xavier, why? Why do you keep leading them to me? Why do you put me in such feeble positions?*

Why do you want me in this so much?

But enough questions. He had to keep them from his daughter. He had to shelter her. Even though she was blocks away, he still felt responsible. His heel dug into the sole of his shoe as he broke from the shop's emptiness and into the hall. He could only hear their cries and guess at their location. Regardless, he would have to find them before they wandered too close. Even if it meant him against four or even a Fallen One. *I will not let them find you*, he swore to himself. *I promise I will keep you safe.*

Things Better Left Unrivaled

"We all, each and every one of us, fall apart eventually. No one is immortal to emotion. It is human to weep, so weep committedly. It is a healing no one has yet to understand."
-Mike Dyrdrik

He hadn't spotted any illusionate. Rather, he rounded the bend and came to an abrupt stop—hand reaching into his sash. He heard weeping behind the crates and broken displays. Carls inched near to one of the large boxes, crouching low to the ground and peering around its corner. A scrawny man sat across the room, head drooped and arms stretched on either side of him. His pants hang loose if at all; his shoes were torn and ripped at their seams. Only threads of his shirt remained, and his skin sagged from his trembling bones.

Long, unkempt hair fell to his shoulders and reeked of forgottenness. His chest beat harshly to his heart, raising and lowering dramatically with every breath. A broken and helpless man, but was he an illusion or tripper? Carls decided to cough to test the man's awareness. But the man seemed too caught up in misery to look his way.

Locke lifted his hand from his sash and slowly stood. He knew the only way to reach them was at their weakest (though that more so applied to a mental state, not physical depletion). He eased forward. The broken man, leaned over and back bent, revealed his frail spine. *What had happened to this man?*

Carls looked about him to ensure there were no traps. The man said something, but Carls could not hear. He moved closer, still saying nothing himself.

143

"*It* wants out..." the man wept, "and *it* wants in... why can't it just leave me be... I can't take it anymore...."

He tried lifting a hand to the man's shoulder, but it was caught. "Don't... tempt... me."

Carls could only imagine what the man was going through. He had to be only in his late teens or early twenties. So weak, so frail... He remembered his wife and how she used to comfort him. He remembered those long, stressful days of work and how she would always just sit beside him and wait for him to take deep breaths.

The man took a deep breath.

He remembered how she would sit beside him just to make him aware of her presence, and so he pulled up a crate and seated himself.

He remembered how she waited calmly and took in such deep breaths herself. It always reminded him to breathe himself. Thus, he took in a breath and let it out.

The man did the same, his body shaking with each one.

Now to just wait.

The man's lungs jumped; his fists tightened. He was fighting something, Carls knew. But it was more than just rage or emotion. It ran deeper. It was something he could not relate to.

"I... can't...." the man wept.

"Yes, you can. Stop this and fight back. Whatever it is that you are warring with inside, fight it." Those words—he'd said them before. The illusionate, the gardens, the flames, the desperation. But this time he had no cards to ruin it all. This time, he wouldn't abuse the hope he had to give. "I am not here to—" The man bellowed with a palm digging into Carls' chest. He flung backward and against the crates. The breathing was harsh and exasperated; the skin a mellow gray and rough scale. The muscles twitched and hands burrowed hard against its forehead. He recognized it as all too familiar.

"Fight it!" Carls yelled, crawling to his feet and keeping his distance. It wasn't helping. The man was breaking; his body mutating under the pressure of something inside of him. "Your name! What is your name?" Carls tried asking in an attempt to distract him.

The man tumbled to the floor—Carls was right next to him gripping the man's shoulders. They felt nothing of weakness; rather, it felt as though the man's veins were boiling. He groaned in his struggle, a part of him letting Carls remain at his side, another trying to tear him away.

"Lara, Chester... all because of me!"

"No! Do not succumb to hate and regret!" Carls beckoned, "Fight it!"

He was trying. His knees shook, and a twitch of muscle sent Locke crashing. But he wasn't going to give up. *Fight this, I know you can. Just calm down. Calm down and think.*

The monster within his skin roared to break free. But the man fought it, every ounce of his being fighting for control. And, slowly, did he recede. The outrage returned to a low moan. Jaws unclenched, fists spread open, and lungs began shaking off their gasps. Tears slid from beneath closed eyelids. On the floor, exposed and frail, the man bundled up and shivered to an unexplainable chill.

He obviously felt ashamed and confused. Carls couldn't tell if the man was aware anymore or not. His senses were still shaken, and he kept to himself. Thus, Carls left him knowing that he had done all he could. He only hoped that the man would come around in the end. That he would change. *Hang in there, my friend. You can yet win if only you keep fighting.*

Clues Found & Paths Followed

Carls hadn't been followed, surprisingly enough. Then again, he actually had the strength to run this time having slept the night alongside his daughter and having had a good meal to eat. The fact that he had been able to reach out to an illusioned one comforted him. It gave him hope of reaching Sherlin's wife. And it relieved the regret he had for his first success—and fatality. Xavier seemed to have had faith in his ability to communicate to the illusionate. Whether that be fate or chance, he did not know. Nor did he care. So what if Xavier expected something more out of him? He had no intentions of staying any longer than he had to. He was only here for his daughter and a favor to Sherlin.

Then again, he had questions about the place. *"You would do them wrong to just leave them."* Those were the words of Xavier. The man seemed satisfied with the role Carls was playing. Was the holograph really more than what he put on? How could he be a tripper and yet... more? What were trippers? How were they even possible?

He stood once again before the entrance of BrainWare Corp. He didn't like the idea of charging in there after some demon. How was he to know if the woman was even still there? Or even alive?

The fact that she had been the one who'd started all this for him caused a tinkling of tension within him. All his loss, all his suffering—all from that pipe.

And now he was trying to help her.

His chest rose and lowered to the heavy breathing. *No, I can't think of it like that*, he told himself. He wasn't here for himself in the first place. He was here for Sherlin. For Dyrdrik.

For Joan.

He could rest assured she would be safe. Though nothing seemed familiar in such a dreaded and unpredictable place, he at least had trust to lean on. *Had* to. Man cannot function without it. His eyes closed; memory flashed:

The cellar showed in flashes of light as its walls stretched down a narrow passage. Moss and slime covered the walls. Along the floor was a channel of concrete through which a steady stream flowed. His own body hung close to the right wall as he progressed down the chasm. Then he noticed that he was not the one moving. Rather, the moss seemed to be pulling back, and the slush in the stream flowed upward and against the current. They seemed to be intertwined with each other and disappeared behind him. He could not turn around fully; his vision stayed before him, the scene still in brief flashes.

Then his body jerked, and the scene changed. He felt as though something was pulling him from behind—a wet string about his waist and arms.

The moss... it was alive?

His body hit the wall and slapped upon the carpet. Not in his vision, but in reality. He saw a glimpse of black as whatever it was bent around the corner and from sight. He felt his waist and saw the smears of black across his coat.

He heard the moan of another presence. Not a moan—*the singing again.*

Somehow, he had been dragged inside the corporation. How or when escaped him, only that he was there and that so was something else. *The boy, he had to be a tripper...*

His hand reached into the sash and felt for the stick. His heart beat anxiously.

I need to calm down, he reminded himself, taking a breath.

The singing faded. His eyes had already taken in his surroundings. The hall met head-on with another, and behind him were closed doors. The *thing* he had seen had peeled to the right. Thus, he inched forward and peered likewise.

Empty.

But something caught his ear from behind. He turned to smolder of ash falling to the floor. *What?* They seemed to have formed some sort of word or phrase. Carls stepped toward it, still trying to memorize his surroundings in case the lights flashed out like before.

They did, and he was left in black.

He noticed that beneath one of the doors a light barely filtered through. He took another breath and raised a hand to its knob. Shoving through, he came to a shocking halt at the blood covered walls. The once-deemed-storage-room was a wreck. Carls pushed aside the pulse to run and honed in on a tape behind one of the crates.

(The voice came in panic) *"It held to a girl! It—whatever it was—I can't fight it! Oscar and Reece were torn in two just looking at it! If this is what* he *warned about, it's certainly* way *above our pay grade. He can hire someone else to find that cursed work, I don't care anymore! No more men to this madness I say! No more blood!"* It was the same man as last time. Presumably an earlier tape, but the same reconnaissance team. *The same ones looking for Norwick's work.*

The melody came again—the hall lights were back on. *What was this monster? What had they confronted?*

Carls stepped outside of the room. The clumps of ash still lie on the floor and wall. He could make out their letters as they faintly called out a phrase to him. "Let not the faint fall."

The same words that were being sung.

None of this is making any sense, Carls thought. *Why would such a creature hold on to her and still slaughter everything else? Why would it be here, as if residing at home? Here—where Norwick had been.*

The thought provoked his curiosity. He remembered the last tape of the same crew. They had tracked down Norwick's whereabouts but had found him already dead. *Already dead.* By what? Norwick himself had mentioned a third party, *not* of Friedelock's, going after him. But who? Dyrdrik knew. He had said so in the conversation Carls had envisioned. Maybe when he got back, having returned the man's wife, he would get some answers.

The child stood before him, oblivious to the dark that held the place. "Come on," he waved and ran through the door further down the hall. Carls pursued. *Was he real?* He didn't have time to question. Nothing was making sense anyways, only that this boy held some relevance unknown to this case.

A Door To The Unknown

The ground beneath him was not there to catch his feet. Carls hit to the floor hard. *Impossible! It was there... the room, the floor—I'd seen it there before I stepped.*

But there was a force much larger at work than his bedazzlement of entry. The area before him seemed vast and open—a tear into the infrastructure of the corporation. Both the floor he had been on and the next five above and below were missing. Along their perimeters hung a very much alive moss that seemed to bend beneath the currents flowing back and forth. *Wind? Inside a building?* But this was no ordinary wind. He'd felt it before. The moist, the chill, the unnatural, the living moss, the broken floors—*could it be?*

The ground shook beneath his palms and knees. *Yes, a Possessioner.*

The black shroud emerged from the crevices two stories above. Carls tried the door behind him. Locked.

"Come on," a child-like voice came again. He looked over the ledge and saw the kid atop a thick moss that stretched as a vein across the vast space. Carls took in a breath and found himself leaping in faith towards the kid. "Follow me," the kid said as Carls' body barely caught hold of the vein. He managed to reach his knees and balance his way toward the desired end. Seeing him follow, the child wasted no time proceeding. Carls yet again dropped to a lower level and followed the kid as swiftly as he could through the tangled mess of overgrowth. His movement was nothing close to fluid, but he pressed forward and down until, finally, he reached another door. A firm hand and quick twist turned everything to silence and before him—a well-lit, carpeted hall.

His breathing was irregular, but he managed. The child was replaced by another figure. *It was the girl!*

"Wait!" Carls called out as she made the bend. He cut the corner just in time to see her take another. "Wait!" *How was she moving so fast if only walking?* He heard a door open and caught a glimpse of which one just as it closed, but came to an abrupt halt.

"Well hello there, my friend," a man said before him with a laugh at his bewilderment. "It's been a while!"

The Dealer?

Serve Per Card was unmistakable with his white table strapped across his back and his plump body somehow carrying it with class and ease. His spectacles reflected the fluorescent hall lights and his tux shone like violet gold.

"That girl, I must—"

"Oh hush, hush. She can wait," the Gambler said, setting his table out and taking his seat behind it. "Come, let us do business. I see you have used your cards? Good! I was worried you'd let them go to waste."

"*You*—who are you?" Carls demanded. "A lady told me you were a *Dealer*, what is that?"

The man seemed surprised and yet already expecting it. A smirk crossed his face.

Carls continued his ramble, "These *Hensers*, what *are* they? Sorcery? Magic? What is their source? Because all I have seen come of them is darkness and corruption!"

"Sloooowwww dooowwwn," the man mimicked. "What is with your kind and their desperate questions? Well, for business sake, let me elaborate more for you. Like I said, they are not magic. Their name, *Hensers*, was given them because of their generalized use: as enhancers. What they can do and how they do it, is nothing of magic. All their power, all their mystery, has origin, and these origins are in Chambers."

"Chambers?"

"Yes, small worlds, you could say, that wield a single substance or material. In the case of Hensers, Chambers are a source of their individual abilities. Think of the cards as... gates to the Chambers. That is why they are so often labeled as dangerous. Rightly so, they are. You witnessed the power of their flames, now imagine its source! When you use a Henser, you are opening the Chamber it is connected to. In the case of fire, you briefly access the Chamber of Fire, and as the gate is opened, the one flows through the other. As for the title of *Dealer*, I trust that you have indeed traveled to the land that uses such a term?"

"If you mean one where waterfalls fall upward, then yes, I have been there. Is that also where you came from?"

"I have different origin, simply put. But I myself have made profitable business there. A *Dealer* is their term for one who sells these *Hensers*. Though that is not the best description of our work. We simply seek out those who we think can wield these gifts correctly and offer them the chance to. As such, I am here now, offering them to you as a friend of business. Here, have this on the house."

"I will have none of it!"

The man looked sternly. "Do you know what lies behind this door?" he asked.

Carls vaguely remembered his intentions before the Gambler had interrupted.

"Behind this door lies a deeper threat than any you have faced. Yes, that means the Nightingale. This *creature*, however, is not summoned as the Nightingale was. It is its *own* being and has gained tremendous power through fusing with another dark force. You seek answers behind the power within Hensers, and surely this goes far beyond that. You will not, in the slightest, have any chance of accomplishing what you came here for unless you put aside your past failure and man up! I warned you what these can do, and you also have seen all too much what they tend to leave behind. But that does not mean they cannot help. You are different from the rest, which is why I think of you as a valued customer. You'd do best not to ignore my offers, for they do not come to many. And rarely are they ever free."

"You claim to only be doing business with me? Then explain their numbers! How is it that everywhere I turn there only lies destruction and so often the ashes of *your* cards?"

The man held silent, as though a part of him felt pity for Carls' temper. But the man was right. If it was anything like that which he'd come to know as a Possessioner, then he had no hopes of fighting it alone. Even with what the Nightingale had left for him. He didn't even know how to use it. A stick? What was he thinking? But a Henser... was that any different? He had sworn he would never resort to them again, and yet here he was about to receive another. *Just this once*, he said. *I only need it this once.*

He took the card from the table. *The Chamber of Ice.*

The Gambler seemed uplifted by his action. "There, there now! Just remember, wield them wisely! And here, you will need more than that if you wish to sustain any chance of victory." He withdrew another card from his deck and flung it into the air. It spun around and fluttered back to the table, landing face up. "The Barrier," he remarked with awe. "What luck! Go ahead, take it, friend, it's on the house."

"Why are you simply giving me these? You have yet to charge me for even one, so what is their cost? Or are you not telling me for a reason?"

He got a mysterious glare. "As I said, there are only a few meant to be *wielders*, less they use these gifts incorrectly." The man snapped his fingers and was gone—table and all—and Carls was left gazing at the door, two cards in his hand. Both of which he had not seen the likes of before.

Finally, A Man Worth Reckoning

For something to occur so suddenly, it was as though the entire scene had already been planned. Carls saw down the aisles of chairs leading up to the far wall. He also saw the dark hands coming after him in a fury of rage and hunger. The fists of the beast thundered into the room's interior as Locke propelled himself along the wall and over the first line of seating. He could vaguely make out the image in the distance. Not of his opponent, but of *her*. His view was quickly obstructed by the monstrosity of resistance far greater than he had expected.

It was a Shem.

The creature had no sense of form in its movements and attacks, it but moved and responded in the instant that its last action completed. A third limb reached out for Carls—the other two merging as its mass corrected to his evasion and struck again. The place stained with his blood and sweat—his bones crashing against the far wall. It had him in a vice grip, but he'd managed to pull the stick from his sash just beforehand. He struggled for room and put all he had in efforts to pierce through the grip that bound him.

POW!

His eyes shot wide to the wave of rippling force shredding from his small stick. His feet touched ground, and the Shem reeled in attempt to regather itself. He looked down. A handle had appeared at its bend, and from its front barrels some blue energy emerged. He fired again.

A blast met with the adjoining parts of the Shem, and it lashed back at him. *Left knee down and shift to the left*, Carls dictated as his body moved.

A thud hit where his body had last been, and he rolled up three feet from it. *What had happened? What was it that the Nightingale had given him?* He held up the gun and fired again—the substance of the Shem's exposed limb snapping under the contact of energy. *But it's only rejoining as I segregate it. There must be some way...* he recalled his first encounter with one. Had Kit actually defeated it or simply warded it off? How could he kill what has no flesh?

He'd made the mistake of thinking too long and underestimating the Shem. Before he could interpret it, the Shem had spread its form across the entire room. *What? It hadn't hit?*

That wasn't its intent.

The walls broke way and room shuddered. The Dealer had been right: this *was* more than a Shem. It had been fused with something else—and he only knew of one other thing to manipulate its surroundings. He shot off another round at its center mass and tried locating the girl. Too late. A splinter of a snapped two-by-four came flying at him. To make matters worse his footing completely gave. The floor beneath him dropped two stories as he twisted his waist toward the splinter and fired.

The wood cracked and showered about him as he hit against an emerging vein. *Wait... vein? Moss? Was this the same as the room the boy had led him through?* He caught his breath as the rejuvenated Shem came rushing at him. It had grown three times in mass—as had everything else. He couldn't believe his eyes seeing the force that emanated from its body, causing objects to levitate in the air and dash toward him at will. *What?*

"Barrier!" Carls yelled, not realizing his hand had lifted before him. The Shem clashed against it and splinters deflected and bounced back. *Had he just summoned a barrier?* Carls looked at his left hand. The card was still there; the gun still dripped in sweat to his right. *Where had it come from?*

The barrier wasn't meant to be circumnavigated. The Shem had broken to the left and peeled around it where it could—lashing its body at him from the side. Carls made a leap for the adjacent vein as the one he had been on snapped. Climbing up, he managed a glance at the card. It hadn't vanished. When he'd used the Chamber of Fire, it had been engulfed. Did they have limits to their use? Or could they be used more when wielded correctly?

"Barrier!" Carls shouted again to his right, and the Shem collided against the clear wall. The barrier was indestructible. *But are they permanent?*

Drop and to the left, Carls processed as his body landed on yet another vein. Regardless, he wasn't getting any closer to beating it. The Shem was learning to read the barriers quicker now too. He'd best not overuse them. *Where is she?* He searched pleadingly in hopes of locating the illusionate.

The ground shook again, and the entire place shifted its terrain. The vein he was on lifted at least twenty feet as one of the walls broke off and formed beneath him. How the Shem was doing this, he did not know. Only that he had to stop it soon before it cornered him. Diving to the right, he flung his gun at the passing mass of dark—the limb peeling from its entity. *Not good enough*, he commented, twisting his body upright at the new direction of attack. The Shem caught his shoulder. At just the moment of impact, it had redirected its entire motion and now came to entangle him.

But Carls wouldn't let that happen. His lungs bellowed in a roar of effort as he dug the barrels of his gun into the dark below. The barrels broke through to a blade of emerald. *A blade?*

He plummeted to the vein below. The Shem retracted and repaired. Yes, the barriers were not permanent. He'd noticed the Shem moving through where they had been—being how it had come at him from all sides just then.

The Chamber of Ice, he reminded himself. The Dealer had also given him that card, and he was beginning to understand why. *The man was more aware than he let on...*

He needed to draw it out. He was unsure as to whether he had just one use or more with the card, and he wasn't going to risk any chances. *High ground*, he observed. With feet in balance and body low to combat the currents, he ran his way along the veins to the opposing end. He needed to be at least two flights higher than he was (the floor he had originally been on). Hands to the wet, vine-like moss, he climbed. As his palms reached the next height, so did the Shem coming at him. He rolled onto the extent of overgrowth and shot his gun twice in the opposing direction.

When had it switched back?

His heart skipped a beat to his surprise. *There*, he redirected himself. The form was barely recognizable, but there the girl resided—arms dangling above her in a mess of vine and her head drooped low. Her body was pale and near bloodlessness. Carls swung his gun at her and, to his need, it formed into a fine point and cut through her bindings. She leaned forward for Carls to catch—but his embrace came empty as his own body hit against the adjacent wall.

A blade to the first limb, he spun and dodged the second, deciding best to deal with the Shem first before her. Though she looked so weak, he saw her awareness returning as her eyes lifted. But to his misfortune, she did not recognize him as a friend. In terror, she pressed her back against the wall and tried to stand so as to flee. "No!" Carls called out seeing a hand of the Shem reach after her. He raised his blade and found that it had returned to its first state—a bent stick. "No!"

Veins snapped beneath his crushing body as he tried landing himself upright (which he failed miserably at). Pain wasn't even beginning to express how he felt. Torture was more like it. He felt every inch of his fall down to the bottom floor. The Shem wasted no time and now sent its entire entity down toward him.

Now.

Back numb and nimble, Carls somehow mustered the strength, flinging a barrier before him and rolling from beneath it. The Shem's center mass collided, and its own previous momentum kept it from altering course in time. *Which was exactly what he wanted.* With all left in him, he forced his weight upward and over the barrier. "Ice!" he yelled from within, his face tensing and both hands shoving outward. The card lit in a cold mist of blue and chill as the entire room before him froze to ice. And as he fell, he drew forth his gun and braced himself.

POW!

The Shem shattered into a million pieces, and Carls landed to the wet mush below him, puffs of air leaving his lungs.

The Return (Arms Wide Open)

The scenery had changed again. Though not to something new. He was back in the hall—his knees pressed to the carpet floor and eyes squinting to the fluorescent lights. The girl resided not but ten feet before him, her body shivering to an internal chill. Just past her, and in the doorway of her attempted escape, stood Xavier. Had he been the one to stop her? But how? He was only a hologram… a tripper…. Though Carls was beginning to think otherwise… Regardless, his attention returned to the illusioned girl. Her name—what was her name?

He staggered his way toward her. He could hear her muttering as she shook her body back and forth. "No, no, no…" she wept.

Carls eased beside her, wary as to not overdo himself.

"No!" she lashed out, body flailing across the carpet as she tried to keep him distant.

"I'm here to help you," Carls called back to her.

"No…" she groaned, her body broken.

"Please, don't let this win you. You don't have to be like this. He's still waiting for you. Mike is still wanting you to return. Don't leave him like this."

Her head shook and hands trembled. Carls knelt low to her level. "He wants you back, miss. I'm here to bring you. But you *have* to fight it for me. For *him*."

"I… can't…" Her breathing hardened. *Time is running out.*

"You have to fight it," Carls reiterated.

She wasn't listening anymore, her back against the wall and palms to her tear-filled eyes. He had to think of something and fast. But she had been illusioned for so long now… He remembered just moments before:

the man on the fringe of becoming a Fallen One. She was nowhere near his state. She could fight it. She had to.

Carls reached into his sash and felt for the vial. It was still there. But should he? *Should he force it upon her even if she didn't want it?*

He looked to Xavier for confirmation. The man still stood in the doorway, arms folded across his chest, just watching. Locke held out the vial for her to see. He wanted her to know what he meant to do. That she needed it. Her body was fighting a million-and-one things, and it would do her best even with just the one. He gazed deep into her eyes and hers locked back to his. For a moment, he caught glimpse of the true person lying beneath the illusion.

"Just hold on there," he said, bringing his hand steadily closer to her outstretched arm. She followed his movements down to her wrists and fought every sense screaming to jerk away. Carls could but hold his breath and hope that she would follow through, the needle touching skin to her vein. He could feel his eyes dry out from the infinity it seemed to drain in the time it took to puncture, but before he could even blink, he felt the grip of another hand grab hold of the vial. It was hers, and she seemed determined to help. Thus, hand in hand, she pressed the needle down and remained steady to the last drop of liquid entering her blood. She did it for herself and for the hope of reaching her husband again. Though a simple feat, Carls was astounded at the significance of her involvement. It seemed as though she were forcing herself to be convicted of fighting against everything she believed. As if she was re-experiencing a change in realities. Only this time, one less feared. This time it was for one that she desired.

The vial fell to the carpet empty of everything, and she took in her first breath of a revived life.

Though not instantly healed, the action had changed her heart and mind, and she once again opened her eyes.

The medicine was fast at work, but her body still far from recovery. Carls drew one of her arms atop his shoulder and decided to carry her the rest of the way—Xavier being the one who led the way, his image flickering from point to point, corner to corner, and hall to hall until they finally broke free of the corporation's maze.

From there, Carls did as any good man would do and carried Sherlin's wife all the way back to him, bearing her weight over his and ignoring his discomfort and pain.

For him, it was enough just knowing he was to see his daughter again.

He was welcomed with arms wide open. Joanna looked livelier than he'd ever seen her. Then again, it seemed she was just three a few moments ago. Time had sped by and he hadn't cared to notice. When it all began, everything went by so quickly. His reality, his daughter, his shock, terror, loss, confusion—his wife. Sherlin noticed his fists clenching at the thought. The man moved from the tent where they had his wife under intensive care. She had been returned, but not all was well for her. Sherlin took a seat atop one of the empty supply crates next to Locke.

"I can't express to you how much I appreciate what you've done," he said. "You must have gone through a lot to get her. I can only imagine the kind of man it took to bring her back. But how about you? Have you come around yet?"

Locke didn't answer. He was stuck in the state of hearing but bearing an inability or desire to respond. It was as though he just stared into space, trying to communicate through the absence of sound.

"I never told you her name, you know..." Dyrdrik went on to say. He looked out across the encampment at all the people that were sheltered by it. "Elpida. It means 'hope'. Quite a coincidence, eh? I don't know who you are or your story, but I do know I have you to thank for bringing me back *hope*."

Hope. What was it about such an ideal that clung to the desperate man's heart? Hope in what? An end?

He wanted to compliment the man on her name but remained speechless. He could only watch as his daughter played in the distance. She'd been getting along with the other kids. They all seemed to love her company. And who couldn't? She was a beautiful, young girl. Just like her mom...

"... if you would like—" Sherlin's hand patted against Locke's shoulder. His reality jumped back, and he looked at the man. He hadn't caught a single word, but the man stood regardless and left.

"Hey, dad, look!" a voice cut in. He turned back to his five-year-old as she came running up to him wielding a toy airplane.

"Wow, that's cool!" he played along, swooping her up and to the side.

She was to her feet and running again. Such innocence. So unaware. He wished she would never have to see what it was like out there, but he would be doing her wrong to hide it from her. He would have to explain to her eventually. But for now, he would let her play. Let her live.

Commotion stirred in the back. He heard some men shouting and saw a figure approach the camp. "Daddy!" Joan called out to him, running to his feet for an embrace. The unease had scared her. He decided to check it out.

"Get out!" one of the men was shouting at the intruder, "You don't belong here! Scat!" It was Jailer, and he had his shotgun waving in the air.

"Wait!" Carls butted in. "Stay here," he said to his daughter as he pressed to the front. "I know this man!"

"We all do," Jailer scoffed back, not hesitant in the least. "He's only trouble, you know nothing!"

"No, I mean I helped him while finding Sherlin's wife. He's changed, he's fine now." It was the same boy he'd left in the crate-packed hall. The same one who had resisted becoming a Fallen One.

Jailer clenched his jaws and shook his head. "I won't buy it!"

"Calm down, Jailer," Sherlin ordered. "Carls, stay out of this. This man doesn't belong here. Not with us. Not with our people."

"So you know him? You can't just leave him out there! He'll die!"

Jailer loaded the gun's barrels. "And I can help that!" He aimed it at the intruder.

"Stop!" Carls yelled. Before any of them could do anything, he had managed to get between the boy and the gun. How *could* he forget the face?

"Carls, back off," Sherlin said, "there is way too much happening here for you to play macho."

"You can't just—" Carls' words were silenced by a deep groan. Every eye before him shuddered. He himself recognized it.

"Please..." the man pleaded behind him, "Please, just a place to stay..."

They were right. He didn't know what was going on. But he knew what was coming. Sherlin ordered the women back, and Jailer pressed past Carls' still body. "Just for you, I won't kill him," he spat in passing.

"Please!" the intruder yelled as Jailer shoved him back and away.

Sherlin gripped Locke's shoulder to prevent any more interference. "Come," he spoke urgently, "we're moving camp. Now."

Hearsay (TAP)

"Where there is an attraction of groups, a business is sure to rise."
-T.J. Lawrence, A Multi-trillionaire Businessman

Joan had been by his side the whole time. Even after they had moved camp, she now rested on his legs as he sat next to the sparking embers of the small campfire. He couldn't tell for sure if it was night or day, but it definitely felt late to him. Time seemed only a shadow of significance in such a place—for he had completely lost track of it. They had barely managed to escape detection of the stalker.

Carls couldn't stop worrying about the man they had left behind. He knew the kid stood no chance against a Possessioner. Not in the state he was in. Not in his weakness. His palms sweat with the guilt of not pressing harder for the man's safety. But Sherlin had seemed pretty set on the decision, and back there wasn't the time to be picking fights. He was still trying to find those he could trust and depend upon.

"Why couldn't you take him in?" he asked against the flames. Sherlin had sat in silence across from him, a stern look on his face. Almost as though a bitterness was attached to the appearance of the man Carls' had helped fight against falling. Carls couldn't even recall his name. He tried thinking back to that moment—to what had been said.

Sherlin spoke. "Next time, when we tell you something, while you're in *my* camp and under *my* wing, you better listen. You could have had twenty people killed back there, easily. This kid, this *Narrl*, is no man we can trust. He... he has only brought trouble."

They both gazed into the fire. "Sherlin, I've been out there, I've seen what it's like. I saw him and what he was becoming, and I stopped it. He is no different—"

"That is where you are wrong, Mr. Locke. Do not think you have the whole picture, for none of us do. Yes, you may have helped him back there, but you didn't *save* him."

"And how can we? If you just throw him out there!"

"Enough!" Sherlin cut, taking in the extra breath so as to not wake the little girl. "My wife... tried helping him."

What? "What do you mean *tried* helping him? Is he not different from all the other illusionate?"

The man's expression was solemn in recollection. "He is no illusionate," he said calmly, the flicker in his eyes showing regret and pain. "He came to us once before, back when Elpida was her normal, beautiful self. We were all wary of him. He just didn't fit the profile of what he knew out there, but my wife was determined to help him. This was, of course, when we were all still gung-ho about reaching out and sheltering everyone we could. We all believed that we could make this into a better place. That if there was a haven for us to live in, then there was a chance we could come out better in all this. We weren't stuck up. We knew everyone here deserved an opportunity to find protection. We felt it upon our shoulders to reach out as TAP secured us a haven. My wife was the fueling rod that drove us to act with such helping hands. We used to count up into the hundreds... we used to believe...

"Well, anyway. Elpida was determined that Narrl was to be no different. So, she began to help him. And that is when she first conducted his illness. I do not know how exactly, only that whatever she did, it wasn't helping the strange case of our new arrival. He was always on edge, and *always* scared—which is the most typical trait of an illusionate. The people began to worry as Elpida slowly picked up the unease. Then, one day, Narrl snapped. None of us had witnessed it before, so we were all too terrorized to react. In a split second, he went from sipping a meal to... to..."

Sherlin stoked the flames to steal the time away. His voice had weighed and throat clogged, but he continued nonetheless: "It was with Jailer's family. In two swipes he had killed both Jailer's younger siblings, a sister and a brother. He alone stood up against the mutating nightmare, biding the rest of us enough time to pack the necessities and flee. However, the delay cost more than any of us could possibly understand. Before we had even the chance to gather ourselves from the inside betrayal, over half the crew had been pounded senseless by the kid. We barely made it, and every one of us with enough terror to never forget the kid's face.

"Afterward, the rest began thinking my wife had conducted the same illness, as she had become rather unstable by then. I refused to believe them. I knew she was a strong woman who would never let herself fall victim to such monstrosity. But she only got worse. Then she started becoming alone. The people saw this as for the best. They knew I couldn't let her go, but that if she wandered out herself... I would... she would just eventually disappear. Her visits back became less and less. I tried nourishing her and bringing her food, but her mind was weakening and soon it became harder and harder for me to look into her eyes and see... nothing. No longer Elpida, but I still loved her. I still clung to her, hoping she would turn around.

"She was beyond recognizing me, and I could only recognize her if I got close enough. My love grew hard and hope fainter. It became harder and harder to find her. Only the clanging of her pipe she had picked up kept me certain she was still alive. Until one day... she vanished. I tried pursuing her, but it was hopeless. Because of Narrl, I had to let her go."

The embers sparked against his eyes. Carls leaned back against the pillar behind him—running his hand through Joan's thin, brown hair. *To think that she would become victim to such illness... to wander off so far having been so strong...*

"But thanks to you," Sherlin added, "she has also made it back. As for Narrl, Jailer would lay his life down to keep him out of here. I reckon you can take me for my word having seen him earlier. And with what he did to Elpida, I cannot say I'd let him either. We're done taking chances, Locke, no more lives for a pointless charade."

"What about TAP? You mentioned them, and I've come across the words a lot. I thought you said they had a place to go."

"TAP... psch. We've long since lost trust in them. It's been at least three months since they went sour, you know. Everything we thought they stood for has come back to bite us. There is no haven, and we care not to wait for it. Might as well make the most of what we have and be satisfied in it than to become dependent on someone who constantly stabs you in the back."

"So, you're giving up?"

"Yes, Locke, we're giving up. Giving up on thinking there's anyone else out there that cares about the lives of those who are actually suffering in this the most. All we would get were requests, requests, requests—and not once did they tell us how far along the plan was coming. We were puppets, and I could take no more of it. They said it was for the best that they kept so private. But who gives hope when there's no trust! No one. It was obvious TAP was using us as pawns to further their work."

"But what is TAP, exactly?" Carls asked, inching closer to the warmth of flame and cradling his daughter's resting head.

Sherlin exhaled his short-winded breath. Carls felt childish for asking so many questions, but he was *finally* getting answers. Maybe not to everything, but at least *something*.

"If you are so interested in their work, then go and find them. I doubt they'd let you in on anything. They even stopped communicating with their own agent!"

"Agent?"

"Yes, Trip. You can find him around the Theatra. At least, that was his last whereabouts. The man's a fighter. A kind fellow, if you get to know him—that is if you can catch his attention enough to slow him down. He was our only link to TAP for the last little bit. But then his messages were becoming vaguer, and it was obvious even he wasn't getting informed much. But be careful out that way. Friedelock's patrols have doubled. We lost contact with everyone in the Delvore Sanctum."

"Wait, there are other groups?"

"Yes, scouting and reconnaissance groups. I may not like TAP or the idea of welcoming everyone in anymore, but I haven't lost heart. Especially when it comes to fighting Friedelock...."

"Friedelock...." Carls muttered.

"Tell me, Carls, how is it you knew who I was? How did you come to find out about Mike Dyrdrik and yet know so little of everything else?"

He didn't like the thought of recalling everything. "Simply put," he answered, "Friedelock took my daughter. She had run off, and I stumbled across a group that pointed me to Friedelock."

"Hold on, this group, anyone by the name Chase?"

"Either I didn't catch it or can't remember, sorry. I did find this map and recording on one of them."

Sherlin immediately recognized it, and grief took to his face. He knew that if Carls had the map, they were dead. "That was one of our more recent teams," he remorsed.

"Then I have them to thank for leading me to my daughter."

Sherlin held a new look as he gazed at the girl asleep on Carls' legs, "Indeed, she has grown then."

Carls took it he knew of what work Friedelock was undertaking. "Tell me," he asked, "why is Friedelock doing this? Who is he? And what has come over this place?"

Sherlin laughed. "You truly are a stray dog!" he choked. "It has been quite some time since so many questions have been asked. Most people here don't care about what happened, they'd rather forget it all. In fact, some of them forced the memory out altogether! As seems the case for you. Only you seemed to have forgotten that you even tried to forget what happened. Truth is, I also do not know. I only played in a single part, most of which dealt with Norwick. But I am not caring to reminiscence over the past. I promised Elpida that it was behind me, and I'll hold to that promise. But do not lose your curiosity. It may have killed the cat, but at least it gave it something to look for rather than become a simple drone of a monotonous life.

"Now, get some rest. If you are serious about finding more on TAP, then you must find Trip. His last whereabouts were sent by that team you retrieved this map from." He waved the map and handed it back. "Rest well. We rise early to move camp out further for safety. I shall wake you then, and then we'll depart ways."

The embers burned out slowly to the narrow halls by which they clung. Carls was swift asleep with Joan gently in his arms. He missed the normal life of day-to-day work and harsh conditions of weather. He missed the smell of coffee in the morning that his wife would have prepared regardless of having to leave to work before him. He missed the sleet of pavement to sewage as he would trudge off of the tram and into his workstation half an hour away from home. But for now, he slept—his mind breaking way to an endless valley of thoughts, hopes, and dreams.

Life Is A Journey Better Kept Moving

"Top of the morning to ya!" the wakening tone pierced his ears, a hand jabbing at Carls' side. "Sherlin said it best for you to wake before we move camp again. He also mentioned you were need of a good meal packed for the trip. Come on over!"

Carls rustled from his stiff position. Joan was still asleep. Pulling himself up he was able to stretch and pull her to his shoulders. She sheepishly adjusted and closed her eyes again. He turned around to see the man who had awakened him already on the move.

"I'm Arnold," the man said across his shoulder, "one of the cooks living amidst dire and troubling times, I tell ya!" Carls could tell already the man liked emphasizing his role in playful manner. He was led to the west wing of the camp.

"I enjoy every bit of it, I must say," Arnold continued. "I also act as head of distribution. So if you need anything in relation to supply, I'm the guy you come to." Arnold seemed proud of his feats, though he wasn't the most built man Carls had seen. The man was just shy of six foot, and his appearance resembled much of a fabric designer, though indeed he was not. His bushy, brown hair turned toward Carls as they came up to a crammed tabletop.

"Here we are," Arnold gestured, "you may have your pick of food, bandages, or whatever so long as it can fit into your sash. Sherlin said you were out to find one of TAP's men. And this is great news to me as I have been dying to hear something new on TAP."

Carls observed the items. He found a crate and began looking through the contents. She rubbed her eyes, trying to recall her surroundings and wipe away the sleep.

"You're not taking her with you, are you?" Arnold inquired.

"I plan to, yes. I can't leave her. Not again," Carls said, taking notice of vials of e-Links. Even Arnold took note of his surprise and hesitation. "How did you get these? I thought they were—"

Arnold raised a finger to his mouth as though for secrecy. "You can take those on me, my man and pal," he said. "Not often do we come across a chance to get them, and Sherlin entrusts me with their proper use! E-Links have immeasurable use, but like anything that makes life easier, it also can slow you down."

Carls held them in his palms. He knew how much they helped, but also that they seemed just *too* good to be true. "I can't," he said and handed them back.

"Here me out man," Arnold said. "I know you have your own interests. Your own reasons. Your own story. We all are trying to just *live*. If there is a chance TAP has found us a safe place, *that* is something I want to help. But out there... it's a mess. You'll get chased. You'll get trapped. You *will* find conflict. Trippers, illusionate, the Fallen—they are enough a hassle as it is. But you also have *her*, and that means two-fold for you: you'll have Friedelock to look out for as well."

He'd forgotten about the man. Especially since he'd sided with Antoinette, he could imagine Friedelock had all the more interest in his predicament. "Why is Friedelock so interested in children?"

"It's not just kids he's after. Not in the least. But for him... man, people lose their minds when their work gets ahead of them. Really, I shouldn't be talking about this..."

"And why not? We're here aren't we—in this demonic mall—so why not tell me what's actually going on?

Jailer approached the two, his arms full of miscellaneous armory items. "Arnold, you give him that Hand-Pal yet?"

"Oh, that's right!" Arnold relieved. "Here, Carls, almost forgot."

The man reached into his apron and pulled out Carls' Hand-Pal. "Your Hand-Pal needed a huge update. These things can actually be really cool." He returned its ownership. Carls could tell Arnold had a knack for these devices. His expression immediately lightened and mouth rambled ninety to nothing. "These retro cells are the bomb, man. Before, you could only receive signals and input tapes, but that was without an NV card. I just so happened to have a spare one for you and put it in. It's a little older but should do. Now it'll not only pick up signals but also take calls, make calls, record messages—pretty much anything with a *Voice*."

"Voice? What do you mean?"

"The NV is a New Voice card. The New Voice was a whole 'nother business funded by Lawrence himself. It's what speaks to you and reads your messages. Granted, calls and recordings will still be in their sender's voice, but the whole interface itself is held by the most current NV spotlight."

"Enough rambling, Arnold," Jailer interjected. "The meat and bone of it is singers sang and people paid. The winner of the competition was declared the New Voice, and hence everyone in support would go buy the latest NV card so they could have her voice on their devices. That's it. Bets were won; portions were lost. Just another business for Lawrence to rack in the dough."

Jailer cleared a spot on the table and began stuffing the items into near crates.

"So, what now?" Carls asked, still not sure of the whole Hand-Pal ordeal.

Arnold picked up the lecture: "It's the pride of Mx3. As their saying goes: 'Putting to memory what matters most.' With the smartphones of *old* having everyone and your aunt able to listen in and be hacked, these things are impenetrable. Practically speaking. Mainly, no one remembers how to hack the old tech anymore. Well, none except the legendary *Todd Whiggins* that is! If you need anything, my station is 43. It's an open channel, so careful what you chime in on the free-waves. It at least gives me a listening post for those who need help."

"Thanks, Arnold," Carls said, shoving it into his pocket. He'd already filled up his sash and now had Joan back atop his shoulders.

"Good luck, Carls," Arnold said, quickly picking up a crate and moving it to the near cart.

Carls made his way across what was left of the camp and found Sherlin instructing Linda and the kids. He was grateful for Linda. She had watched over his daughter well while he'd been away, and Joan liked her. It was when Linda turned to leave that Sherlin noticed him there.

"Ah, you're awake, good. Arnold return your Hand-Pal?"

"Yes, and thank you."

"Good. Well, I hate to ask this of ya, but if you see anything out there, please give us the heads up. When you need refilling, we'll try to help you in exchange. Our scouting teams grow thin and we haven't heard from the area you're headed to. If you come across anything, I'd like to know. And good luck. Especially with your daughter."

The people under Sherlin's protection had given him shelter, but even now he knew there was something more to be discovered. He was not satisfied with settling down and forgetting all that surrounded him and its cause. He did not wish to become as the people there had: content with just living. Sherlin himself had shown their loss in flame—something every man needed for a drive to live. He wasn't about to just sit and watch the flames grow dimmer. The fire needed stoking. The heat needed a story to its burning. He wanted answers. TAP was a step in that direction for him. According to Sherlin, they had a key to fixing this problem.

Whatever the problem was.

Enlightened & Unaware

The halls were much vaster when walked alone. He knew he would have to yet again pass through dreaded territory to reach the Theatra of which Sherlin spoke. The stillness and shroud haunted him. He found himself thankful for once that the lights were dim, though why so he did not know. The place had been so alive, so filled, when he'd first arrived with his family. He remembered the crowded shops and restaurants—his mind could even picture it vaguely as he walked. But it all lay in ruin. Deserted and wrecked as chaos stripped all it once held of order. *What had happened here? What was this place?*

He could feel Joan stirring and let her down. He remembered first hearing about it. The very day was still clear to him. Bill had told him it was the perfect vacation spot. Full of activities, scenery, and astounding feats. It sure was astounding. Everywhere he had read up on it said it was the attraction of the century. How this was possible, he did not know. They had been in such an economic crisis and devastation that it seemed impossible for such a place to emerge from the ashes. And yet it had. Amidst the depression and struggle of countries abroad as companies went bankrupt, governments crashed, and powers fell, somehow the Grand Attraction had been made. Then again, everyone was looking for an escape from the loss. All they needed was hope of an illusion, and they would flock to it. Carls had. Bill had. And everyone in this place had. Whatever the birth was of such an idea, it had worked.

Joan had slipped through his fingers and ran out before him.

"Joan!" he called out for her to come back. But it was too late. She turned with innocence in her smile, her hand outstretched. His body froze and eyes shot open. Literally.

Elairah held her hand—having suddenly appeared. All around him people hustled and noise sprang from every corner. *What is happening?*

He felt a panic surge through him. "Joanna!" he shouted, reaching for her. As his skin touched hers, everything vanished but a single thug coming from behind. He felt contact to his back and spun with a fist.

It met nothing but a dodging figure as the man ducked and came from another angle. Carls swept up Joan by her waist and shoved his body between them. He tripped on the man's heel and hit with his back to the floor. "Get up!" the man yelled while swinging his foot. All Carls recalled was pushing his daughter to the side and taking the brunt of the blow—his body skidding across the floor. Another man entered the scene as the first disappeared.

What?

Carls swung a fist at the opposer, but it went straight through. *What was this? Some hallucination? Or were these just trippers?*

He took a boot to his rib cage and hit to the near support beam. There were more now, and he was swinging in every which direction—his knuckles meeting the concrete of the pillar where he'd thought one to reside. The blood trickling sent him reeling to his senses. From behind, a form emerged.

A Fallen One.

A trap. Joan stood lost at his aimless actions. Something about her... could she not see any of this? Was he just a maniac in her eyes?

But now wasn't the time. He turned to face the six-armed beast. Just the mere size of its body had made climbing to the second floor easy.

"Daddy, what's going on?" her little voice came. Just like Elairah's voice. He couldn't help his breathing, nor the firm grip on his little girl. He could not fight it with the illusions still spitting at him. He grabbed her and ran—rounding the corner to yet another sterling surprise. Body dropping low, he barely managed to evade the pounding force of awe-striking, masonic forearms of a Shem. *Two?!*

The downward momentum slid him out of reach as the Fallen One drove its weight into the Shem. The two met with force and temper—the Shem somehow also lashing at Locke. But its efforts were hindered by the larger threat—Carls wasted no time, instead crawling to his feet and making a break from it. Down the halls, he ran with his daughter tight in his arms. One of the trippers was following him.

"Daddy, who's that?" her hand stretched to the side. Carls followed it to a figure just fading from within the near store. It couldn't be!

"Not now, Xavier!" he yelled, not caring for sympathy at the moment. *How had she seen him?* But now he realized the man's intentions. His image flickered hard to the left and down another hall. Despite detesting his own desperacy, Carls followed.

The shop immediately caught his attention. *City News!* was etched across its entrance, and TVs buzzed beneath its roof next to paper-filled racks. The doors to it were hard pressed, but he managed to shut them tight. The glass at least dampened the sound.

"Daddy, I gotta use the bathroom!" Joan piped, completely oblivious to the dangers outside. At least here, for the time, it was safe. And there were restrooms in the back. He leaned against the front post of the bathroom and waited. If she had been nearly trained at three, at five he hoped there to be no problem at all. Her high-pitched voice bounced off the walls as she sang at the top of her lungs. "I was right, you know," came Xavier's deep voice from behind the counter of the shop's reception.

"Why do you keep appearing like this?" Carls asked. "Every time I see you, even though you help, I know they're coming. So why do you?"

"Do you really think she is safer just being with you?"

Carls had to push aside the guilt. The man was right. Bringing her wasn't the safest thing. But as a father, he couldn't trust her in the hands of any other. "Mine will have to do," he said. He could still hear her singing. Must have been a song the other kids had taught her because he'd definitely never heard of it before—but one phrase caught his attention: "... *Watch as the petals drop and learn from their song to let not the faint fall.*"

Let not the faint fall. Those had been the same words etched onto the carpet and that the boy had sung.

"She has quite the wild imagination it seems," the man commented.

Carls could feel the steam rising within him. *What did this man know? What was he keeping secret?* "What of her?"

Though his form lay hidden behind the bend of the bathroom walls, Carls could tell he was smiling (who knew what all the man was actually aware of).

"Know this," Xavier began, "there is a difference between becoming aware and being enlightened. Remember Antoinette's words. And I must say, you are far from a full awareness, but indeed you have something of value worth fighting for. Both for my and your sake."

Antoinette's words—they were coming back to him. "*Your eyes are still but opening to what lies beneath. Do not overstep yourself else you be swallowed up like the rest. The illusions are powerful. Do not think you are yet free of them.*" His eyes were opening. Did that mean Xavier was calling him enlightened? Was that what set him apart from the rest?

"And she's aware..." Carls said beneath his breath as the toilet flushed behind Joanna's emerging form. "You are either a genuine friend or filthy deceiver—and I need to know now. I can't be putting my daughter in anymore treachery and yet here you are helping me."

"Just take a look around, my good friend. I shall leave you for now. And do not worry, they will not be finding you here. Not if Whiggins indeed left his mark."

Whiggins? He could almost remember the name.

And now Xavier was gone.

The City News! Shop

Posters were all along the walls. The largest hung above the main display—one of a lady in white clothes standing on the balcony of the Hanging Gardens. Above her, in forties fashion, were the words *"New Babylon Rises from the Rubble!"* Her curled hair hung in the ominous wind her hand was reaching above. *New Babylon?* The term was on every cover in the shop, and the lady's picture covered the front of nearly every magazine and newspaper. He stood next to the display and observed the many articles. They all spoke of this "New Babylon" as though a paradise city. *Is that what they called this place? New Babylon.* It was then he noticed the TVs no longer blurring, but they played a recording. The words hit him from every side as he watched—his daughter too carried away with all the posters and comics to notice.

The cartoon figures resembled the sixties as a voice narrated their story. The figure on the left had his hand on a suitcase and wore a suit and hat. "Too busy these days? Been working non-stop?" the narrator said as the figure broke into a sweat. "Need a break? No worries!" The figure then turned to the second—a man in straps with a cigarette looking at ease and fame. The smoke rose above them, and the narrator spoke the forming words, "Come to New Babylon!" The two met and shook hands, the second taking the man's suitcase and patting the man's back. "We have put aside all the struggles and work you've been abused with and offer a break from it all! And if you want, you can even make us your new hobby! Forget those back-bending days of coming home to barely a bowl of rice and milk... we offer you the life you've dreamed of! Fight the depression— join the sensation!" The figures raised their hands to their viewers, and the screen blurred out.

If this place was supposed to be an escape from it all, he wondered how it had ended up so wrong.

"Daddy! There's a big hole in that room, and I found this! Can I have it?" his daughter jumped in waving a comic through the air. A hole? A comic? A smile lit his face. To think that amidst such abandonment and ruin his daughter could still be entertained by a simple comic. You could never shove aside such innocence. And for her, he walked up to the cashier and pretended to exchange with her, acting as the store owner and sharing the laughs and imagination. The register slid open beneath his movements, revealing what bit of currency remained within its cold chambers. It was no presidential figure that was imprinted upon them, but that of a familiar face: *Bill Childs.*

His mind flashed back to that first moment—to the e-Links he would always find lying about. To that newbie who seemingly caught on to things almost too quickly. *Yes, he remembered Bill. He remembered what he had said, only now the severity of how he said it was becoming all the more significant.*

He had wanted Carls to come. He had known something more than what he'd first let on. Looking back, Locke knew he should've known it sounded too good to be true. But was Bill to be the one to blame? The man spoke so confidently...

And how was he now the one on the currency of such a place?

Carls shoved the register closed again and looked at his daughter who was sitting with her legs crossed on the floor and looking through the comic for the tenth time already. *Bill Childs... who was the man?*

The Maintenance Bays (Sub-City)

A figure knocked upon the glass—a man in his fifties; white hair, blue eyes, and spectacles. He seemed urgent to be let in.

Only, *where had he come from?* Xavier must have been wrong. If Whiggins' mark was indeed to keep them secure, it sure wasn't working. Just as quickly as he had noticed the man, so did he the flicker of its image. Carls' hand caught the collar of his daughter as two beasts tore through the adjacent hall and shattered the front glass of the *CityNews!* shop. He must not have noticed the cart the first time through, but he was quick to flee to the back room as the gas tanks rolled across the floor—hissing. Then came the roar.

The *Fallen One.*

It was the same one he saw raging against the Shem earlier (which explained the tripper). Carls had just the time to shield his daughter as he dove for the shelter, narrowly escaping the tumbling wreckage as the entire front entrance crumbled to the explosion and rage. He'd made it into the bathroom—Joan was screaming in his arms. The hole—she'd mentioned a hole in the bathroom. Maybe it was an escape.

Sure enough, he found a massive hole in one of the stalls. It was a clear path through the white brick and down another passage. A dark one. But at least it held better hopes of escape. With his daughter close and his eyes aware, he stepped into the crevices of the small passage, eager to escape the beast raging behind. Down and just a little farther he saw that it met up with another pass—one with lights.

Piping lined the four corners of the tight walk-space. He guessed a system similar to this ran through the entire infrastructure. It was obvious this place had been used frequently with the metal cross-grips wearing thin.

Carls hadn't yet come to ease in the inconsistency the lighting gave. His daughter was scared. He was scared. His ears still rang from the explosion.

His footing slipped. Joan had been calling out to him, but he'd been too dazed to notice. Some sludge seemed to be following them. *Sludge?* He looked at the walls and rail flooring. Indeed, it was not a simple factor of being unmaintained. They were distinct. They were *aware*.

He cradled her closer to him, not quite sure yet how to respond. *What are they?*

Their forms seemed unsolidified. They morphed and moved as though completely manipulated by their surroundings. He saw them change—from sludge to an attempt at arms. The one he had stepped on seemed more agitated than the rest. It had reemerged from the depths of the railing and spread itself like a cobweb. Carls stepped back.

The creature lashed out at him—a single thread catching his arm and twisting about it. Not wanting any risk, Carls withdrew his stick and hacked at the strand—tearing himself free. Spinning on his heels, he grabbed hold of Joan yet again and ran, taking more heed of his steps in the inconsistent lighting. One of the panels gave and he crashed down.

"Daddy!" his daughter cried as her foot caught the vise-grip, drawing blood.

He realized now that below them were the sewers—a place he could not afford for his daughter to fall into.

He looked intensely into her eyes, trying to calm himself as he climbed up. "Wanna play a little game, Joan?" he asked, brushing her up as more web splashed past them. "How about hide-and-seek? Okay, dear? You go hide, and I'll find you, ok?" He set her down, and she looked at him. For some reason, for some bizarre and unknown purpose, she seemed to understand, and turning, she left. *Could it be? Was it the Trust Seal of Bondage that she acted upon? Was it simply trust that a child would listen and obey amidst such odds?* She was past the next junction by the time Carls felt the grip on his ankle. He twisted his body toward the slime and thrust his heels at the mass of it. "Come on!" he yelled, frustrated that his gun was not working. *Why was nothing working when and where he needed it?*

He didn't have time. Kicking at one of the joints, he busted a pipe and shoved it at the—whatever it was—before him. Muddied water spewed everywhere, and he momentarily broke free. The other creatures were beginning to get agitated as well from the commotion. *Great, more is the last thing I need.*

Carls took three steps to clear the bend and see his daughter behind the desk of an opened maintenance room.

"Look, daddy, I hid!" she said at the sight of him.

"And you did a good job too!" he said to her, jerking the drawers open and trying to keep the conversation. *But how were you supposed to convince a five-year-old that there wasn't more to the situation?*

Found it.

"You just stay there, ok? I'm gonna find a place to hide too."

"Is someone else playing?" she asked, but he was already back around the desk—some sort of maintenance gun in his hand.

"Just stay there," he said and disappeared.

They covered the lights. *So, they liked to crawl and mess with everything? No wonder they preferred the sub-system.* Carls held the gun close to his chest, trying to cling to the walls and increase his stealth. He could hear their slurring—or at least he thought he could—it was hard to differ from the dripping pipelines and short-circuits.

He fired off to his left—a spark of light ricocheting off the walls. He heard a shrill and dissipating liquid. *What kind of gun was this?* He held it up now and outstretched, feeling slightly better of himself. His breathing was heavy; his eyes were wavering. A drip touched the shoulder of his coat, and he shot upward—

Nothing. Just a jolt of electricity as it followed the water down to his skin. He tumbled backward and strained to see into the dark. He could not see anything.

"Daddy?" his daughter peered from her cover as he reemerged, his shoulders weak but body still composed.

"Joan, are you okay?" he asked, embracing her and caring for her cut. The bleeding had stopped, but the flesh about it was swollen. *Not good for such an unclean atmosphere.*

"Did you get found?" she said.

"Daddy was, but now the game's over. Let's go."

He'd searched the cabinets and drawers twice over for ammunition. Whatever the actual use was for, he was thankful to God that they had such a device down here. The battery packs it took were heavy, but it was the brand name that held his attention. *BrainWare Power Cells.* Always BrainWare. Did they have some monopoly on the industry? Or was the market within New Babylon geared around monopolies to begin with? Friedelock, Antoinette, Lawrence, BrainWare—all held an edge above the rest. Mx3 included.

He came to another maintenance bay. There seemed to be a lot of such winding paths. Not that he cared—it was a break from the close-tight passageways and hissing pipes. This one was larger. The cut on Joan's leg made it hard for her to stay focused, but she neither complained. For a five-year-old, he was astounded at her self-control. Or rather, thankful for it.

"Daddy, did you get cut too?" she asked, pointing to his own leg. He looked down, eyes widening. Same leg, same length, same spot—*what?* He pulled his pants up. *How? There had been no tear in his pants?*

It now was noticeable. The pain of its depth spiked as he touched to feel if it was real.

It was, and the only thing making sense of it was the card. He remembered sharing her pain under Friedelock and guessed it to work the same still. Which was both beneficial and risky. He took another look at his daughter's cut. *So long as it helps you*, he said calmly to himself, smiling at her curiosity.

"It's fine, Joan. If you're big enough to handle yours, then I guess I'll handle mine as well."

Such conviction in her smile. She believed in him more than he believed in himself. He brushed aside her hair and held her hand. *I will die for you, Joan. Never forget that.* And who wouldn't lay their life down for such innocence? It was for that that he kept moving. Her trust, her dependence, her need—it was all that he had left to fight for. And for that, he was willing to give to others the hope she gave him. For that, he was wanting to find Trip and whatever it was TAP had been working on. These people needed a haven to go to. They needed a reason to stand against the illusions that possessed them.

He could only pray that Trip still had ties to TAP or at least leads. *I will fight for these people*, he assured himself. *I stand for those whom none else will.*

A single latch rested atop a rusty ladder in the far corner. He had been in the sub-system long enough. It was time to emerge once more. Lord willing, he was closer to his destination than when he'd started.

Trip, A Man Worth Seeking

Trip held his spot at the structure's edge. The bait was set and target approaching. Three days now had he been tracking this beast down—this master of illusion.

He was not the only presence, of course. Trippers and people alike walked the expanse before him. He could see them—the people—but not separate them from tripper or real. Regardless, those that were real walked the fine line between naivety and awareness. He lifted his hand to his watch that fell just a couple seconds short of the new mark.

Fifteen seconds.

He held his breath and took a second look at the crowds. Seventeen figures, only four of which were real, or at least that he could tell. Something about the Theatra Amusement Park seemed to draw out the bridge or whatever it was that separated the aware from the unaware. Only, instead of separation, it somehow bled between them. He checked his watch again.

Nine seconds.

He stepped from his cover and walked past the large tent selling overvalued merchandise. His hand caught the edge of the curtain entrance and cautiously drew it farther aside. He needed them to see.

Four.

He now stood in the center—the seventeen in full view. *Two.* His right palm turned and lifted into the air—body dropping to one knee and a handheld device smashing into the tile floor.

One.

A disc shot up into the air, a pulse suddenly emanating from it. The surge of energy gave him a glimpse at the trippers as their forms flickered to the wave. There were five—five real ones.

The sound came from his right—and faster than he had expected, but he had the five already memorized. The massive black was unmistakable. Weight to his fingers, Trip had already propelled himself as the Shem dealt a heavy blow. The crash obliterated his last position as the creature bent its mass and momentum in the new direction. Trip had rolled next to one of the pillars. There were several that extended beneath the protruding display floor. Just what he needed.

He drew his gun (and no ordinary one, mind you), and he leaped for cover—a shot at the pillar leaving a small attached device. *Five more.*

The gun only held two shots, and he'd already fired the second at an adjacent beam. It was hard enough evading the Shem as he concentrated on placements. But he had waited for this, longed for this.

The Shem seemed aware of their presence too. It knew Trip wouldn't stand for their awakening. The creature stretched out two of its limbs as though forming a multi-headed beast. Trip dug his boots against the tile. He couldn't allow for any unwanted awakenings.

A javelin shot from his wrist, and he was flung toward the middle-aged man just in time. His body hit with the flesh of the Shem and forced it off course by an inch—just enough to avoid. But he wasn't quick enough to stop the second limb from coming through. Relentlessly, it tore through its victim, sending shrills through the dying air.

The other four awakened. Panic flooded an old man as his coffee cup dropped to the floor.

I have to finish this, Trip nudged himself to his feet as the retracting limb slid toward him. Gun reloaded, he fired a distant shot. *Six shots, six pillars, one path. That's all I need.*

The black swept beneath his feet, and he hit hard, but his tailored-ops suit took the most of it. He looked up. A girl. Mid-twenties. High socks. Bright shirt.

The Shem crashed into her as it tore toward Trip's still body. Or rather, *was* still body. He'd picked himself off the floor and launched to the side and behind the pillar from which the Shem came. The posts he needed were in the opposite direction—a distance he wished to not have to recover.

A switchblade was in his hand—his body in the air and rotating above the force. The blade acted simply as a pivotal point. He spun and landed on his feet as the Shem took to another form and rounded back at him from the front. He'd just the time to place a single shot before needing to reload. He stopped, dropped, and rolled with a thud in his wake. *Right side, third clip*—he had the movements memorized. He decided to take the risk and make a break for the end. The Shem, like a serpentine rhinoceros, shook the ground as it wove through pillars and back around. Trip fired off to his right. *That's five. One more.*

His body hesitated. Before him was another girl, her eyes wide pressed, mouth gaping, jaws tight.

A tripper.

His body dropped and back bent more than he'd known possible. The limb had broken through the illusioned image and nearly taken him by surprise. His only warning—the Shem had already claimed her at the pillar. This one was fake.

But he knew the Shem more than capable enough of changing momentum and sending itself crashing down upon him. Palms to the floor, he forced his body to the side as the darkness pounded his vacantcy. Body still bracing for impact, he saw as the limb broke from before him and joined in with the mass from behind. He had no time for any worthy escape. It was now or never.

He took four bounds to the last pillar and lunged himself past it—turning mid-air and placing his last shot. *Now.*

From his waist, he drew a single trigger and—back hitting to the tile—he pulled.

The sets acted as pulleys sending wire spiking through the aligned Shem. The spikes reeled as they tightened and lit up in a rippling flash of static. The creature roared as its attempts to squirm fell apart and its mass turned to a dreary liquid on the floor. Trip stood on his feet and inhaled a long-awaited breath of satisfaction. *Finally.*

He spun around—a second gun drawn (this on loaded with bullets). Behind him stood the remaining two that had awakened. A man and his little girl. But they seemed different.

Especially the girl.

Why There Are So Few Witnesses

Carls Locke held tightly the hand of his daughter—and his breath. He didn't dare to make one move against the drawn gun that was pointed straight at his face. It held steady and firm, not wavering one bit. Indeed, Trip was a man worth seeking.

"Name?" the man spoke commandingly.

"Locke. And this is my daughter, Joan. We were told you could help us."

"By who?"

"Sherlin."

Trip lowered his gun, looking him square in the eye. "I don't remember taking requests from Sherlin. Since when did he stop taking people in?"

"He said you could tell me about TAP."

Trip's expression changed. "Come with me," he said, turning away. Carls noticed a man crouched in the corner that he hadn't noticed till passing. The old man seemed broken at heart and mourning inside. *How long has he been here? Has Trip been ignoring him?* He couldn't get his mind off the burden he felt to kneel down beside the man.

"Don't bother, Mr. Locke. He's in shock. Everything he knew reality to be was just torn away from him. Don't think that you would understand."

As if. Carls knew all too well what it felt like to suffer the shock of losing grasp on one's perceived reality. He looked back at the old man. "You're just leaving him?"

Trip seemed challenged to prove his point. "The man is in denial," he put simply. "Try as you may, he won't be doing anything for a while. It's best to just leave him, and he will decide his next step."

Trip seemed confused that it had taken Carls this long to notice. It was such a familiar circumstance to Trip that he wasn't used to explaining. Nor did he like second-guessing himself. It was just something he never did. He didn't want the responsibility of looking after someone. He'd failed so many already. All he had left to drive him was the journey and fight to the bitter end. He strode into the large, red tent. Locke watched as the man quickly sorted the valuables and took his leave.

"Daddy, isn't that stealing?" Joan asked, pointing at the stranger.

Carls was oblivious as for how to respond. Thankfully, Trip did it for him. "It isn't stealing when it no longer belongs to anyone. They left it here for us. I'm sure they won't mind."

And just like that her attention flung towards a rack of stuffed animals on a display cart. "Hey, daddy! Can I take one?" she asked, jumping up and down.

Carls had to take a second look. He recognized the cart. *The same one that...*

It couldn't be. There was no way. He just shook his head to the notion.

"No, Joan. We don't need it, and it's not ours. It still isn't good to take things."

"Please? I need it really bad!"

"Sorry, maybe another place and time."

Trip made his way to the girl, kneeling to her level. "I'll tell you what. You take this money and place it over there, and I'll get ya whichever one you want, ok?"

She leaped with joy. Trip looked up at Carls, "Sorry, don't want to be going against your word or anything."

"Now can I get one, dad?" Joanna peeped in.

Carls found himself struggling to contain the memories that cart brought back. *Her laughter. The fun they had pretending to chase down the wild clown.*

The moment she disappeared and the moment he went unconscious.

She would have no idea. He didn't like the sight of it at all, nor the thought of carrying a part of it with them wherever they went. In fact, he detested the thought but reached out nonetheless and took from the top a small, stuffed, red teddy bear. Joanna took it with arms wide open— completely oblivious to the significance behind her request. *For Carls at least.*

"You mentioned TAP," Trip jutted in from behind. "Why?"

"I didn't come here to have everything I know shattered to pieces, and I am sure no one else did either. People need a haven—a refuge—from all... delusion. If there's a safe place here for people to go, for my daughter too, then people need to be told."

"It doesn't just work like that," Trip reluctantly replied. "You got a safe haven then you got security. And, for most, security is just an excuse to get comfortable. You get comfortable, you get careless. Such a place can't risk being destroyed from inside out. That's why it wasn't open to everyone. That's why even *now* TAP's exact location has been kept from the outside."

"Wait, so you don't even know where it is? I thought you worked for them?"

"You don't understand TAP and the way they operate, do you? Just because I work for them does not secure any inside position on my part. I was simply their messenger between rally points and distribution centers. It wasn't my job to lead people to the place."

"Then what happened?"

"They went silent, and I've been spending these last few weeks just trying to figure out why."

"What do you mean silent? Sherlin mentioned them just cutting off communication. I wouldn't expect them to be so cold as to abandon everyone if their goals had been to save them in the first place."

"As I said, I don't know why. All I know is that something forced them to shut down from the inside."

"So, this whole talk of a *safe place* is just made up? It doesn't exist, does it?"

"If you are just as curious as I am, then I suggest you pitch in. I don't have all the answers—just the fact that I lost connection is proof enough. However, it *does* exist. I know it. It has to. The men I know to have helped start it wouldn't turn against such a vision so easily. Help me find them, and maybe we can finally start getting some answers."

"If you were left out of the loop, then how do you know about them?"

"I haven't been dormant if that's what you're implying. I'm not just chasing down monsters and putting lives to rest. I believe in what TAP was undertaking, and I want to finish it. But I can't as a one-man team. If you want to help, then help, but I can't be wasting time trying to catch up every curious mind on the happenings."

Carls glanced at Joanna as she played with her bear. All he wanted was for her to get out of this. He'd been reunited with her for the present, but now he wished to secure her future. If lending an arm and foot to yet another cause was a means of doing that, then he would. Not just for her, but others. For the rejected and the helpless.

"I'm in," he said.

A spread of relief filled Trip's face. He put aside his gun and leaned against the near desk. "Then it's time you hear as to why there are so few witnesses."

The Lost Scientists & Their Work

"A voice as beautiful and lustrous as hers, she would win every Challenger from henceforth."
-Sponsor of NV singer Samantha Childs

"There are few who have lived past the exposure of TAP. Not in the sense that TAP eliminates them—but there are those that wish TAP dead and gone. You should know that going into this. My brother and closest cousin both died for this. Friedelock is the primary. That man is a demon in disguise I just know it. Countering him was one of Sherlin's primary tasks when he'd signed on with TAP. But it seems he couldn't take it anymore, or it was just too much. Regardless of any of Sherlin's efforts, TAP seemed to be getting more distant still. I don't know how Friedelock could be such a force against them, but somehow, he managed to war on two, if not three, fronts. He single-handedly pushed back Sherlin's men while somehow chasing down all of TAP's agents as they were being exposed. On top of that, he runs his own campaign. The man makes no sense. His abilities are far underestimated.

"It is my guessing that Friedelock was getting too close to full exposure of TAP's intentions. Thus, to protect themselves and their work, TAP went silent. By the time I had caught onto this, it was already too late. They hit our small outpost without warning. Not just the hired hands but the Shem as well. Though *they* didn't care for telling Friedelock's men apart from the rest. Everything on the hinge, I fled. Not as a coward, but in an attempt to bury any leads possibly gained from such a raid.

"I also uncovered something that interested me: a name of a man I knew them to be pursuing desperately. It seems that TAP, at its top, is run by a bunch of scientists, or at least they held the majority, and Friedelock hated them. His trail wasn't hard to miss, seeing as Friedelock's men were forcing him to think on his feet and be sloppy in doing so. I never did reach him... but I uncovered three tapes in his wake—from which I have since been searching high and low for answers. Everything keeps hinting at four names—names I doubt Friedelock hasn't already uncovered as well. Regardless, I *must find them and what's left.* They are the key to unveiling whatever it was that TAP had accomplished in its time. Is it obvious their work is at a halt and hiding from everyone? Yes, but it is also on the fringe of being lost altogether. Those few remaining that do know anything are being slaughtered one by one, limb by limb.

"If you wish to help, you can start by finding Tenius Morphela—he is the first I came to uncover. You will reach him in the Delvore Sanctum if my findings are correct. Go there and find him. You *must* get whatever he has left. While you do, I will be pursuing leads to the rest that you might find them also. If we do this properly, I do not doubt in the slightest that we can uncover this *haven* that you and I both know to exist."

Carls found it hard to comprehend everything but swallowed the mounting questions anyhow. "Tenuis Morphela... how do I find him?"

Trip reached beneath his belt and withdrew a tape. "This analog is all I have on him thus far. Hopefully, it'll help you get off on the right foot. But be careful, Friedelock's men are all over that place—enough so to have pushed Sherlin's contacts out of the picture, it seems."

He took the tape.

"Whatever you do, keep your eye on her as well." Carls knew what he was referencing to. He knew that Friedelock would try to take her again. He knew that being so close to the man, he was putting her at risk again. Nausea suddenly filled him as he began doubting his steps. But he couldn't be. Not now. No second guessing. *Just close your eyes and trust,* he told himself. But half of him was missing from the painful loss of his first love. Joan reminded him so much of Elairah, his beloved wife. At times, he would have to remind himself that it was, indeed, Joan and *not* her.

He had no idea the character behind Trip. Only that if this *haven* were to be found, Trip was his only way. For the moment, he stashed the tape into his sack and looked back to his daughter. *Friedelock will not have you again,* he pledged to himself. *I will not allow it. Not less over my dead body.*

"Carls Locke," Trip's hand gripped his shoulder, and he jerked back to reality. "Thank you. It's been a while since someone has actually helped. This means a lot to me. And *her*."

"Don't mention it," Carls replied, calling Joan to his side. "I expect you to have my path cleared for the next one when I'm done with this."

Trip chuckled. "Yeah, if you make it alive. Just watch your back."

And just like that, his meeting with Trip was over. The man parted way, and Carls once again faced the unknown with but some far-stretched hope of finding solace and answers.

Beneath What's Known To Man

Carls was beginning to see things previously kept unknown to him. But not just see. Hear. Touch. Smell. Almost as if something had once held grasp of his mind and kept him from knowing. *Was this what Antoinette had meant? Was there some illusion that had wrapped its way around him only to now begin unraveling?* He was even more cautious with every step as the realness of everything slowly came to him.

The halls truly were empty. But he could hear the vents and flow of cool air sweeping around the place. The entirety of the Theatra Amusement Park seemed... different. For some reason, as though the rapture itself had occurred, the place was left alone. Empty, the lights and attractions still carried on their work. The machines still turned their wheels and shone their shows—but no one was there to encourage it on; thus, all sense of attraction was gone. Well, at least for him. Joan still found the rides amusing and longed to go on every one of them. To her, everything was normal. *Somehow.* To her, the people were still there. She could still see the flickers—and it terrorized him so—but she would only smile.

The carousel wound itself around for the last spin. He stood silently behind the retaining bars, but she laughed playfully in the seat as it moved even at its lowest speed. She was happy. At least that. *I don't know what has happened to you, Joan. I am sorry, but I am glad you at least don't have to see things for the way they really are. Just play for me. Laugh, run, play—just do not lose your innocence.*

Every time he touched her—every time his skin met with hers in fear—the images came. Her reality would clash with his, and he would also retreat from it. For some reason, he did not wish to see things how they were...

He could not bear seeing Elairah while knowing she was...

Her laughing broke the cause for tears, and he looked up. The ride had finished, and Joan was waving her arms around. "Look, daddy! Look! A clown," she said, pointing to the distance.

But what he saw was completely different, and it was only a matter of a heartbeat before his shoes reeled from the ground, and he rushed toward her. "Come, Elairah!" he said, catching himself. But her buckle was snagged.

No, you're not Elairah.

And that was no clown.

Carls felt nausea flood his gut at the sight of the Fallen One charging through the small metal rails of the adjacent attraction as though they were just stencils. He struggled with the last buckle and pulled her tight to his chest—his knee dropping to the floor and twisting as bent bars flew above his head. Joan was confused and frightened at her surroundings—clinging tighter to his form. He could only imagine what she thought of his rash movements and the tension across his face. The Fallen One drew closer. Where she saw crowds, Carls saw the appearance of illusionate rushing towards him. Ducking low he was able to evade the first, and a flying chunk of pottery struck the second aggressor approaching him. *Did the Fallen One throw that?* His eyes strained to see two tents in the distance, a kitchen tent and fireworks display. Perhaps he could lose them there....

But had the Fallen One intentionally hit the illusionate?

He didn't know, nor did he care to second guess the situation any longer. He'd only the time to run behind the cover of a fireworks display tent—though he wasn't the only one to have made it. The Fallen One tore through the opposing side as the ground shook and air intoxicated with firecrackers.

Carls could feel their flares as they rippled through the air all around him. His shock turned to terror as he noticed them crashing toward a kitchen tent, specifically the *gas tanks.*

He lunged behind a concrete block of a hall square—shielding his daughter with his entirety. Everything went slow for a time. He could see from the corner of his terrified eyes a shimmer of light spark across the vast space between tents. It was beautiful against the shadows of desperation. Where the darkness once held, light now shone vibrantly. Yet following the flash, Carls felt the pounding in his ears as the ground trembled from the forceful wave. The Fallen One toppled backward, and shrapnel covered the floor. Just like that, fire began to spread. The Fallen One was outraged and confused and tore toward the flames, pulverizing everything in its reach.

Carls had noticed his footing too late. Before he could escape the collapse, his stance gave and he tumbled downward.

And back into the sub-system. The wreckage had left him no option but to press deeper in to avoid clashing with the beast. The explosion had caused the ground to give under the Fallen One's fury. But the chase wasn't over. An illusioned one had also fallen in after him.

"Run, Joan, run!" he said, pushing her behind him as he drew his gun with bleeding fists. He raised it to the charging figure. *I cannot kill this one,* a voice spoke from within him. *There are just like me—human.*

He hesitated, and the illusionate hit into him. The pipes gave no comfort as he retracted from the pain and shoved the figure off.

"You don't have to be this!" he yelled as the man grabbed Carls' arm and dug his nails into Locke's exposed skin. Carls could just end this altogether but fought the urge, knowing all too well they were one and the same. "Please!"

The man seemed struggling to convince himself to fight on. Something inside him was making him force his hands against Locke. His power was overwhelming, but his old age was hindering him as well. Carls dropped a blow to the man's thigh and redirected the man's frail fist into the pipes. It sprang under the pressure, and the man dropped to one knee—weeping.

"Please," Carls whispered.

The man's bleeding hands rose to his forehead in pain. He hadn't felt the fractured bones, only that which was inside him.

Carls felt pity for the man as he lashed out in frantic attempts to satisfy his confusion.

But now the illusionate seemed to be fighting itself. Its steps were faulty, and it continuously crashed into the piping and tripped over the grid paneling—soon to cower against the wall.

Carls' wrists stung to the tainted air from where the man had dug in. He could just leave the man, abandon him to his mindless game. But he also felt a gentle touch to his own hand—an image of the same figure Trip had deserted flashing before him. He nearly jerked away before noticing it was his daughter's touch. *Was he* that *close to the edge?*

No, he could not just leave the man. Not again. Not like this.

The old man was pale and every nerve shuddered under breaking sweat. Carls knelt beside him, still keeping out of reach. His daughter's face barely reached into the light from the cracks in the flooring above. The wreckage before them made it hard to go back.

The illusioned, old man had his attention at the time. His lungs fought desperately for anything that was real, but he was changing. *Somehow.* "Would you like something to eat?" Carls asked.

The man's head shook every which direction as he fought for the words to come out. "Yes."

Carls reached into his sash and withdrew a small wrapped granola bar. The man took it as soon as it was offered to him and began fiddling with the wrapper to break in. His dry lips devoured the small bar and wrinkled themselves to the dryness.

"Would you like water?" Carls then asked.

The old man shivered. "No, not the dirty water. It tastes disgusting and dirty and black."

"Not this water. It is clear and clean. Please, take it." Carls held it before the man.

The eyes of thirst could only stare for so long before the man became convinced. It seemed as though in one gulp the man had finished and now wiped his mouth clean of stain. He leaned back against the wall and rested his head, breathing in and out.

But at least breathing slowly now. The man's eyes were still shaking with fear and regret. "Please... don't leave me," the old man pleaded.

Carls knew he couldn't take the fragile man with him on his journey. The man's age was not fit for such a task—and how he'd managed such strength only moments earlier still astounded him. "Listen," Carls began, "I cannot take you where I am going, but neither can you just stay here. I know you are weak and exhausted, but you must find Sherlin."

The man shook his head, not wanting to accept the thought of being on his own. "He's not... like them, is he?" he asked.

"No. He is like you and me, and he can help you. He runs a small encampment up the alleys. If you're quick enough, you might catch him in time, but you must hurry."

"I can't," the man answered. He was still shaking from it all. Still questioning his grasp of reality.

Carls knew he had to convince the man to make it. That he could have safety. "Here," he said, holding out his shaken hand the man had once grappled with. "Take this gun with you in case you feel threatened. But use it wisely. There are many darker things here for you to yet discover, but know this: I did not fire upon you just as you should not so easily fire upon others. They are just like you—human—but confused. Illusioned, you could say. You pull that trigger and you are sending them to a point of *no* escape. Protect yourself, but also try to help them as you were helped. Remember that."

The man took the gun, eyes wavering for a moment. He was grateful beyond words. "Thank you, kind sir," he said. "You have saved me from this demonic possession. But I must ask, what happened here? For one moment I was with my granddaughter and the next I am alone..."

That is something you must answer for yourself, he thought to himself—the same words Xavier and Antoinette had spoken to him. "I do not have all the answers, those will come in time. For now, you must focus on getting to Sherlin. Are you up for that?"

The man looked up at the light filtering through the wreckage. A hole just large enough for a man to crawl through if helped up. He nodded, holding the gun close to his chest for a sense of security and courage.

Carls reached a hand to the man's shoulder for comfort. "Just one thing. Why were you after me?" Carls asked.

"You had something," the man said. "Something that I wanted. I do not know what or why, only that I was willing to do anything to get it. I wanted it so badly, and all I knew was to kill you for it. I'm glad I did not. I'm glad you stopped me before any harm came to you."

Something I have?

"Will you help me up?" the man asked. With a shove, he crawled through to the surface. "Thank you, sir. I won't forget what you did for me. And please, do not forget me either. The name's Hardy. I hope to see you again."

Likewise, Carls said to himself as the man slid away. He had finally helped a man, and for that, he felt a wave of confidence and hope infiltrate him as never before—once again from the touch of his daughter. He looked back down at her and to the dimness beyond.

Unlike Hardy, they would be sticking to the tunnels. For better or worse, they would pursue this scientist Trip had spoken of. This *Tenius Morphela*. Having tasted that there was some hope in such a condemned reality, he was determined to find this *"safe-haven"* that TAP was rumored to have constructed.

PART IV

ESCAPE

"It's a simple intent that drives man the deepest. In all manner of the phrase: there truly is nothing new beneath the sun. We may try to convince ourselves otherwise, but just the thought itself has already undermined the attempt."
-Mike Dyrdrik, In Search of Life's Mysteries

Penetrating The Surface

The long, narrow passageway was turning into a nightmare to decipher direction. The tunnels were vast and winding. He'd uncovered their blueprints from a maintenance hub, but making sense of it was a task in and of itself. Not to mention that the etchings on the walls and emblems engraved on the piping made him shudder to what might *actually* lie within the chambers he passed through. Whatever cultish group they were, they spoke feverishly of their convictions. The *Wakers* and the *Shylow*—who were they? Why were they?

He'd come across them before, having been led by that mysterious boy in the Holstein Sector. At least the *Wakers*. It had been the *Wakers* that cried out for restlessness and that had been deprived of everything. "*Don't sleep,*" they had written, "*don't eat. It is their poison; turn from the Resolute.*" But what was the *Resolute*?

It all was upon the walls and mingled with countless others. But in contrast to them, the *Shylow* ringed out their calls of *the Dark*. "*The rain is falling,*" they wrote, "*it's the Dark calling.*" Unlike the *Wakers*, they seemed to praise the closing of eyes. Their graphic pictures of blood portrayed a darker conviction of pursuit and possession. "*Holstein is in the Dark*"—did that that refer to a tangible presence? Were they worshiping a demon of sorts? A Fallen One?

For *Dark* worshipers, there was a lot of *dark* for them to worship. But there was no better of the two. It was not light versus dark in the sense of good against bad.

Both held convincingly to their beliefs; both were convicted of their ways of survival.

Both were *dark*.

But why would they be hiding down here? Why wouldn't they be spreading across the entire city? Were they a result of what had happened or a cause?

Carls' nerves twitched to his senses going wild. Joanna didn't like the feeling either, only she still held onto him for safety. It wasn't an illusion—there was something following them, and he didn't like the thought of what. He could not explain how the dim lights still shone down in such an overrun place, but he was grateful. With nothing but a stick from his sash, the light helped him not feel alone. But that did not mean someone or something could not still sneak up on him. It was in this eerie stillness that the twists and turns of the adjoining passages seemed to come alive. In every direction he looked he felt as though it was just behind him that eyes lurked in secrecy.

Joan's arms tightened around his leg. "Dad..." she nudged.

He turned.

A cloaked figure stood not but six paces from him. A black cloak and from beneath it a dark red shimmer of a gloating smile. The figure mumbled something in a language Carls did not understand. A word and an echo and his hands rose. Carls' body shook from a force that was overwhelming him from inside. He found simple functions coming short. *What?*

His breathing hardened and focus blurred. *I got to get out of this!* His mind yelled, and he dropped, hand and knee, to the railing. *This is ridiculous, I can't move anything. And my breathing has slowed. Come, Locke, breathe!*

"Daddy?" Joan called out to him. The girl's voice seemed to agitate the man's attempts. *He's not affecting her...*

But of course, it was the card again... the Trust Seal of Bondage. Carls forced his attention to his lungs. He had to be breathing if he were to do anything else. He found the strain required for such a simple task laborious but had no choice to do otherwise. Whatever and whoever this figure was before him, his presence was crushing Carls from the inside out.

"Who... are... you?" Carls forced out of himself. He could still move his mouth if he tried hard enough. The man's pose tensed, and Carls' head bent even lower. *I... can't... do this!*

Every muscle in his body was focused on fighting against the hidden restraint. His breathing was coming back to him, but only as he constantly drilled himself to inhale and exhale. He wasn't used to making each breath happen. The day-to-day functions such as breathing and calculating every step seemed preposterous to do. *Move, Carls, move your foot!*

And it did. His balance was thrown off though, and he tumbled to the side—his daughter still trying to hold on to him. *Joan!*

The man seemed outraged at his daughter—his arms suddenly jolting to the side, and Carls quickly found out why.

The man was possessed. He had to be. Nothing of man did Carls know to be capable of breaking pipes without a touch. Only a Possessioner could do such things.

Or so he had thought.

The water spewed everywhere in outrage. As soon as Carls was free to move, he grabbed hold of Joan to shield her just in the nick of time. He still felt weighed down tremendously from the figure's presence alone. His movements were slow—but at least moving.

The cloaked figure bellowed out another chant, and from his hands a shroud seeped. His blood-red smile seemed to glare from beneath his hidden face. He released a puff of air and soon vanished beneath the light.

The light cracked.

Carls couldn't tell if the man was gone for good or was just pulling another surprise card.

Card. Carls hated that word. Ever since he'd come to know of Hensers nothing but bad had come of them. *Except one....*

His body froze again.

The figure was before him with a darkness rippling against his cloak. Whatever the power that flowed through him, it was trembling to behold.

"Sleep!" the man gloated with hands raised. The lights around them burned with ferocity. From the corner of his eye, Carls saw the faint flicker of another form—one that completely took the Shylow's attention. A flash of force pulsed down the passage in the intruder's direction. The lights all burst, and in brief darkness Carls found himself free of his oppressor. He fiddled to his feet and strained for focus. He would have made a break for it but another figure suddenly appeared before him, this one both surprising and quite a relief.

Xavier.

The man meant to lead the way, and once again Carls followed, little Joanna close to him. He could not question the help, though he knew this meant far from being safe. He had to take Xavier at his word and that he was no deceiver. In trust, he followed. In trust, he put aside the doubt he had for the man.

How? Why? Xavier seemed to be both a blessing and a curse—somehow always having a role in assisting Carls. *Who was this man? What was he?*

They had escaped the utter darkness and fled into tunnels now dimly lit, and Carls and his daughter were soon led to a single ladder that wound its way up. Carls penetrated the small trapdoor that broke cover to the surface. He breathed in the air of a place less damp than where he had been. It wasn't all too refreshing, but at least he was out of the sub-system.

Under New Ownership (Tenius Morphela)

"I can't recall the events leading up to now. Everything seems to be a blur to me. First, it was the rumors, and now everything is falling apart. Of them all, I will be least capable of escaping the cursed shadow of the Big Man. Friedelock is on to me. All my leads are toppling. Only so many can know of what is really going on here; only so many can fully comprehend. It is thus that I must bury the work—no, I can't. I'm too close. My part in this is nearly complete. If only I had the time... if only I had the safety of the Protector. No, too late now... I must finish before they come. I can only pray it is done in time, and that—"

The room was a wreck. Files and loose office items were scattered everywhere. The portraits that had once clung to the walls were ripped from their frames, and every inch of secrecy had been ravaged. Carls felt a wave of heat infiltrate his mind. Something about the place hurt. His daughter thought it a game to skip between the miscellaneous junk, but he took to it rather seriously.

This had been a man's life's work. This had been his joy. For the most part at least. The fact that he had been with TAP made his position dangerous to begin with. The cults, the dark, Friedelock—everyone was after them. *But why? How?* The tape he had just listened to made him wonder. Remnants of a scientist's work were all over the room. If this was indeed Tenius, the man had run out of time. But from the sounds of it, he had expected as much. Whatever he had been working on wasn't there anymore.

Xavier posed at the unhinged doorway. "Why him?" Locke pointed to the flickering image as though for an answer. He knew Xavier wasn't one to give answers. In fact, he didn't even know why the hologram of a man was even here.

"Isn't it obvious?" Xavier answered, "He had something. Something someone else wanted."

"By why all this? Was TAP conspiring against Friedelock? I thought they were trying to fix this?"

"You've thought a lot of things, my friend. That is why I like you: you still think. And you still ask questions. Keep it up, you're beginning to stand out from the rest like a sore thumb."

"What if I don't want to? I have my daughter at stake."

"You've chosen this far, you might as well finish it. So why do *you* think they came to this room? What were they searching for? Who were they?"

Carls looked blankly. Those were the questions he was supposed to be asking, not Xavier. *If they were wanting Tenius... but why?*

No, they were after his work.

But what?

His eyes shut, mind leaped, and conscience awoke in memory. Everything about him was in a blur of a poorly lit room. Four men were present. To the far wall stood two in coats, both wearing hats of the finest material. Across from them was a white-jacketed figure and another sitting in a chair.

"We are running the line," one of the coats began, "The risks of ruin are on either side of our path. I pray we all understand the significance of our independent work."

"Indeed," cut in the white-jacketed figure, his tone a deep, throaty response.

The man in coat continued: "If *anything* threatens the secrecy of this matter, all ties to this project must be cut. It would do no good to announce a false hope. Only when the work is done can we unite arms. Of all, this is key." The man pulled out a small chip of the sorts that Carls could not make out. "This is the last time we shall meet. For your safety, for *all* of us, any further discussion of this must cease. If the project is to succeed, it must be done in silence."

"You're meaning abandonment?" one of the others asked (the other white-coated figure).

"It is in their best interest, yes. Many may wish to help, but our enemy's spies are many and are increasing in their methods of deceit. Trust no one less you be knifed in the throat."

"Then tell me," came the hoarse voice of the figure seated in the corner. "Tell me how this might come together if neither of us knows what the other is doing?"

"Someone will come, my old accompanist. One will come that is able to see past what devices have been put out to keep this silent. One might come who might hear the voice to which we all speak...."

Pain. He felt pain in his forehead and knees—just realizing he had dropped to the floor.

"What was that?" Xavier asked.

Carls studied the room about him once more. He was back to reality. *It had to have been another vision. What exactly had Antoinette done to him in that observatory?* The visions seemed like migraines of schizophrenia. *And how was it that they seemed to always apply to his situation?*

More questions. More mystery.

He looked up to his daughter who ran to his arms. Across the COMM came a dreaded voice. "You... you think you can just betray your word and not pay the penalties? I will have you know that I am aware of what you did with what was *rightfully* mine. And now you are meddling with matters that are even more so none of your business! Mark my words: you *will* pay your dues. As for your little friend, Tenius, I recently paid him a visit for you. I know you wanted to meet him, so I prepared a place for you two to meet—in *my* grounds. Come to my place... I'd hate for you to keep him waiting...."

It was Friedelock. He had Tenius—or so he claimed. Carls felt torn within as to what he should do. He knew the dangers of going back. He feared for his daughter's safety—for her life. She had already suffered so much. It would be unfair to bring her through such yet again. But if Friedelock was speaking the truth... then Tenius *was* there.

But he knew it just as plainly to be easy bait. He hated the thought of another life to be used as such. He hated that after all he had been through it somehow came back to confronting Friedelock.

This time, however, it would be different. He had his daughter; he had his clarity.

He despised the thought but knew, with all he had been through and all that he hoped to accomplish, to proceed meant to find Tenius. Even if he was dead, even if it was a trap—he had mends to meet with this ever-so-feared *Andy Friedelock.*

I will find you, Friedelock, and if you even perceive of laying hands on her—I will end you with all that is in me.

The walls rose high above him as though some impenetrable barrier within his mind were making it real. It was real, but the feelings he got from just the sight of it were over cumbersome. The large doors to Friedelock Industries slid open once more; this time he entered knowingly. It was a clean absence of sound that irritated his skin in the way one feels that at any moment the walls can close tight in a death-grip. For once there were bright lights. It was hard to find any secrecy in movements with the exposure from white, open halls. Doors aligned either side of him and his daughter as they progressed. Joan's weary body had climbed onto Locke's back, and he carried her. The steam leaking from the venting systems made him grow weary as well, but his conscience was too aware to fall victim.

Before him, just a few feet farther, the hall had been barricaded. Friedelock's voice came upon the COMM at this point: "Ah, it seems we're still down for maintenance on the main hall. Strange, isn't it, what gets moved down on the priority list when your employee list begins to wither. No worries, there happens to be a scenic route I have prepared for you...."

The door to Carls' left lit up green. He moved toward it and peered through the small window into the dim-lit room. He saw at the far corner a hole had breached the brick wall, and light filtered from it. *Friedelock wanted him to go through there? Why was he doing this again?* It seemed he just couldn't keep his daughter close enough to him.

The room smelled of bleach. Chemicals painted the floor tiles, and bags of powder dusted the counters. Joan stirred to readjust herself—her small form far more susceptible to the leaking gases. It was probably better she slept through this. He wouldn't want her ingesting more unknown chemicals than he needed to. Especially with what he knew the research of Friedelock to be. Still, he looked with curiosity at the faded papers and ink-marked cabinets. *It's in the serum*, the words faintly read. *Serum*—could it be Norwick's? And what? What was in the serum?

"You know what, I'm beginning to find you not so strange after all," the COMM clicked again. Carls didn't like the idea of being watched by someone. Especially Friedelock. Every move he made, every expression he carried—Friedelock was watching. The man continued his monolog: "I find it fascinating. Your curiosity. That you would be so courageous as to return to me *knowing* that you owe me something that *you* now have had a part in stealing. My war with you is not with whatever it was you were looking for in that room. I couldn't care less why you wish to speak to this Tenius fellow. I just don't care. That's why I'm fine with the two of you meeting. I just want what was mine... *back*. And *you* kept it from me. I know you had it, oh stranger of mine. I can see the look on your face. Yet here you are, and your daughter with you!"

He couldn't take it much more. His breathing got heavy—Joanna woke. "Daddy, I gotta use the bathroom," she said, swinging her legs to be let down. "Where are we, daddy?"

He could hear Friedelock's mocking voice over the COMM but chose to ignore it this time. Instead, he focused on holding his daughter's hand and moving through yet another door. The room before him was... wrecked. The light still shone brightly over the ravaged items and scientific work. "Daddy, who's that?" little Joan asked, referring to the COMM. But Carls wasn't listening to it, his attention had been drawn elsewhere. A small tablet lay upon the red-stained table. His daughter could not see it, thankfully. And behind it, he saw the attempts of a fleeing figure. The body was absent from the scene, but the fingerprints obvious. As for the contents of the small screen—they were somehow familiar to him.

His mind tumbled backward in time. Back to a moment in which he was desperate. Back to when he had entered into Paradise Suites. Yes, it was there. The same message—same note—but on this tablet: *317.* Reaching, he grabbed it with a shaking hand. He remembered the room.

He remembered the terror.

"Daddy!"

His body twitched to the sudden darkness. The light had blown and scared little Joan. She gripped tightly to his wounded leg. His injury from the tunnels was still there. But at least hers was nearly gone.

"It's okay, Joan," he reassured, placing the tablet into his sash. It had to contain more, but now was not the time to check. Friedelock was watching, and he needed to keep moving. The sooner he could get out the better. But how was he to know what Friedelock had in store for him?

He held the little angel in his forearms, bending low to clear the last hole in the wall of another passage. It was a hall again.

"Good," the COMM echoed, "You've finally made it to the hall. Quick now, your friend is waiting for you three doors down and to the left. Hurry, I don't want you to miss the reunion...."

This wasn't going to be good. Carls knew that much for sure but in no sense could he have prepared himself, or his daughter, for what he was about to see.

He'd heard the TV as soon as the door had cracked open—the broadcast flickering light throughout the otherwise dark room. He saw the TV hanging above the figure of a man, under which its shadow he sat slumped in his chair. His daughter buried her head into Carls' shoulder as he stepped in shock. Literally. The TV buzzed with the electrical current beneath it. The man had been electrocuted to a brutal death.

"You see, Stranger, no one messes with my business and gets out clean!"

Locke's eyes were back upon the TV. *Was that Tenuis?* The same man he'd watched before? How? Why? Who...?

His heart was pounding. Friedelock was meaning to kill him too—his voice reverberated in his ears. "I believe you owe me something, Stranger, and so did Tenius!"

He was out the door and down the hall before the room lit up once more with static. The full tape of what he'd uncovered back then had been playing, the words of Tenius Morphela ringing out strong: "*Time is getting short. TAP can no longer function as it did. They're getting too mischievous for us to outmaneuver; we must do it without them. Friedelock has gone mad in an attempt to uncover it, we have to stop him. As for these kidnappings, we can no longer help. Leave that to TAP. Andy Friedelock is stepping up his game, and we have to as well.*"

Answering To Friedelock

"Where are you going?" Friedelock mocked over the COMM system, still nowhere to be seen. "You should know by now that if I want a guest to remain, then remain he shall!" Sure enough, he'd locked the doors from which Locke had come. The fact that little Joan was scared in his arms made his already-wild senses no easier to control. He stood vulnerable in the hall, staring down its endless passage. *Where to run?* It was about now that he regretted giving away his only gun. Still, he had the Nightingale's stick.

"Hold on, Joan," he said, swinging her to his back and reaching into his sash. His sweat-dripping hands felt for the stick and withdrew it—he moved quickly down the hall.

"Try as you may, you can't leave this place," the man said. "Besides, I think we were introduced improperly last time. I think a proper meeting is due, wouldn't you say? Only this time, try not to ruin it."

The COMM hissed and Carls caught his step. He'd been trying the doors but knew Friedelock would not allow it. The light flashed green overhead one of them. *Does he mean to meet me face to face?* Carls' mind rushed him. He couldn't risk meeting a man in the state he was in. So much rage for his daughter's safety—so much fear for her life—he would not be able to contain himself.

He took a calming breath. *God help me not to kill this man... and to keep him from killing us.*

The door pressed open.

It was him. "So, we finally meet again..."

"What do you want with me, Friedelock?" Carls imposed.

The man smiled wickedly. Carls felt the strange sense of a darker presence. The man before him stood postulated and tipped his hat. "You see, we can still do this as men, you know? I feel ashamed that we have to be enemies, but that does not mean we must kill each other—I'm sure this is just a big misunderstanding, my strange Stranger."

Something didn't seem right. The man was too... something.

"So here is what I propose," Friedelock proceeded, "First, come closer. Yelling across this vast space is doing pain to my lungs. Don't worry, I don't plan to kill you."

Carls noticed the gun in the man's hand. How could Friedelock mean *anything* he was saying? Carls hated being manipulated. He could run, but that put the barrel to his daughter's back. He could back out, but that put cowardice to his name. Either way, his host was armed, and he was not.

Carls stepped forward. His eyes blurred to the beat of his heart. Something was etching at the very points of his nervous system. *It couldn't be Friedelock. It couldn't...*

"There, there, now. See? Isn't it much easier for us both if we keep this civil like?"

"You killed Tenius."

"Oh, pity party, he deserved it."

"Why? Why did he? Why did all these people here? What are you trying to accomplish?"

"Don't you see? There's so much more at stake here! Mind you, I did not wish their lives to be cut short, but they pushed my hand to end it. My work here is not to take life but to prolong it. Man is far more capable than the individual is let on to know. The place I have here is meant to be envied by man! Not regulated by some superficial government. Here, man is free of mind! No longer bound by his natural tendencies, by his body. Here, one might obtain the supernatural!"

"Which nearly killed my daughter!" Carls answered.

The man scoffed, "Your daughter's fate was brought upon by *you*. I still wonder myself of the scene your presence had brought. Such magnificence!"

"She nearly died!"

"Oh, hush, hush," Friedelock cautioned, his gun waving through the air. "I'm not the one you should be blaming. I assure you that my intents are pure—"

"But the means unjustifiable!" Carls cut.

"I said HUSH!" Friedelock bellowed, a blast from his barrel ricocheting off the walls. The man was struggling to maintain his professional composure. They both were. Joan held fearfully to his shoulders. *I have to think of her first,* Carls reminded himself. One false move could easily put her in more danger.

"What do you want, Friedelock?" Carls asked, hands up so as to show he was submissive.

Friedelock stepped forward, brushing his rustled vest. "I... I want you to give me what is rightfully mine. You have it with you, don't you? I know it was more than enough for just your daughter. The files—hand them over."

Antoinette had them.

"Well, hand them over!"

"I don't have them."

The man's eyes widened. His obsession with whatever had been within those files was great. Carls recalled the events he'd uncovered. "I. Don't. Have. Them." he reassured.

"I don't believe you. Give them over. Now!"

The man stepped up and shoved against Carls' exposed chest. Leaning back, Carls gripped the man's outstretched arm and swung back in— they hit against the wall in an arm lock. Joan still held tightly to Carls' shoulders, and he quickly remembered the gun in Friedelock's hand. He was shoved back and stared at gunpoint into Friedelock's black-filled eyes.

"You don't have to be doing this," Carls cautioned his steps backward. The man was overtaken from within, and his chest beat harshly. It was then that he saw it. The silhouette of a figure left the man, and his eyes regressed.

"Friedelock, stop this madness. You've been overcome by the same darkness that's taken everyone else. Don't let it destroy you—"

"Enough!" the man bellowed, his nostrils inflamed with disbelief. "I will hear of no such nonsense! I rule my own mind, my OWN body, and never shall I fall for their demise!"

Carls couldn't believe the scene unfolding before him. This man was practically denying himself. The figure behind him stood massive and resembled the shape of the man he had possessed—only no detail, no identity. Just *dark.*

He felt pity for the innocence that had been consumed. But the man's actions were nonetheless unjustifiable. He had *fallen*. He had killed. His hands were drenched in a blood so dark and terrifying that he had *chosen* to ignore its existence. He had *chosen* ignorance.

"Friedelock, please—"

"No! This is foolishness! You are in no position to point. Hahahaha, yes! No position... see? *I* hold the gun... haha...."

In a matter of seconds had Friedelock's composure been completely shattered. Carls could tell of something he feared. The man laughed to himself, holding his head up, and turned.

Carls but watched as Friedelock fell to his knees—for he too now saw the silhouetted figure that had come out from him. His hands trembled and every pore breaking way to sweat. *Knowing far more of the figure than Carls...*

And from his side did the gun raise.

From his hand did the gun shake.

And from his throat a desperate utter: "I failed..." –a sound of thunder.

As Man Falls, So Do His Dreams

"Get out of there, Locke!"

If not for Trip's voice breaching over the Hand-Pal, Carls would not have been pulled from the shock still reverberating between his ears. Friedelock had dropped cold to the floor in red stain. Joanna was buried in his side, and he quickly covered her eyes in embrace—tearing himself from the scene and back down the hall.

The entire place shook.

"Quick, Locke! Before the whole place comes down!" *What? What was happening? What had* just *happened?* He wanted to ask but had not the time to pull the Hand-Pal from his pocket.

Sure enough, the wall to his right blew. Shrapnel and smoke were the least of his worries as the drums in his ears all but burst. He fell backward just barely managing to brace Joanna from following.

"Locke!" Trip's voice yelled over the COMM system now. Carls struggled to his feet. "Good, you're alive. I made it to the Main System and should be able to lead you outta here if we do this right. Now, quick through the hole that was just made. Once through, there's a door on your right—yes, right—that'll lead you into a storage cell. Get in there and find the trapdoor."

He was already moving—adrenaline fueling his body just as it had done so many times before. For a moment, he almost could not tell that his beautiful angel still resided in his arms. For a moment, he could feel no pain. Thought nothing. Only focused on the steps given to him.

"You there? Good, now input the code: 317...."

Carls looked at the combination lock. Sure enough, it was a

three-number combo. And he thanked God it worked. The latch clicked and rose upward revealing a ladder.

He was back down into the sub-system.

"You there, Locke? I'm getting a weak signal from here... it must be the damaged sensory system. Listen, Locke, you have to reach Bay 43. It should be down your left. I'm getting crazy readings, man, so you better be careful, and you have *got* to move quickly!"

The COMM cut out. Obviously, Trip had enough to handle for himself as well. *Left*—that was all Carls was focused on at the moment. *Left and 43.*

Only now he could hear the sounds.

"I hate sounds..." he mumbled to himself, bracing his daughter even closer to his chest. His arms were getting heavy, but he chose to ignore. He was to the left and dodging pipe breaches to-and-fro. To his dismay, the numbers slowly rose in count—31... 32... 33...

A form flashed before him. The already sparking lights of alarm momentarily went dark. *Not again...* He stopped.

All he could think of now was getting to that bay. He had to make it there quickly but knew he had not the ability to fight whatever darkness lay ahead *and* ensure his daughter's safety. But he had to try.

A force knocked his first step right out from beneath him. He hit hard, and Joan slipped from his grasp. "No!" Carls yelled out, reaching for her—a form suddenly blocking the way.

A dark form.

A familiar one.

Once again, the hand stretched out, and Carls was frozen in place. *Not... now...* he beckoned his body, focusing every bit of his being to fight the powers about him. Somehow (for not even he knew), his hand slipped into his sash and grabbed hold of the stick. The eyes before him flashed a dark red and then was swept to the side.

Not by Carls—but another force that nearly blinded him. No longer petrified, his hand slipped back out, and he rushed for his daughter. Lifting her from the dripping pipes beneath which she'd hidden, he preceded to run.

34... 35..... 38....

He could feel the ground shaking beneath his feet. Trip was right—the whole place *was* coming down. *But why? Who? That man... that shadow... who was he?*

40.. 41... he was almost there. What to expect once he reached it—he could not even speculate. Nothing made sense down here. All he cared about was getting *out* of the sub-system. *42....*

What? Where was 43? Carls felt a swirl in his stomach as he stared at the blank wall. *The door should be right there!*

His body jolted back—his daughter just barely slipping from his fingers as they both plummeted.

Everything stopped. It had happened so quickly he had not the time to even take it all in. A light had flashed... but just before it had, everything around him seemed to collapse. His eyes opened to an endless white about him—nothing expanded below, above, or to either side. All he could make out was a few chunks of concrete and the relief of his daughter not too far from him. She was unscathed with her hair twisting and winding as though a gentle breeze swept past them. But he felt nothing. Externally. Inside, his body felt a wave of something so surreal he had no idea of how to begin describing it. He looked and saw his wounds closing. The blood and sweat faded from his clothes; the rips in his shirt closed shut and the pain in his bones and bruises on his skin left him.

He'd nearly forgotten about his coat. Such a mystery as to how he had received it. A place so bizarre one would either remember everything or disregard it all. In his case: he remembered. Yes, he recalled.

"Pamella..." his voice whispered from within. Such a strange character. It was almost as though he could vaguely see her amidst the white space. So willing. So caring. So...

His eyes awakened to everything but a sense of surreal. The shades around him, the dim reflections of dying light, the cold touch of some dark aura—it all embraced him as his hand pushed upward through the latch. The next thing he knew, he was pulling his daughter up from behind him and from a dark descent of unknown from which he also emerged.

He heard the fading stampede of crumbling below him and cleared the tunnel way. For a moment he simply stood, breathing. Little Joan behaved as though having no recollection of what had occurred. Just like any five-year-old, she was drawing upon the walls of the alley. Carls leaned up against the side, taking into account the healed wounds and mended clothes. How, who, and why remained a mystery to him. But he was thankful. Grateful. *Thank you, Lord*—for there was no one else to give credit to at the time.

"Carls? (It was Trip on his Hand-Pal) Is that you? I thought I'd lost you in the collapse. I know you've been put through enough wreck already, but I need you to meet me outside of Theatra. Be careful, there's a lot of ruckus from that collapse. You're lucky to be alive—please just keep it that way. I've tried detouring most of the commotion but I can't guarantee it's all clear. I'll be waiting for you there."

Great. Not only had he fallen short of getting to Tenius on time, but he'd only found more questions than answers. Right now, he didn't seem to be helping any bit.

Wait—the tablet. He reached into his sash and pulled it out. *317.*

Seeing Past The Illusion

"Take caution in your steps, my friend, and heed my words. Your eyes are still but opening to what lies beneath. Do not overstep yourself else you be swallowed up like the rest. The illusions are powerful. Do not think you are yet free of them."
-Philis Antoinette

It had been a while since he'd felt so much strength flow through him. For so long had he not slept, not eaten, not tended to his wounds. His last good meal had been at the encampment, but whatever had happened to him earlier—the white space he had been enveloped by—had made him feel satisfied within. So long had it been that he nearly forgot what satisfaction felt like. He could step now without limp. He would breathe now without liquid filling his lungs and choking him.

And he could notice how much he had previously become accustomed to the coarse air. The place was thick and cold—the air polluted with some substance. Even in the vast halls of the mall, he could feel the dampness upon his skin. And it was cold. He could imagine how these halls were once filled with warmth and people. Indeed, now vacant, the vents simply brought about a chill. And almost, just briefly, could he see them. *People.* The scene unfolded before him in a manner of no alarm. To his right smiled his beautiful wife. His nerves trembled at the very sight of her. Her smile... her laugh... the look she gave—his legs nearly knocked out from beneath him. Joanna had grabbed hold of Elairah's hand and was running about her bright colors. The whole sense of an unexplainable peace swept about him. It was just as when he'd first arrived at the so-called "Grand Mall". Light filled the place. People filled the place.

But it wasn't real. It couldn't be. He tried opening his eyes, but they wouldn't wield. He tried shutting them but could only blink. And with every cover of his eyelid, the scenery flashed to reality until, finally, it shattered.

He saw his daughter fall (for whom she had been grasping was no longer there, but an illusion). His senses sparked. He could hear the steps closing in and quickly saw them. "Joan!" he called, reaching out for her just in time. A thud hit behind him.

What?! He still didn't know what happened, only that now he was fighting for his life. He'd managed to stand ground between the offender and his daughter and now grappled with the powerful force of an illusionate. They were everywhere and rushing toward him. *How?!* He knocked the male figure before him to the ground, stumbling backward, shielding his daughter from a faulty projectile. These were people, not illusionate. They were just as human as he was—only at the moment, his daughter's safety was of more concern than theirs. He reached into his sash and withdrew the weapon. It glowed a vibrant blue and either of its sides extended into a staff. He wielded off another two—feeling his back pressed into a corner. His movements were being hindered by the clasp his daughter had upon his thigh. He picked her up and tossed her upon his back (a burden he would gladly bear).

He had to reach Trip, but with this many illusionate he doubted his ability. He made a break for it—the cover of a dress shop would have to suffice. He peeled behind the glass doors and braced their handles with his staff. The pale forms hit up against the glass mindlessly and craved. He saw the smudges left by their stained forms; he saw the bloodshot veins of their eyes; he saw the drying skin upon their necks and limbs.

No different from me... he thought to himself, remembering exactly how he also felt, and remembering the words Xavier had spoken, *"Your pain, your hurt; your doubt, your fear—they too had struggled with it all."* Indeed, he'd been there and ever so closely. But why was he different? Why had he retained his sanity? *Why had God spared him from such depravity, and yet others fell all about him?*

And why were there some still like him?

Your eyes are still but opening to what lies beneath. The illusions are powerful. Do not think you are yet free of them—that had been Antoinette's heeding.

Their hoarse breaths just barely reached through the glass barrier. Carls, his daughter clinging to his leg, felt numb to the vibrations of the frail protection before him. *How did it all come to this? Why do I feel so much burden for what would otherwise harm me? Why do I struggle so much to swing any blow at them? Why...?*

The front-most figure jolted to the side, ravaging to break past the gathering horde. Something else had caught their attention as, one by one, they began peeling from the glass doors of the dress shop. In but seconds, Carls was left to watch the last of them escape his view. He stood in momentary silence before removing the staff which had long since returned to its original state.

Mistaken Agenda

"If only one could learn from another's mistakes and act upon such valuable knowledge—maybe then history would not so often repeat itself."
-Mike Dyrdrik, In Search of Life's Mysteries

Trip stood amidst the vast hall running adjacent to the Theatra. His composure was steadfast, his eyes gazing forward to the appearance of two—a man and small child. Locke had managed to maneuver his way undetected for the most part. He now was before Trip, curious for answers; worried about his shortcomings.

Trip crouched low to Joanna's level, holding out a candy cane, "Here you go, I got it just for you."

Little Joan smiled and looked up to Carls for the "okay" before running out to retrieve the candy.

"Thank you," Carls said to the man, more appreciative of the smile his daughter bore than the treat smeared all over her face.

"Thought I'd lost you," Trip stated, shoving his hands back into his tight pockets beneath his heavy-loaded belt. "Did Friedelock find out anything? Listen, Locke, I don't know what business you had with him, but it could have cost us everything. Going in there was risky, and you know that—you nearly came to your end."

"He had Tenius."

"What? And you still went?? He's a murderer of any scientists in opposition to his work. I thought you would know...."

"Then tell me what I don't. Because, as far as I can tell, I still have something to lose and I'm not about to risk my daughter for something I am uncertain if even exists. And Friedelock is dead... he shot himself.

There was something *much* more twisted in that man than anyone, you included, had warned me about. What. Is. Going. On?!"

Trip held silent. Carls could tell he was holding something back. It didn't seem to fit the man's character to hold to such privacy. Trip finally broke.

"You're right, and I'm sorry. There is a whole lot more going on here. But to be frank, I am just as confused as you, and giving you every detail will still leave you with countless questions. As for Friedelock, he's inevitably why TAP fell apart from the start. Friedelock broke the chain. Friedelock fell. As for what the reason, I can only speculate. Some say it is because he works with the Big Man...."

"Works with? I saw the Big Man or something so close I couldn't tell the difference. Friedelock was being controlled by him, not used. And when he saw this—"

"The tape!" Trip cut, "You still have it?"

Carls reached into his sash.

It wasn't there.

Trip clenched his jaws. Carls handed him the sash, and he searched for himself. "Before it all came down did he manage to take anything? How close was he to you?"

"I was at gunpoint—" Carls remembered. He recalled thinking of his daughter. And he could still see the expression Friedelock had carried. A sudden change in character—a split personality. And it was then that whatever had been inside him, the Big Man, had stepped out.

"*The Big Man...*" Carls mumbled. *He'd somehow grabbed hold of it.*

"This isn't good, not one bit good...." Trip stepped back, hand through his hair. "Friedelock was trouble enough, I can't even *begin* to imagine what the Big Man would do if he found out TAP's intentions. This couldn't have gone more wrong—"

Trip had his gun drawn before Carls could blink. But it wasn't pointed at him, rather to the left at a familiar face. "Kit..." he relieved tension. "What are you doing here?"

Carls' Hand-Pal buzzed. It was Antoinette. "It's been a while, my friend. There's been a slight change in plan." The voice was choppy with hard lungs of the old man. "I need *you* to come to my place ASAP. As for Trip, you are needed elsewhere."

Trip seemed astonished at the recognition of the speaker's voice, but before Carls could ask why, Antoinette added, "Time is flashing zero, we must act *NOW*. I know where it is, but we cannot delay in detail at the moment. The numbers are few, and the pawns must be set in place quickly. So come, Mr. Locke, that we might act quickly—" Carls had to dodge the swing of a barrel as Trip suddenly twisted to behind him. Another figure had emerged.

One that neither he, Trip, nor Kit would have guessed to make an appearance.

"Trip, don't! I know this one!" Carls demanded.

"A lot of people do, Locke, and I can't risk it!" he tried pushing past Locke, but Carls held his ground.

"Trip, he's with me! Stop! Narrl is with me."

The words held him still.

"We don't have time to quarrel," Kit put in. "Leave him be. Least you can do is respect the man for what he's already sacrificed for you... and everyone else."

Trip stepped away, steadily lowering his judgment. "I'm trusting you, Locke. Rather, I *trust* you, and I'm gonna hold you to this."

Kit was already gone—Trip close behind him. Carls could but turn to see the shy figure stammer in the distance. So weak... so frail... so....

"Why are you here? How long have you been listening?" He could tell Narrl was without excuse. The kid was completely broken. "Why do they fear you so?" he asked.

"I just want to follow you..." the tender voice came. His long hair dangled about his face as he knelt, bracing his forehead. "I can't do this alone... please.... I promise I won't get in your way, I'll help you. I'll even carry your stuff...."

Carls felt a strong sense of pity for the man. Everyone hated him. And it wasn't without reason. There was something about the young man that gave even Carls the chills, and yet he saw a genuine heart. He tossed his sash across the distance—a valuable asset to him entrusted to a yet-to-be-determined ally. "There is water in there if you desire."

Narrl shook his head, simply placing the bag over his shoulders. Carls didn't know what to think of his actions. He hoped it wouldn't come back to haunt him.

Getting To Antoinette

Narrl had a sense of expertise when it came to avoiding the wandering illusionate. Each time they drew near, his body seemed to surge with such an inner pain that he would nearly flee. The fear wasn't of *them*, but something within himself—a pain that raged constantly and that he devoted all his strength toward hiding. Insecure, yet stable enough. They had reached the main hall to the e-Company in a short matter of time. He still held securely to the baggage Carls had handed to him to carry. It was as though he found recognition in it, and to it clung for acceptance.

Carls pressed gently to the edge of the corner, peering down the hall for roamers. Joanna was holding to his thigh as she always did. He knew she needed rest. But that was not a comfort he could offer at the moment.

There were three.

Why can't this ever just be easy? Carls pondered. If they crept closely enough to the walls, he wondered if they just might go undetected from the cover of pillars rising to the floor above. The hall expanded all four floors and an ominous light dared to shimmer through the smogged glass. *Yes, that would have to do.*

He looked to Narrl, gesturing for them to move. Narrl cleared the corner first and crossed to the first pillar. Carls stepped out and held his daughter close. *One pillar down. Just about fourteen left.*

They crept to the second—Narrl was surprisingly alert. "I... I don't like this," he whispered back as he braced behind the sixth pillar. He was shaking his head at Carls. Something was up.

Carls peered back into the hall. Two illusionate were across from them and the third a bit more down. Narrl was right. Carls was getting the feeling too.

He heard a thud, and glass shattered from the floor above. A black mass hit the tiles and roared. Carls' first thought was Joan. He had to protect her. Narrl had pick-locked the shop across from them, signaling for Locke to follow him. Carls made one step before finding himself lunging backward by the second one. An object hit across the window display and glass burst. He'd just enough time to shield his daughter's face but could feel the cuts against his—his coat protected the rest of him. With what little time he had, he made a break for the shop, finding Narrl in the back, grabbing hold of a small pot. *Yes, they had stumbled into a pottery for their refuge.*

The Fallen One was tearing to shreds anything its vast hammer-arms could touch. The illusionate acted helplessly to overtake it, for some reason deciding not to run. And they were being crushed. More came and yet again failed at subduing the monster. Narrl took the pot and chucked it across the hallway into an adjacent shop. Glass broke, and the Fallen One ravaged its way toward the sound. A dangerous maneuver, but it gave them just the time to advance—

Carls ducked beneath a fist of an illusionate. It'd come from nowhere and was now clawing at his coat. He couldn't move. Joan had stumbled just from his reach and turned to him scared—a form rising behind her with clamped fists.

"No!" Carls screamed, his face being pounded into the floor. All he heard was a grunt and through a trickle of blood from his brow, he saw a figure wrapped about his daughter—Narrl was shielding her.

Carls did his best to drive an elbow into his offender's jaw. The illusionate released and stammered backward. But before he could do anything else, another illusionate pounded him into the wall. "Narrl!" he choked, a hand outstretched. Narrl was busy enough dodging for himself and the little angel he held to, yet, in a brief twist of favor, a small object landed perfectly between Carls' fingers....

Hammer met bone unforgivingly as Carls thrust the tool into the illusionate's ribcage. He was clear of bondage and could not catch up to Narrl and his daughter. But now they had another problem. A barreling bench crashed across their path to the roar of a powerful foe. They broke hard to the right and into the denounced store—illusionate quickly on their trail, as was the Fallen One. The beast came through the entrance as though a man punching through a plate of dry mud. The isles of displays were made alive in flying shrapnel. The illusionate were piling upon it, and the creature soon lost control of its course—its weight and force more than enough to break through the barrier of the two stores.

The hole in the wall crumbled in disturbance as the Fallen One proceeded to lash at the little pests to which its attention was drawn. Narrl was unexplainably terrified. His whole body shook, and every bit of him was in sweat. Seeing her dad, little Joan slipped from the fear-stricken hands and into those of her father. "Narrl!" he called out, making a move toward the hole between the two shops. The commotion had moved back into the vast openness of the hall, leaving them just the space to pass by the last few pillars. And to their relief, the doors opened just quickly enough to mask their escape. They were inside Antoinette's protection now (if one could even call such a place safe in of itself).

The Final Words Spoken: A Warning

"Glad you could make it," the COMM spoke to them. Light filled the bay room, and a single elevator door slid open. "There is much to warn you about and little time to speak it. Come now, that we might speak face-to-face; man-to-man. However, you must come to me alone."

Carls was hesitant. He glanced over at Narrl and saw him seated atop a crate and playing hi-five with his daughter. Despite her young age, it seemed she was the one doing the cheering up. Carls walked toward her and knelt down. "You okay?" he asked her while giving a warm embrace.

She held tight.

"Thank you," Narrl spoke shyly.

"I think I'm the one supposed to be saying that," Carls said to him. "You saved her, and I greatly respect you for that."

"No... I meant 'thank her'. *She* protected me...."

It didn't make any sense to Carls. Thankfully, Narrl proceeded to answer. "If not for her, I would have lost it. She gave me strength to fight."

Carls felt a wave of relief and pride. He knew exactly what strength he spoke of. The strength to keep fighting. A desire to fight simply to protect.

Something worth fighting for.

"Joan, I'm gonna need you to stay here, ok? I'll be right back for ya, ok?"

Narrl looked up at him, a surprising expression across his face. "You... trust me enough?"

"Should I not? Watch over her. I'll be right back, and when I return, I wanna see her exactly how I left her: here and unharmed."

The old man still slouched in his wheelchair from behind the glass.

It was the same room they'd first spoken in—the same mechanism that he'd awoken to with such bizarre images. He stood before the glass looking into Antoinette's observation room. The man wheeled his chair around and coughed.

"My age is catching me, my boy; I can't fight it much longer. Not with such presence overwhelming my conscience. Look here," he pointed to the glass which suddenly displayed a large screen from which a single picture resided. *A box with silver linings.* "Do you know what this is, Mr. Locke? This is a Wishing Box—a very, very valuable artifact... or tomb, if you so wish to call it. Many years have its contents been wondered at. It has the power to grant a single wish, the deepest desire of the heart, to whoever opens it. It was thus sealed and guarded for many centuries due to the fear that one with a dark desire within might open it."

"But this picture," Carls began, "It's already opened...."

"Indeed, it is. And you may not believe all the powers at work, but believe me when I say they are vast and *very* dark in their corruption. We do not know for certain when it was opened. Whoever did also had shut it quickly after. Some say it was a child, some say a poor man. Still, only speculations. However, they did know that upon this Wishing Box had also been placed a curse. A dark one. One of utter destruction— not even I know its extent, only that it is coming and doing so ever so quickly. A *Shroud*, some call it, a cloud of darkness that possesses all and consumes all."

"But... how? How could something like this exist amongst man?"

"It isn't from here. Now listen to me, you fool! Something is emerging here that goes *far* beyond just man and this planet. I do not know how this came to be possible, but I can certainly guess that it is coming from *this* box! You. *Must.* Find it! Darkness is swelling in, and it is not of this world, this *realm*." The man's cough worsened, and the screen cut off revealing his desperation.

"The serum..." he coughed. The door to his chamber slid open, and Carls moved quickly to find a slot against the wall where the serum lay. He grabbed hold and rushed toward the choking figure.

But Antoinette's firm hand stopped him. "No... it is too late for me. This serum is for you." With a shaking hand, the man closed Carls' clasp on the vial. "Hear me now and heed my warning: the reign is coming; the storm has moved in; darkness is upon you, but you *must* shine through it. Pull it down to its *own* depths and leave it there to rot! Too long have I lived in the grief of this. Too long have I done my best to forget. Fix my wrong! Find the box and return it and put to rest the name of Grevious."

The man's hands went cold; his eyes rolled back and head dropped against its supports. Antoinette was dead. Carls looked down at the vial he had been given. It glowed a rainbow of colors and rested warmly on his palm. Across its surface a single label: *N.S.*

Too Close To Call It Safe

"A man once told me: If you can't convince one to change his own mind, then try manipulating his reasoning and he will come to convince himself. For business is won in the mind— where man boasts he is secure in his own right."
-T.J. Lawrence, A Multi-trillionaire Businessman

The box, the vial, the illusionate, TAP, the Hensers—nothing made sense to him as he took to another hall. As far as his leads went, the encampment had moved out past even the Holstein Sector. Narrl was still carrying the sash and leading the way. He knew this place rather astoundingly, but it wasn't helping that they'd been pressured into such a fast pace from the beginning by the gathering wanderers. Something about the place felt dark... and it was stirring the life from every crevice it once hid.

He wouldn't be able to hold this pace must longer, not to mention the drastic rate at which Narrl was beginning to slow. *We just have to make it a little farther... we might be able to lose them on the second floor.* He looked to either side and found an escalator that was tattered in dust. "Narrl," he motioned upward. Narrl's form clambered up and against the rails for support. Carls was close behind him, realizing the threat increasing. He grabbed Narrl by the arm and helped him past the last few, nearly draining his own strength. The footsteps were drawing closer. They had to reach the elevators *now* if they were to have any hopes of making an unseen turn. He saw them just down the second floor. Just past a rum shop. *What? Rum?* An encampment used to dwell upon this location. Carls could make out the crates of piled supplies (mainly rum) along with sleeping bags and abandoned fire pits. *Obviously, a wild crew that left rather quickly, but an attempt at home nonetheless.*

Narrl dropped to the floor. Carls turned around to grab hold of his arms, and Joanna crawled down from his shoulders and began helping (as all children do, though not actually helping much). He doubted they'd be able to reach the elevators—it was already too late.

The illusionate had reached the top. Just one. Its breathing was heavy, eyes lusting for prey, but itself was terrified of everything about it. Carls, Narrl, and Joan had taken cover behind a stack of crates with but a small slit to peer through. The illusionate was shortly joined by another. They prowled, obviously aware that Carls and the rest were near. But it wasn't *them* he was worried about. The noise was getting louder. *Not just feet, but pounding.*

The look on Narrl's face wasn't good. His face was pale and skin beginning to sweat so much that it was forming salt. And his eyes....

Carls froze. Narrl had been looking at something, and he now noticed it himself. A dark paw slid across one of the upper crates to a low growl. In but a moment, a second paw stretched across their small bunker, revealing a fanged face behind it. A panther—but more fearingly: a Shem.

It was too close to dare reach for his weapon, so he remained still, a shaking hand over his daughter's eyes. The beast crossed over them (large enough to expand the gap in which they hid with but two steps). Everything grew silent as the hunter approached its prey. Carls was losing sense of everything but sight as he gazed forward. The Shem lashed out from its waist—paws doubling in size and forming a net-like choke.

And then the ground shook. Not from it—but the Fallen One that had emerged from below. The massive forearms crashed into the groaning floor, and the Shem's attack came to an abrupt halt. The Fallen One roared as it beat its chest and pounded away viscously. Their own cover was blown as Narrl kicked his legs and attempted scrambling away. The beast was looking directly at them.

The Shem hit back. Carls wrapped himself about his daughter as the massive form crashed overhead of them. The Shem had now taken on a multi-snake form swinging its body against anything it could to lunge itself forward. The Fallen One braced one of the heads and tore it limb from limb but allowing the Shem to wrap three others about it. In a powerful force, the raging horrors tumbled off the bridge—leaving Carls to the now full-pursuing illusionate. "Narrl!" he called out wishing his weapon, but Narrl had his head buried in his hands and jaws clenched hard. Something was terribly wrong with him.

"Fight it, Narrl! Fight it!"

Carls took the first blow. But he wasn't the only one they were after. His daughter cried with tears as she knew of nowhere to hide. A second was approaching.

Despite how much power he felt surging through him, he could do nothing to lift the illusionate off his body. They were just as strong as him—with added madness. *Not Joan*, he bellowed within himself, letting out every rage a father would bear to save his own daughter.

A fist dug deep into his foe's chest, and a cry answered it. Knocking the illusionate's grip from beneath it, he quickly found himself atop, and with both arms tugged the savage through the air and against the second. Carls dropped to one knee, his right arm cramped—at least one illusionate senseless. It killed him inside to not welcome his daughter's embrace, for he still had to ward off her foes. More had appeared now—like ants to a kill; a spider to a trapped moth. The distant figure of Narrl beat hard against the skull of his own struggle. The illusionate flew off the balcony's edge, and another skidded ten feet across the floor.

Carls was speechless.

He knew exactly why now.

He knew why everyone feared and hated Narrl.

Not the Narrl that had saved Joan... not the one that had provided Carls an escape from behind the glass of the small dress shop... not the one that refused to become a monster—they hated the beast that for so long warred to get out of him, to control him. They hated the actions of his weak suppression. To them, he was incapable of rescue, but to Carls....

"Narrl, you *must* fight it!"

"Ah!!!!! I... Can't!!!!" With one grasp had Narrl managed to toss an entire barrel of rum into an opposing illusionate. He was beginning to draw their attention. More came.

"Daddy!" Joan called from behind, her little hands reaching out for embrace. Carls looked at her, biting his lip to tell her to stay. And she did.

He hid her quickly behind a single, battered crate and made a dive for his sash—he wasn't about to let Narrl fall.

"Narrl!" he yelled, a blaze of blue from his tri-barreled gun. Every fiber of his concentration was at stopping the illusionate from reaching him. Narrl screamed from within as his own hands dug into his forehead like a man on the brink of atomic explosion. His joints were jolting in every which direction as his muscles expanded and retracted violently. "Narrl!" he cried out again, another blast from his barrel and glass shattering to its wake.

"I'm…. TRYING!!!!!!!"

Carls felt a knee to his thigh and tumbled back. The gun turned to a blade and pierced the form clawing at his face. The figure slid to the side pulling the blade with it as another illusionate piled atop of Carls' exposed form. "Well that's not good enough!" he bellowed, shoving off the third blow to his face. Hand back upon the blade, he found his reach extended to either end as he swung the pike around. He saw a glimmer of hope hanging upon the pillar before him. A vial dispenser.

Stay with me, Narrl! Keep fighting it!

He broke the wave of four pressing toward him, a beam of blue shooting off to Narrl's aid as pike turned to gun again. And with its hilt, he leaped forward and pounded against the dispenser's lock. Vials hit across the floor. He didn't care which his touch grabbed hold of, only that he prayed it would work. He grasped the nearest fist to his and clenched, digging the needle into it quickly. The illusionate cried out hoarsely and tore free of Locke's hold. *God, help me please*, he prayed to himself, lifting his gun to the injected illusionate and firing. The form collapsed dead but was just as quickly replaced.

He'd forgotten about the Fallen One.

The beast climbed up to the floor on which they fought—ignoring the illusionate that clung to it in attempts to bring it down. It seemed focused upon one—vitory over the Shem staining its flesh and now hungry for the struggling suppressionate.

"Narrl! No!" Carls yelled as Narrl locked eyes with the beast. He charged, still bearing his small form but with the courageousness of a hulk. The one he fought was the same that they had seen together before, and the two seemed acquainted.

The massive fists of the Fallen One were its only disadvantage. Its strength far exceeded that of the suppressionate, but Narrl had agility.

But not enough. The beast clamped tight a fist that pounded into a miscalculated lunge, sending Narrl tumbling across the expanse of space. Carls knew he had not the strength to ward off the Fallen *and* suppress himself. But to what extent would he sacrifice his sanity?

The Fallen One charged with relentless force. Narrl was still against the wall. Time was wearing thin; he had to delay it.

The trail of wake fled his barrel as he pushed off from his pillar of safety—full intent of taking on the Fallen One. The beast toppled, twisted, and turned until its eyeless face raged straight towards Locke. Carls sent off another round just awhile diving between the gap of the creature's arms.

He was unlucky.

The corner of the beast's fist caught his coat and flung him to the bridge's edge. He felt his lungs bursting, but it wasn't blood that covered the floor before him—*insects?*

He heard the Fallen One coming at him, body too exhausted to react quickly enough. But Narrl had. His mutating form ruthlessly hit into the Fallen One, and they crashed onto the bridge, both roaring at each other. "Narrl..." Carls could but cough out.

The arrow came from nowhere against the exposed beast. Narrl was on hands and knees, his head lifted to the crates beside him and to the eyes of a small, terrified girl. And at that moment, his muscles relaxed and color of skin returned to him. As for the Fallen One... behind its form emerged a much-anticipated figure—one he had hoped for. It was Kit, and the man seemed to know exactly who it was that had broken into his investment.

A smile spread across the man's face as he spoke: "You are lucky the circumstances deem otherwise...."

An Unwelcomed Sight

The encampment lay upon the top floor of the mall and just behind the overlook of massive panes of glass forming a mosaic once proud to man. Now it was dim, and only a glimmer of light shone through its stains and gathered dust.

"Carls?" It was Arnold. "It's about time. A large man with a table strapped to his back left this for ya. I know not its contents, only the address. May it do you well, and thank you again." At that, Arnold disappeared back into the commotion from rising panic. Carls looked down at the small package wrapped in cloth—he knew exactly whom it was from. Sure enough, a collection of Hensers lay within the wrapping. *What the Dealer meant of this, he did not know, only he hoped to not have to use them.*

Carls looked about to the people surrounding him. He saw Arnold and Sherlin nearside the supplies trying to load them into a cart for their departure. He also recognized Linda and the kids, and Jailer directing most the commotion to proceed orderly. Trip was there also—which explained how Kit was able to reach him in time, for he had just arrived with Trip at the encampment moments before.

But now the air about him was growing noticeably thick. He soon found himself fooled by the wind of small insects swarming past. Not thick enough to see clearly, but he knew it to be them. Though why them.....

"Daddy! Look! The wind!" his little girl yelled, pointing to behind the encampment. Sure enough, the walls grew black and a thick breeze had gathered and was proceeding their way.

"That is no wind..." he said, grabbing hold of his daughter's hand.

"Run!" a man in the distance yelled as his wagon tipped and boxes spread the floor. The current hit hard and loud. Somehow the insects managed to create such wind beneath their movements that it battered against the tents and clothes. *This was no ordinary wind indeed.*

"It's *him!*" Jailer called out, fist pointed at the distant figure of Narrl.

"Hold it, Jailer," Carls cautioned. But it was of no use. It took both Trip and Kit to hold the man back.

"This is no time to quarrel!" Trip tried reasoning, a scream off in the distance catching everyone off guard. A second wave hit the camp, only this time not alone. From its cloak came a sight so unexpected that for a moment all but stood in shock.

Which was to the Possessioner's advantage.

Kit was the first to act—a white beam leaving his forearm and penetrating the *dark.* But he was unable to cut the grasp it already had upon one of the caravans as it was tossed like a doll into the eyes of a petrified couple. Carls had to tear his gaze away from the nightmare to react any. *Why here? Why now?*

The Possessioner had taken control of Arnold's booth—the once inanimate displays now came to life. Trip was already moving toward it, leaving Carls' attention to wander to the massive cluster of insects forming far down the hall where the large panes of the mall met the gloom of the outdoors. Through the crevices did they come and nest themselves in a single drive toward the encampment. Carls wrapped his daughter in his cloak and withdrew the only thing he knew to save them—a small barrier formed before them. But the bulk still proceeded toward the mass of panicking eyes.

Behind him, a greater barrier shielded them. Carls could hear the insects' rage, and he turned to see the vibrant barrier that had deflected them, not of his own doing, but of one he could hardly believe.

"Go!" Pamella yelled at him, her hands moving to every which side the hordes struck—along with the Possessioner; it was already a match for her to reckon with. Her palms were stretched to their fullest; her hood glowing in a most vibrant ocean blue; the gold trim about her expanding its ribbons to the force of her energy.

The *dark* had turned its gaze now upon him.

Thus, he ran as quickly as possible—sweeping his daughter up into his arms and fleeing with Narrl close behind toward the only thing that made sense. The worn figure was undoubtedly loyal to Carls and his daughter, and for that, he found the strength to keep moving.

The glass panes began cracking under the pressure of the swarming insects. He saw the expanse still before him and how it seemed to grow farther away.

He ran even harder.

And harder.

The doors all about him opened their floodgates of illusions and illusionate. Carls was fighting his mind to keep track—adjusting his tracks as ground unknowingly gave way and roots unexpectedly formed pathways and bi-ways. *A web of illusions to distract.*

His heart pounded. The illusionate were gaining upon him and Narrl.

Narrl! He glanced behind him and saw nothing. "Narrl!" he shouted, daring himself to stop for a better look. The thickness behind him made it difficult to make out, but he was there—illusionate piling about him; his eyes looking to Carls for last hope, and then closing.

Carls knew exactly why.

The pass between them split, and new terrain formed. Narrl raised his forehead and smiled. He was going to give himself. "Narrl!" Carls yelled again, trying to stop him.

But it was too late. The beast emerged.

Carls hated himself for turning away, but he was wasting the time Narrl had sacrificed for him.

To have felt the wind and seen light but only darkness follow was truly a haunting chill amidst the shroud that sought to overrun the encampment. Fleeing, helpless, and desperate, Carls lunged towards the fractured glass panes of the great mall's southwest entrance—his daughter shielded within his coat.

He broke the clasp of that grand mall, feeling the weight of its attraction against his bitter judgment as he did.

The force of black wings, ever so immense and numerous, obliterated what remained of the once elaborate mosaic display. Carls felt the *dark* surround him as he warred against the gravity of his fall, doing all he could to cushion the blow for the child he cherished so dearly in his protection. His back hit hard to the concrete, barely able to move but forcing himself a footing against the torrents of the *dark*. He stood and watched as the black regathered itself and hung monstrously in the sky above him.

He was outside the holds of the mall, yet no joy was felt in the cold, bitter breeze against his skin. He took it in regardless, but bitter it was. He had to swat away at the insects he dared to inhale. His hands lowered down to the shoulders of his daughter who still clung tightly to his waist. *Her pain had been given to him.*

But her grip soon released as she gazed into his eyes. She knew what it was he was asking of her, though he had said nothing, for the bond between them began to show as he took upon himself her worries and fear.

And shaking he stood, his eyes cast down upon his beloved daughter. So innocent. So pure.

So strong.

She stood there—her attention only upon him as though all that was around her had never existed. She stood still, not against will, but because she believed in him enough to throw her life in whichever direction he desired. She entrusted him with her fate, even though she was too young to understand its significance.

The *dark* was approaching. The small trails of it still gathered from behind and brushed about him, digging into his eyes. He stepped back and held out his palm to which a Henser showed.

I need you to live.... he whispered to himself as the card began to glow.

Golden bars shot from it and formed around her a cage of impenetrable power. It was just large enough for her to stand in. Should she touch its edges, it would disappear, but while inside, nothing could harm her.

Nothing could touch her.

Which led him to turn his gaze upon the dark that rushed towards him. He was quick to draw the second Henser, though the cloud was far swifter and collided with far more power. He was surrounded, his footing trembling beneath the force—countless biting from relentless insects wherever his coat was not.

But through the heaps, he could still see the cage in which his daughter faithfully stood.

"I will not bow!" he yelled out to the demon he fought, a torch lighting from his hand that wielded another Henser and a blast of heat erupting in splendor, lighting up the earth. The Chamber of Fire unleashed its full fury and, in its wake, only ash.

Carls felt the flesh of his own fingertips burning. Above him, the sky thundered at the flame he had brought. His skin was cracking, his pupils drying, but he pressed further from his daughter until he was sure to have the *dark's* attention. And there, while the storm gathered its reigns yet again to take him, Carls looked down at his own hands.

All I wanted was for you to be safe, he told himself, speaking of his daughter. *I would give my entire world to ensure that. And now, I must hold to that promise.*

The blue glow of the bonded thread emanated from his form to that of his daughter's.

The Trust Seal of Bondage—had the Dealer meant it to come to this? All that time ago, having given him the card to use, had the Dealer truly known it would come to this?

He then held out the Nightingale's staff—that which he had fought so desperately for—an ocean-blue revolver. A unique gift it was—a weapon of situational evolution.

All my life, I thought that if for all I strived for, I would at least be blessed with a family. Well, God gave me such, and He nearly took it all away. But now I give it all to Him. He's blessed me with my wish, now I must finish on His behalf.

Time felt still to the bolt of energy which surged from that Nightingale's single barrel. It projected itself toward the link that bound his daughter to him. The Trust Seal of Bondage was an interesting affair to say the least, for it gave one's pain and suffering to another. In exchange for utter trust, the holder was responsible for any burden and shared two-fold of it.

It had kept her safe.

It had kept her close.

And now... it was to keep her away.

He needed only have the peripheral view to feel the fear in her awakened eyes as the thread snapped—her body falling forward and through the golden bars, having lost consciousness.

But she fell not to the concrete, rather into the arms of a surprising figure.

The Dealer?!

Their eyes met—an indescribable command from Carls' gaze to that of the Gambler. He knew not whether the *Gambler* was to be fully trusted, but that was not a thought he could doubt at the moment. The echoes of his demon forced him to accept it.

A burning current ruffled through his clothes and jacket and singed face as he looked into the ominous force that sped towards him as a javelin to a paralyzed victim.

And in that thought, his eyes shut, and he took his last breath for all he knew.

FROM THE AUTHOR...

*"The stroke has touched the paper—now all that
is left is for the picture to unfold."*
-Kalian, the Scholar

To The Great And Wondrous Reader

I am excited to share with you the Grand Series. This is but the first four parts, and there are many more to come. Act I will entail four books, so buckle up: they are forthcoming. The events uncovered thus far will only compound upon in what truly is going on.

The Grand Mall is nothing of what you've come to expect, nor what you thought you knew. Carls may not be "prophesized", but he sure as anything is determined to keep his daughter safe. For that, he is willing to delve into the madness and disdain lurking even farther beneath the shadows of what is known to man.

There is much yet to say of the scientists—of what they have done and are still doing and of where they have gone and why.

More of Sherlin's men.

Of the illusionate and Antoinette's plea.

I am overjoyed to leave you with but a snippet of what is to come. The curtain is only just beginning to open.

The show is only getting started (as you will find in the preview to Part V). The mall is only the beginning piece. The world is still moving outside of the Grand Attraction. The Board is still struggling every bit to sort out the chaos. Carls has not left the world—it is still living and breathing, trying to make its own way.

There is so much more to say, but most of all: thank you for reading. *You* are the most significant part.

More Of The Euphora Realm

If the Euphora Realm—you know, that city within the mall—intrigued you, there is much more to be told of it through the adventures of Mr. Fauldon in *Fauldon's Dream and the Karier of the Task.*

There are countless mysteries within that world. Those of new and those of old. Even still are its histories unfolding through the works and efforts of the Great and Wanderous Nomadicus. Even Pamella has a story of her own and an origin still unfolding.

Euphora also has problems and struggles, mind you. It was of no coincidence that Carls appeared there either. There was no shortage of urgency in his need and the severity of it upon the people of Littlerut, having given to him the Tarsh lilies. The ramifications of everyone's interactions affect everyone.

But keep in mind, Fauldon's Dream preludes Carls' appearance and the events of the Grand Attraction. While the stories do intersect, they are not dependent upon one another. No "one" character (less Keyno, perhaps) is of more importance than anyone else. Carls is not a figure "prophesized" to redeem everyone and everything. They all have stories to tell. They all have roles to play.

Big or small, everyone pitches in to the story of time unveiling.

Even you are a part of a much greater picture. Your role is invaluable. And it is what you make it.

Our Stories To Be Read

"Everything you do, every jot and tittle, will be read by someone else, for the sum of your acts is always written and never overlooked. Time is the great reader of everything. Time is always reading. Time will read you. Time will tell. Time will remember."

Such are the words of one you have yet to meet and at a point you have yet to reach in the Grand Series. The context, however, is taking place in Act II.

Yet it makes one think of the sayings "nothing you do goes unnoticed," "time will always tell," or "someone is always watching." Growing up, that was usually used as a cautionary phrase. "Better behave well" many a father has said to their son.

Now, however, one might find the hope in that. Yes, there is immeasurable power in being true to yourself and image even in shadow and secret. But how much more so is there encouragement in knowing you are not an overlooked speck?

That feeling of insignificance and valueless purpose we often depress ourselves into. That feeling of being void and pointless in existence. The emotions that swell when feeling abandoned and isolated—be it surrounded by loneliness or stranded in an ocean of strangers speaking a different language.

Your life is worth something. There is no written justice to the pain and suffering felt through depression, depravity, and desperation. The very itching surface was but scratched in the Grand Attraction—the portraying of an illusionate's state of digression into illusion and longing for that which they feel incapable of experiencing.

There is hope. Carls Locke did not just find clarity. He did not just reach enlightenment, he chose to create for himself words that would resound with hope for others who not only would eventually read of his acts, but those who were even as it happened.

You will be read. Concentrate on bettering the now. Find hope, and if you can't, look for it in others. Read others.

If you have found it, put yourself where others might read.

We are all suffering. Even in joy, we all have struggles.

To every man his struggle is the greatest. That is a mantra worth treasuring on to. You may work at the desk; you may work in landscaping—each has struggles just as real and difficult as the other. Only in sharing them can we be reminded of what we have overcome and appreciate it.

Life is appreciated together. You are never alone because, in time, our stories will be read.

There is hope. There is remembrance.

A Glimpse Into The "PÔRTRƏT RELMS"

"Well, Mr Fauldon, as you said: I brought you here from another place, just as Grevious was once brought..."
-Sir Knowington, Fauldon's Dream, Scene XI

"Imagine a single portrait from which many look upon in splendor. It has different colors, traits, and scenes throughout, yet still is known to be one image as a whole. You are looking at this picture from the front as though standing in a gallery. Now, imagine yourself stepping closer, noticing that the portrait is actually a puzzle of many pieces fitted together to look as one when, indeed, they are but pieces. Now, say you stepped slightly to the side of it. It is then you realize that none of the pieces are actually joined, only positioned to look so when viewed from the front. The picture once "whole" becomes instantly complex and layered as the pieces spread forward and back so that none touch, but all would otherwise fit perfectly.

"Each of those pieces of the puzzle, of that grand portrait, is a realm so to speak. Where you came from, where Grevious came from, and where you both are–all are different pieces. They are meant to be kept apart, never touching, yet forming one picture. It is when parts from one piece cross into another that there is a brief tip as the two pieces experience a brief attraction. It is during this period that a brief imbalance occurs. If the alien part does not return in time, the tilt of the two pieces begins to draw nearer—leading to what you have been hearing as the Overlap."

So are the words of sir Knowington to Mr. Fauldon as he tries to explain the significance of sir Grevious' recent actions. What actions? Well, using the Violstone of course! What's that? My, my, my–so many questions. Almost as many as Mr. Fauldon! But let me elaborate upon that which sir Knowington speaks of first, for the other answers lie within the book *Fauldon's Dream and the Karier of the Task*.

The Pôrtrət Relms are the pinnacle of the Grand Series. These "realms" all have their own unique settings, plots, characters, and creatures. They are only bound by the limit of one's imagination. Thus far, two realms have been officially introduced: Remedii and Euphora. There is also the Realm of Nim that has only been but mentioned, and a more confusing realm it is. The scale that is to unfold is a "portrait of realms" and that each piece is individual and yet just as essential. The first installment of this series will only touch on a small cluster of them—but there are plenty more to come.

There is also the Realm of New Tarnor, a far more ancient realm long desiring to reveal itself. It was once "Taylor Tarnor", though the events of the Arc Wars and the Amotu and Utoma have since reshaped it into the next era. Throughout the story of Carls Locke, there are also countless other characters being spoken of. The Gambler being an example. While popping in and out, he also has a story-line just as significant and greatly in need of being told.

Thus, while Fauldon's Dream serves as a more youthful short, understand it as an example of the scale to which the Grand Attraction is addressing. After all, the Wishing Box to which Antoinette speaks came not from the realm of Euphora nor of Remedii…

A PREVIEW INTO PART V

REMINISCENCE...

Back Into The Lion's Den

It was in one of those moments where one finds themselves in an ever-ordinary place only to have the mind explode into unfathomable creativity. Much like that moment when you look up from what you're doing only to ask what and where and why on earth you are doing it.

The concrete broke like puzzle pieces, and the vacant cars of that great mall's parking lot all lit up. Carls felt the wisp of a gentle breeze on his numbing skin—exhausted, bewildered, and breathless did he gaze upon the brilliant hexes of indigo.

A man had appeared beside him, one in a bright suit with a spectacle lifting to his eye. With only a single outstretched hand had the man summoned the blue hexes to shield them, though the prowess of the *shroud* was about to break through.

The stranger of familiar disposition held out a card to Locke, "Take it," he said, "and hurry now if you don't mind."

Carls knew not who the man was, nor where he had come from, only that he resembled the composure of those whom he'd met in Euphora. But neither was he hesitant in grabbing the card and waving it before him.

The same instant in which his body teleported from the closing field an ominous force of the *dark* crushed over his vacancy.

Bone and flesh met with the hood of a car as his back arched to the impact. He coughed his lungs into submission from the pain while struggling to retain his sense of direction. The *dark* sped towards him again, this time taking form as an ever-shifting tentacle tearing through its terrain to reach him.

He still wielded the Nightingale's staff and knew nothing more than to hold it before him—its energies forming the smallest of shields to deflect the overwhelming blow.

His back hit yet again against an unmovable force—this time of the mall. He dropped to his knees, his eyes cast upward to the massive panes through which he had finally broken free from the clutches of that wretched mall.

That fatal attraction he had fallen so easily for.

I dare not go back, he tormented at the thought, desperate to take in the air as much he could. He knew he would forget what it felt like.

He would miss its imperfection presently perfect to him.

The suited figure had appeared before him once more to deflect the blow—almost as though the man wielded Hensers with no cards in hand.

Truly such power was not conceivable, not plausible, not viable.

"Go now," the man said to him, a ricochet of the *dark* smashing the weakened glass of the grand, south-west entrance. Carls was dismayed at the sign, and the hesitance met him with force as the field broke and found him ill-prepared.

He knew not how he'd lived that moment, only that the suited figure stood the pathway as he slid across the ever-familiar dread of cold marble.

He was back inside the mall.

Back inside his cage.

Back inside the lion's den.

Printed in the United States
By Bookmasters